W9-CCW-604

BALLYKISSANGEL

A SENSE OF PLACE

Ballykissangel

A SENSE OF PLACE

Hugh Miller

Based on the public television series
created by Kieran Prendiville

First published in 1998 by BBC Books, an imprint of BBC Worldwide Limited.
First North American edition published 1999 by Bay Books, an imprint of Bay Books & Tapes.

for the original BBC Books edition:
Executive Producers Tony Garnett and Brenda Reid
Produced by Chris Griffin
Directed by Paul Harrison and Dermot Boyd
Book Design by Harry Green
Typeset by Keystroke

for the Bay Books edition:
Publisher: James Connolly
Art Director: Jeffrey O'Rourke
Managing Editor: Clancy Drake
Design: Patrick David Barber
Proofreader: Sabrina Rood-Sinker
Cover photography by Patrick Redmond © BBC Worldwide
Insert photography pp. 1, 4, and 8 by Patrick Dowling © BBC Worldwide
Insert photography pp. 2, 3, 5, 6, and 7 by Patrick Redmond © BBC Worldwide

Library of Congress Cataloging-in-Publication Data:
Miller, Hugh.
Ballykissangel : a sense of place / Hugh Miller.
p. cm.
"As seen on public television. Based on the TV series created by Kieran Prendiville."
ISBN 0-912333-63-4
I. Prendiville, Kieran. II. Title.
PS3563.I385B35 1999
813'.54-dc21 97-49050
CIP

Distributed to the trade by Publishers Group West

Printed in the United States of America

10 9 8 7 6 5 4 3 2 1

This book is published to accompany the television series *Ballykissangel*, a Ballykea Production for World Productions for BBC Northern Ireland.

HUGH MILLER was born in Scotland but has lived for more than twenty-five years in Warwickshire, England. He is the author of a number of books, among them the acclaimed Mike Fletcher crime novels and *The Silent Witnesses*, a study of the work of forensic pathologists. He also wrote the bestselling *Casualty*. His books have been translated into most western languages. Hugh lives in Warwick with his wife, Nettie.

KIERAN PRENDIVILLE, a former journalist and broadcaster, has been a television scriptwriter for ten years. He has written for many popular drama series, including *Boon* and *The Bill*. As well as *Ballykissangel*, he also created *Roughnecks*, the hit series about life on a North Sea oil rig. He is 48 and lives in London.

ONE

ON A SUNNY Saturday afternoon, on the common ground opposite St Joseph's Church at the north end of Ballykissangel, the entire village turned out to support the charity slave auction. There was cheering and laughter as the young landlady of the local pub, Assumpta Fitzgerald, allowed herself to be led around the cordoned-off parade ring with a halter round her neck. On a platform behind the ring, Brian Quigley, a hard-eyed local entrepreneur, performed the function of auctioneer.

'Come on,' he shouted into the microphone, 'who's going to start me off? Do I hear five pounds?'

'Thanks a lot,' Assumpta muttered.

'Come on!' Quigley harangued the crowd. 'What's the matter with you?'

'Too much!' shouted big Brendan Kearney, the schoolteacher.

Padraig O'Kelly, owner of the filling station, yelled, 'Lower!'

'Ah, come on, this is a fine specimen . . . '

'I am not a specimen!' Assumpta hooted.

'Young, fit, strapping,' Quigley went on.

Assumpta glared at him. She was certainly young, definitely fit, but her figure scarcely deserved to be called strapping. That was a description that fitted Siobhan Mehigan, the vet.

'One or two question marks about her temperament maybe,' Quigley added.

Assumpta put up a warning finger. 'You are barred,' she told Quigley.

People were enjoying themselves. By the barrier Father Peter Clifford, the youthful English curate, stood with Brendan, Padraig and Siobhan, the vet, loudly egging on the auctioneer and gently disparaging the slave currently on offer.

'Five pounds,' Father Peter bid.

Assumpta threw him a look of contempt.

'I have five pounds,' Quigley shouted. 'Any advance on five pounds?'

Somebody in the crowd bid a tenner.

'That's more like it. Let's go. Come on, look at her, she must be worth more than one of Eamonn's heifers.'

Standing in the crowd, the farmer Eamonn Byrne, who resembled a scarecrow in dress and stature, pondered that remark, then shook his head.

Niamh Egan, standing by her husband Ambrose, the local policeman, waved at the auctioneer, who happened to be her father. 'Fifteen pounds,' she shouted.

Assumpta put on a hurt look and told Niamh not to go mad.

Father MacAnally, the parish priest, pushed forward to the edge of the ring and held up his hand. 'Twenty,' he called.

People were surprised. The long-running animosity between the parish priest and the landlady of Fitzgerald's was well known. Assumpta herself looked wary.

'I hear twenty pounds,' Quigley cried. 'Any advance on twenty pounds?'

'Throw in the bar, you've got a deal!' Padraig shouted. The crowd laughed.

'Assumpta Fitzgerald going once for twenty pounds,' Quigley said. He glanced at Father Mac with the trace of a wink. 'Do you know what you're doing, Father?' Quigley held up his hands. 'Going twice for twenty pounds . . . Gone for twenty pounds to the parish priest!' He brought his hands together with a crack.

Amid the cheering Assumpta stared uneasily at Father Mac. He smoothed his silver hair and gave her his kindest smile.

The rope was removed from Assumpta's neck and dropped over the shoulders of Peter as he stepped into the ring. Assumpta pushed her way through the barrier and over to Father Mac.

'If you think for one moment – '

'Ah whisht child and calm down,' the priest said.

'What do you want with me?'

'All in good time.' Father Mac smiled again and walked away.

Peter was meanwhile being led around the ring and Quigley was back at the microphone.

'Come on now,' he coaxed the crowd, 'think what you could do with a curate for three hours.'

Niamh responded with a sensuous little moan.

'Niamh!' Ambrose, her husband, was shocked. She had noticed he was always more easily affronted by her when he was in his police uniform, as he was now.

'I just meant, think of all the Novenas you could get through,' she said.

'Come on now, all in a good cause,' Quigley said. 'Who wants the priest for three hours?'

'Who wants the priest for three minutes?' Assumpta shouted.

Padraig bid a tenner.

'Ah, come on,' Quigley groaned, 'the man has feelings.'

Niamh had switched her attention to another man who had joined the crowd around the ring. He was tall, somewhere in his forties and good looking in a gaunt, rangy way. He wore a wide-brimmed hat, jeans and cowboy boots. Niamh believed she recognised him. She nudged Ambrose.

'Is that Enda Sullivan?'

'Who's Enda Sullivan?'

'Him over there.'

Ambrose looked. 'I don't know. Do you want me to arrest him?'

'Dark Rosaleen,' Niamh said. 'The band. He used to play guitar.'

'Dark Rosaleen . . . ' Ambrose looked again. 'Oh God, yeah. Them. I think I will arrest him.'

In the ring Quigley was trying to shame the crowd into making bids. 'Come on, how often do I have to say all the money raised goes to the Ballykay Hospice? Ten pounds for the curate – is this the best you can do?'

Peter put on his saddest little-boy smile.

'Go on then,' Assumpta said grudgingly. 'Twenty pounds.'

Brendan Kearney turned and looked at her. 'What is it with you and the clergy?'

'Whatever Father Mac wants with me,' Assumpta said, pointing at Peter, 'he can do.' She walked off.

'Sold to Assumpta Fitzgerald,' Quigley announced to further cheering.

Niamh was looking at Enda Sullivan again. 'Is he in the auction, do you think?'

'He is not coming to live with us,' Ambrose told her.

Niamh continued to gaze thoughtfully at Enda. She began threading her way towards him. Ambrose had his attention distracted by Brendan Kearney, who was waving to attract Quigley's attention.

'What about yourself, Brian?' he called. 'Fine figure of a man.'

'Yeah, go on, Donal,' Siobhan shouted to one of Quigley's employees, who was holding the rope. 'Throw the halter over him.'

Quigley laughed uneasily. 'How can the slave-master be up for sale?'

'Read about it in the local paper,' Brendan said. 'Go on, Donal.'

The loop was dropped around Quigley's neck.

'And who's going to do the auction?' he demanded.

'I am,' said Padraig, stepping into the ring. He got up on the platform and adjusted the microphone. 'All right now, ladies and gents,' he called in his drink-matured voice, 'what am I bid for Mr Quigley here? I can understand your reticence. I mean, what purpose exactly does he serve? But then again you could say the same about a bad-tempered old dog. He might bite your arm off but you'd miss him if he wasn't around.'

As Padraig continued to entertain the crowd at Quigley's expense, Niamh sidled up beside Enda Sullivan.

'How are you?' she said brightly.

Enda smiled at her absently and produced a pen. With the other hand he took her programme from her.

'Who to?' he said

'What?'

'Who do you want me to sign it to?'

'Oh. Ambrose.'

Enda looked at her.

'My father wanted a boy,' she said. 'Look, I don't want your autograph. I like your music but I wouldn't know what to do with your signature.'

'Sorry, force of habit.'

Niamh didn't believe that for a second, and she let Enda see she didn't.

He shrugged. 'All right, wishful thinking.'

Niamh watched his eyes track Assumpta as she walked away down the hill, her dark red hair swaying on her shoulders, counterpoint to the swing of her hips.

'What would she want with a priest?' he muttered.

'Assumpta? She's a big fan of yours.'

'Go away.'

'Oh yeah.' Niamh paused, gauging the strength of his attraction to Assumpta. 'Would you like to meet her?'

Enda tried to look indifferent. 'Sure.'

'Stay here. I need you to do something for me first.'

Back in the parade ring Quigley was grouchily allowing himself to be led round by the neck.

'Ah come on,' Padraig appealed to the jeering crowd. 'Fifty pence? For an ox like this? It's an insult.'

Liam, the other of Quigley's employees, said he would bid a pound.

'What?' Quigley glared at him.

'I was thinking of your dignity,' Liam explained.

Quigley told him to concentrate on his own life expectancy.

'Going once for a pound, ladies and gents,' Padraig said. 'Ah come on, have a heart – '

'Get on with it,' Quigley snapped.

'Going twice, still for a pound.' Padraig waited, his eyes beseeching another bid. None came. 'Going, gone.'

The crowd cheered. Liam smiled at the scowling Quigley and sidled over to him. 'Your ass is mine,' he said.

Quigley looked grim, but he said nothing. Instead, he got back on the platform and resumed his duties as auctioneer. It took less than five minutes to sell Brendan Kearney to Siobhan.

'He's all yours,' Quigley told her as she counted out the twenty pounds. 'God knows what a vet wants with a human being.'

'Experiments,' said Siobhan.

She led Brendan away as Niamh approached her father. She had Enda Sullivan in tow. She whispered something in Quigley's ear and he nodded, smiling. Enda looked bemused.

†

Ballykissangel sat snugly alongside the River Angel in a hollow of the Wicklow Mountains in County Wicklow, south-east Ireland. The long main street sloped down to the river bridge for half a mile and rose gently again at the other end of the village. There were rows and clusters of small houses, tidy shops and regular patches of green common land. The houses thinned out across the rising land behind the main stretch of the village, with smallholdings and farms and wooded hillsides beyond.

Fitzgerald's pub was at the lower end of the main street, opposite the point where the road turned right across the river bridge. The bar was cosy but roomy enough, with a good long bar, a fine selection at the pumps, and enough in the way of domestic touches – armchairs, framed pictures, shaded lamps – to make people respect their surroundings without feeling restricted.

Half an hour after the auction Peter stood in the bar listening as Padraig and the hill farmer Eamonn explained the rules governing those sold into slavery at the annual charity event.

'Whatever she says you have to do, Father, you have to do,' Eamonn said.

Peter could never conceal how much he enjoyed days like this. He was still a relative newcomer, but already his sense of belonging was powerful, and it grew with the smallest pleasures. There was his sense of place, too, an understanding and harmonising with the character of Ballykissangel. Since falling so heavily for the place and its people, he had kept a scrap of verse tacked to a corner of the pinboard in the sacristy at St Joseph's.

God gives all men all earth to love,
But since man's heart is small,
Ordains for each one spot shall prove
Beloved over all.

'No one has ever refused their owner's command,' Padraig was saying in his fine bass voice. Peter reflected that Padraig – it was pronounced Poraig – with his dark curly hair and mildly debauched features, was the precise epitome of the man who could hold his drink.

'I can't refuse any order she gives me?' Peter said.

'Such a thing would be unthinkable.'

'She owns me?'

'Yeah, I own you,' Assumpta said, coming along the bar. 'You talk too much.'

'Then you have to feed me.'

'What?'

'If I'm your slave,' Peter said, 'I'm your responsibility. Tuna mix in a granary bap, please. Easy on the mayo.'

Assumpta narrowed her eyes at him. 'Do you know what we do with slaves around here?'

'What?'

'Did you ever see the film *Mandingo*?'

'I know that film,' Eamonn said. 'Didn't a dog run off with a baby in Australia?'

The talk drifted back to the auction and what a laugh it was, and how it was a better way to raise money for the hospice than the amateur dramatics they used to have. The problem, Assumpta said, had been that Father Mac's idea of challenging theatre was a dramatisation of the Lives of the Saints. Peter believed that amateur dramatics, properly handled, could pull in the punters and raise plenty of cash for charity.

'We just need something people would want to watch,' said Peter.

'Yeah,' Assumpta nodded. 'Videos.'

Siobhan came into the bar with Brendan behind her.

'A bottle of Harp, Assumpta, and whatever my man wants.'

'Oh,' Assumpta grinned, 'so you've bought one, too?'

'Yeah. Have you given yours a test drive yet?'

Peter and Brendan exchanged weary looks.

The door opened and Assumpta's Irish Setter, Finn, bounded into the bar, followed by Padraig's ten-year-old son Kevin. Several people bent down to pat the dog, then backed off sharply as a foul odour rose from the animal.

Assumpta was behind the bar and didn't understand their reaction.

'I don't know what you've been feeding him,' Siobhan said, 'but it doesn't agree with him.'

'Oh, that's right . . . ' Assumpta came round the bar and knelt by Finn, 'blame the dog.'

Padraig looked at her. 'You think it's the priest?'

'I think it's Kevin,' Brendan said.

Assumpta patted the dog and suddenly her own expression changed.

'See?' Padraig said.

Assumpta bravely stayed beside the dog, patting his back. 'Don't mind them, Finn. You're only doing what comes natural.'

Padraig shook his head. 'That can't be natural.'

'He needs exorcising,' Brendan said.

'He's just had his exercise,' Assumpta said.

'Not exercise, Assumpta, exorcise. What Father Clifford does.'

Peter stared. 'Are you sure you want me to drive out another one of those?'

Scowling and trying to ignore the laughter, Assumpta led the dog away to be fed in the back room. As she returned to the bar Niamh and Enda Sullivan came in. Ambrose Egan slipped in a second later, glaring at his wife.

'Happy birthday, Assumpta,' Niamh said.

'What?'

Niamh pointed at Enda. 'This is your birthday present.'

'It's not my birthday.'

'I know, but when is it – soon?'

Assumpta looked at the tall pseudocowboy. 'What is he? A Chippendale?'

Enda looked wounded.

'This is Enda Sullivan,' Niamh said. 'I bought him.'

'Who's Enda Sullivan?'

'Dark Rosaleen. The band.'

'Yeah?' Assumpta did not look impressed. 'What were you?'

'Guitar and vocals,' Enda said.

'He sings and he plays, free, for you,' Niamh said. 'That's your present.' She paused, looking for a sign of reaction. There was nothing but faint embarrassment.

Niamh turned and flounced to the door, leaving Enda standing. Ambrose hurried out after her.

Enda remained where he was. When it was clear that no one was paying any attention to him, he gave a little cough.

'You'll have to audition,' Assumpta told him.

'What?' Enda looked insulted.

two

LATER THAT SAME day Father Mac called at Fitzgerald's and found his curate working behind the bar. He demanded to know what was happening. Assumpta explained that she was getting some value out of the clergy for a change.

Father Mac insisted that Peter could not work there, it was a violation of the dignity of Father Clifford's calling that could not be countenanced, charity or no charity.

At that point somebody asked Peter for a glass of stout.

'He is not serving glasses of stout,' Father Mac said.

'Pint of lager, then,' said the man.

Assumpta laughed. Peter asked her if perhaps he could do something a little less controversial, like turning water into wine.

'Go on,' Assumpta said, releasing him from his obligation. She pointed at Father Mac. 'Take him with you.'

Father Mac shook his head. 'We have to talk, Assumpta.' He nodded for Peter to leave. 'Go on, Father.'

Peter got his jacket and left. On the street outside the pub he was intercepted by Padraig, who was carrying a dog-eared manuscript.

'Father Clifford, can I have a word?'

'Go ahead.'

'I won't keep you.' Padraig held out the manuscript. 'Would you read this?'

'Sure. What is it?'

'A play you might like to consider. For the Dramatic Society.'

Peter read the cover. '*Ryan's Mother*.'

Padraig nodded. 'I wrote it.'

'*Ryan's Mother?*'

'The prequel.'

'Oh. Right.' Peter tucked the manuscript under his arm. 'I'll check it out.'

'Thanks, Father.'

Peter walked on, struggling to keep his face straight.

Back in Fitzgerald's Assumpta was serving Father Mac with a pot of tea while he fished unsuccessfully in his trouser pocket for some money.

'Forget it,' she said.

'You're very kind.'

'Let's have it, then. Your pound of flesh.'

Father Mac frowned. 'You take a dim view of humankind.'

'Just a certain kind. What do you want?'

'I want to book three rooms for the weekend of the twenty-fifth. How are you fixed?'

'Busy weekend,' Assumpta said. 'There's a convention in Wicklow.'

Father Mac said he knew that. Assumpta said she hoped he didn't expect the three rooms on the house. He assured her he did not. She pulled out her ledger from under the counter and opened it. She looked at Father Mac again and watched for signs of shiftiness when she asked him if this was absolutely all he wanted.

'Your debt to me would be wiped out,' he said.

Assumpta shrugged. 'I think I can help you, in that case. Who are the rooms for?'

'Some friends of mine.'

Suspicion dawned on Assumpta. 'What kind of friends?'

Father Mac's mouth went very small for a moment. 'What do you mean, what kind of friends?'

'You know very well what I mean.'

Father Mac sighed. 'They won't be dressed in robes if that's what you're worried about.'

'Robes?'

'One of them's a bishop.'

'A bishop.' Assumpta felt herself turning white. 'And the other two?'

'Humble parish priests on a golfing holiday – '

'Not under my roof.'

'– for whom I promised to find accommodation.'

'You left it too late,' Assumpta said, her voice rising. She took twenty pounds out of the till and slapped it on the counter.

Father Mac stared at the money. 'What's that?'

'What you paid for me.'

He shook his head. 'It doesn't work like that.'

He turned and walked out.

Later that day Assumpta told Siobhan, Brendan and Eamonn what had happened. They were not sympathetic.

'You can't do that,' Brendan said. 'The whole thing falls apart if you do that.'

'Ah, grow up.'

'It's tradition,' Brendan insisted. 'How do you think the tradition survives?'

'If someone pays money for you,' Siobhan chimed in, 'you do what you're asked.'

Eamonn was nodding. 'Did you see what Liam asked Brian Quigley to do?'

'What?'

'Unblock his drains. A real blockage, mind, one where a man has to get down into it, as you might say.'

Assumpta flounced out of the bar.

'And he's doing it,' Eamonn said, his voice hushed with respect for Quigley's sacrifice in the name of tradition. 'He's working up to his neck in – '

'Yeah,' Brendan said hastily, 'all right, Eamonn.'

Siobhan turned to Brendan, smiling faintly. 'You don't know what I want you to do yet.'

†

Late in the afternoon, having read Padraig's play, Peter talked to Brendan about it. He told him he liked the play, he liked it so much he would really like to put it on. Brendan said he couldn't believe Peter was serious.

'I certainly am, Brendan. You should read it.'

'I've read it.'

'And?'

'Father, Padraig is my oldest friend and I'll not hear a word said against him. His play, on the other hand . . . '

'Yes?'

'If it was a fight they'd stop it. If it was a lame horse they'd put it out of its misery. If it was – '

'OK, OK . . . '

'I can't believe you want to produce it.'

'It's not that bad, and he's a local author – '

'He's a local chancer.'

'It's a good play!'

Brendan looked squarely at Peter. 'No offence, Father,' he said, 'but what do the English know about literature?'

Later still, Peter spoke to Brian Quigley about possible sponsorship for the play. The conversation was rather too one-sided, because Quigley was down inside Liam's drain at the time and his concentration was not at its best. Nevertheless, when Peter spoke to Padraig next day, he told him he was cautiously hopeful that patronage could be mustered to mount a production of *Ryan's Mother*.

'That's fantastic, Father, brilliant.'

'Well, hang on, Quigley didn't say he would, I just think he might.'

'Brilliant.'

'Now listen.' It seemed important to keep Padraig's enthusiasm within bounds. 'I don't have a cast yet. When did you write this anyway?'

'Ten years ago now, I'd say. I sent it up to RTE but it was too raunchy for them.'

'Yeah. I wanted to talk to you about that.'

'I thought Assumpta'd make a great Mary,' Padraig said.

Peter considered that. He nodded. 'And I can think of one or two people who wouldn't mind playing the priest.'

'What about yourself, Father?'

Peter swallowed his response. Instead, he said they would really have to talk about editing out certain parts of the play and toning down others.

Padraig agreed, but he didn't want to be bothered with fine details right at that moment. 'Sure we'll get the casting sorted out,' he said, 'and then we'll worry about the script.'

They went to Fitzgerald's, outlined the play to Assumpta and put their proposition to her, trailing behind her as she emptied ashtrays and wiped tables.

'Mary?' she said finally.

'We can change the name if you don't like it,' Peter assured her.

She still looked uneasy. 'It's not really my thing, you know.'

'Don't give me that,' Padraig said, 'you did this at college.'

'Padraig, at college I did *Playboy of the Western World*, *Juno and the Paycock*, life-enhancing works of art and power. *Ryan's Mother* was not among them.'

'It's a community project,' Peter said.

'Oh yeah?' Assumpta looked from Peter to Padraig. 'Who else is involved?'

'Are you kidding?' Padraig said. 'They're beating his door down to take part.'

Assumpta couldn't help smiling at their enthusiasm. 'Yeah right,' she said, 'I'll read it, OK? No promises.'

Peter and Padraig left. Peter wanted to get straight down to some editing, but Padraig was still intent on assembling a cast for the play before they did anything else. A male lead had to be found and Padraig had no doubt who would be perfect in the part: Enda Sullivan. Peter had his doubts.

'Come on, Father, it's a great idea.'

'How do you know he can act?'

'He's a performer, isn't he? Anyway, he's a celebrity, he'll get the punters in.'

'Assumpta had never heard of him.'

''Course she had,' Padraig said. 'She just didn't want to look impressed.'

'All right, but don't you need to be local? If it's a community project.'

'He is local,' Padraig said. Noting Peter's sceptical look, he added, 'In the sense the Irish Football team is Irish.'

Peter drove them out to Enda Sullivan's house that afternoon. It was a small neat farmhouse along a country road to the north-west of Ballykissangel. Peter and Padraig stepped up to the front door and Peter rang the doorbell. There was no answer.

They took a quick look around the sides and back of the house, then Peter rang the bell again. A window opened above them and the naked torso of Enda appeared.

His hair was mussed, but he didn't look as if he had been sleeping.

'Sorry, Father,' he said, 'have you been ringing for long?'

'No, no. Do you want us to come back?'

'Ten minutes,' Enda said. 'How's that?'

'Sure,' Peter said. 'Fine.'

The window slammed shut.

Peter and Padraig walked back to wait in the car.

'Finishing a song,' Peter said.

Padraig nodded. 'That's what it'll be.'

They got in the car and sat watching the cottage. A few minutes later an attractive young woman in her early twenties slipped out through the front door, pulling on her coat.

'Ten minutes,' Peter said, sounding impressed.

'Maybe he had writer's block,' Padraig muttered.

They went back to the cottage and Enda invited them in. They stood in the kitchen while Peter and Padraig explained the project, and the reason for their visit.

'I'm not an actor,' Enda said, 'I'm a singer. And your woman in the pub doesn't think I can even do that.'

'That's just her way,' Padraig said. 'She likes you, really.'

Enda asked if she was involved in the project.

'Oh God, yeah,' Padraig said. 'Female lead.'

'And what would I be?'

'Romantic interest.'

'Playing the priest?'

'It's that kind of play.'

'Bang up-to-date, anyway,' Enda said. 'No offence, Father.'

Peter shrugged. 'None taken.'

'I like that Assumpta, though,' Enda said, warming to the idea of the play. 'Know what I mean?'

Peter and Padraig swapped a look. They knew what he meant. By the time they left, Enda had agreed to play the male lead.

As they drove back to Ballykissangel there was the sound of a mobile telephone ringing. Peter fished it from his inside pocket.

'On approval,' he explained to Padraig, putting the instrument to his ear. 'Father Clifford speaking.'

It was Brian Quigley. He said that having now had time to think over the proposition, he was prepared to back Peter's production of *Ryan's Mother*. On one condition.

'Name it, Brian.'

'I've had Father Mac on about Assumpta Fitzgerald. You know what I'm talking about.'

'I can guess.'

'Here's the deal, then.' Quigley said. 'Make her do what's right and the money's yours.'

When Quigley hung up Peter pocketed the phone and drove in silence for a while. Finally he told Padraig what Quigley had said.

They decided it was worthwhile trying with Assumpta, anyway. They went to Fitzgerald's at six o'clock and piled on the pressure. Siobhan and Brendan were at the end of the bar, listening. Assumpta listened, too, and she resisted.

'Why should Quigley care?' she said.

'Why?' Peter said. 'Because after spending hours up to his neck in . . . '

'What's good for the roses,' Padraig offered.

' . . . he's just a little cheesed off you won't do something that costs you nothing.'

Assumpta stared at him. 'You have no idea what it would cost me.'

'I can tell you what it'll cost us,' Padraig said.

'If you don't change your mind,' Peter said, 'we don't get the money.'

'The play doesn't happen,' Padraig said, and saw Brendan join his hands in an ironic prayer of thanks.

Assumpta stared at the bar for a moment. Finally she said, 'It's a good play.'

Brendan looked startled.

'We've got Enda Sullivan,' Padraig said, soothingly.

'Come on, Assumpta,' Peter coaxed.

'For God's sake!' She was clearly wrestling with her dilemma. 'The clergy is one thing, but he wants me to put up three of them!'

'I know,' Peter said softly, 'and one of them runs a diocese. Assumpta, you're blowing this all out of proportion. It's just one night, it's such a little thing.'

'As the publican said to the bishop,' Siobhan muttered.

Not long afterwards, Father Mac sat in his study, talking on the telephone, nodding and smiling as he listened to the responses at the other end.

'Absolutely, Your Grace. Three rooms, no problem. Not at all, she's only too pleased to help.' He listened and smiled broadly at the mouthpiece. 'And you, Your Grace.'

THREE

IT TOOK A WEEK to get the project properly on the rails. After much argument and compromise between Peter and Padraig, a revised version of the script was prepared. Copies were delivered to the principal actors, so they could have a read-through before trying out their lines in front of other people and each other. Niamh agreed to do regular stand-in duty at Fitzgerald's for the duration of rehearsals, and Peter re-scheduled his parochial duties to leave space in the evenings for him to take up his role as director.

The first rehearsal took place in the village hall eight days after Assumpta had acceded to Father Mac's wishes. Dress rehearsals would come later; for the time being Assumpta and Enda played their parts in their ordinary clothes. They faced each other on the platform, scripts in hand, watched by Peter and Padraig in chairs at the front.

'In your own time,' Peter told Assumpta.

She glanced at her script, then looked at Enda. 'Go now, Matthew,' she said. 'If they find you, they'll kill you.'

'I'll be back,' Enda said sternly.

'No,' Assumpta cried, 'get real.' She interrupted herself and turned to Padraig. 'Look, call me picky, but I don't think they said "get real" at the turn of the eighteenth century.'

'I know they didn't,' Padraig said haughtily. 'I'm trying to give it a contemporary resonance.'

'It's got all the contemporary resonance it needs.'

'Hold on, hold on,' Peter interrupted. 'I'm the director.'

'And I'm the writer!' a voice called from the back of the hall. Brendan strode in, glaring at Padraig, brandishing a copy of the script like a club. 'You thieving swine!'

'What?' Padraig shot to his feet and backed away as Brendan advanced on him. 'What do you mean?'

'This is my play! My words, my script, my play!'

Now Peter was on his feet. 'What?'

'What are you talking about?' Padraig demanded.

'You know very well what I'm talking about, you duplicitous, unscrupulous plagiariser!'

Peter stepped between Brendan and Padraig.

'Just hold on,' Padraig yelled, 'who are you calling a plagiariser?'

'If the cap fits!'

'Enough!' Peter shouted. 'Stop it, the pair of you. Back off, Brendan. I thought you said you hated this play? "If it was a fight they'd stop it", remember?'

'Oh, very nice,' Padraig grunted.

'I hated his play,' Brendan said. He held up the script. 'I've only just seen this play.'

'Well . . . ' Padraig shrugged. 'It's not all yours.'

'Wait a minute,' Peter said, 'you mean some of it's his?'

'Bits,' Padraig said, 'bits here and there.'

'Bits?' Brendan said, glowering. 'Bits? Great big colossal thundering slabs, you cheating, pillaging, word-embezzling bandit!'

Brendan's voice rose so sharply the village-hall cat scampered away.

'Oh, that's good, that's really good,' Padraig said, 'coming from a man who opened a scene on top of a house with the words "it is a roof universally acknowledged".'

'That was satire!' Brendan said. 'Do you not know satire when you see it?'

'Satire? What are you talking, satire?'

As the two continued to barrack each other Enda turned to Assumpta. 'I don't think there'll be any more rehearsals tonight, do you?'

'Nope.'

'Fancy a jar?'

Assumpta smiled. 'Why not?'

They turned to leave.

'Hang on,' Brendan shouted to them. 'Where are you going?'

They stopped and stared at him.

'Who told you you could go?' Brendan demanded.

Assumpta looked at Peter. 'What is he? The director, now?'

'No,' Peter said firmly, 'he isn't.'

Everyone waited for his word of command.

'Go,' he told Assumpta and Enda. 'You're clear. I'll talk to you later.' He turned to Brendan and Padraig. 'In the meantime, will the real writer please step forward?'

As Brendan's anger went off the boil and Padraig stopped being so defensive, both finally agreed that they had written the play together. The problem, at the time, had been that they argued endlessly, so very little was put down on paper. They wound up writing separately and showing each other afterwards what they had done. They shook their heads at the memory.

'So both contributions were terrible,' Peter concluded. 'But between them there's a half-decent play.'

Brendan threw a look at Padraig. 'Did you think I wouldn't find out?'

'Brendan, I took so little . . . '

'So little?'

'Enough,' Peter warned them again. 'Are we going to do this play or what?'

'Damn right we are,' said Brendan.

'OK,' Peter told them, 'but the sexy stuff still has to go.'

'Over my dead body!' they said in unison.

'We both wrote that,' Padraig said.

Peter shook his head. 'Assumpta won't play it.'

Later, Padraig and Brendan went down to Fitzgerald's and asked Assumpta outright if she would do the controversial scenes. She said no, she would not. Siobhan seemed to approve, but Niamh, standing with Ambrose, looked mischievous.

'Not even with Enda Sullivan?' she said coyly.

'Not even with Jack Nicholson,' Assumpta said.

Brendan looked huffy. 'I thought you liked this play.'

'I do like it. I just don't like what you're asking me to do. There are other ways of . . . of communicating passion.'

'Such as?' Niamh said, shocking Ambrose again.

Assumpta started to say something else when the door burst open and her dog Finn ran in, followed by Padraig's son Kevin, who had taken him for his evening walk. Everyone froze as if a gunfighter had just walked in, then they all, with the exception of Niamh and Ambrose, stampeded to the far side of the room as the dog trotted up to the bar.

'Come on.' Niamh, wild-eyed, grabbed Ambrose's hand and rushed him out of the door.

For a moment Assumpta looked shocked, then everyone burst out laughing.

'Yeah, yeah, very funny.' Assumpta knelt by the dog, patting him. 'Don't mind them, Finn. They have a retarded sense of humour.'

She stood up again sharply, her face stiff from the need to stop breathing. Foul gas wafted up over the bar as she led the dog hurriedly through to the kitchen.

'Mother of Jayz, Assumpta,' Padraig shouted, 'will you not get that animal seen to?'

'He looks healthy enough to me,' said Siobhan. 'Bring him in tomorrow, Assumpta, I'll take a look at him. Through a telescope.'

Again the pub erupted with laughter. Finn appeared at the kitchen door, eyes shining, tail wagging happily at all the commotion.

†

Brendan and Padraig gave in to the vigour of Assumpta's moral stance. They cut the offending passages from their script. Revised versions were distributed at rehearsal the following evening. Peter, Brendan and Padraig sat together out front, preoccupied with the action as Assumpta and Enda read their lines and went through the movements. Standing in the wings were Quigley's men Liam and Donal, who had been drafted in to work the lights and the curtains. Near them as they stood watching was young Kevin with the dog Finn.

'Oh, Matt, why did you come?' Assumpta said.

'I had to,' Enda said.

'The soldiers are everywhere.'

'I don't care.'

'What about me?' Assumpta sighed.

'I care about you.'

They embraced and kissed. In the process, Enda's hand came to rest on the upper slope of Assumpta's left buttock.

She pulled back her head and glared at him. 'Do you mind?'

He looked at her with wide-eyed innocence. 'What?'

'Where your hand is.'

'What?'

'Keep it where I can see it, please.'

Brendan stared at Assumpta. '"Keep it where I can see it, please"? Oh, very passionate! You do realise you're about to sacrifice your life for this man?'

'My life maybe . . .' Assumpta cut herself off. 'How many directors have we got around here?' she demanded.

'I am the author,' Brendan shouted.

'We're both the author,' Padraig amended, just as loudly.

Peter threw back his head and roared, 'Are you all quite finished?' Everyone looked at him. 'Right,' he nodded to Brendan and Padraig, 'you two. Have you ever heard of a silent partnership? You're it. Sit.' He turned to the stage. 'Assumpta, this is a play about passion. Without passion, it's nothing.'

'But you were the one – '

'We've got rid of all the sex,' Peter said. 'It doesn't mean you can't have physical contact.'

'Yeah, but he doesn't have to be so close!'

'What?' Enda looked bewildered again.

'Of course he has to be so close!' Padraig snapped. 'Where do you want him to play it from – Kilkenny?'

'Quiet!' Peter shouted.

Everyone was startled by the volume, including the village-hall cat. It ran across the stage.

'OK,' Peter said, his voice softer now. 'Let's just calm down and see if we can't find a compromise.'

The dog saw the cat and shot across the stage after it. As Enda turned to see what was happening the dog ran into him and knocked him off the stage. He landed on his side with one leg doubled under him. He let out a cry of pain, clutching his foot.

'My ankle!' he howled. 'That is a dead dog!'

As the cat tore across the hall pursued by Finn, Brendan and Padraig wrinkled their noses at a sudden terrible odour.

Later, the local doctor, Michael Ryan, examined Enda's ankle. He declared the patient unfit to perform, unless the structure of the play was adaptable enough to let him do his scenes from a wheelchair. If that wasn't possible, then the production would be looking for a new leading man. No one had any idea where a stand-in could be found in Ballykissangel.

Late the following afternoon, Brendan and Padraig sat talking in the pews outside the confessional at St Joseph's. Brendan, an irregular churchgoer, admitted that this was the only church that ever had the effect of lifting his spirits. It was bright and well tended, with polished, gleaming wood and brass. The floor was always spotless, and when the season allowed there were fresh flowers in every vase.

The general effect of the place on Padraig was to make him whisper, even when the church was deserted. He believed that was a throwback to childhood when the tidy, well-kept homes of relatives were places where you whispered, or you got a smack on the knuckles for making a noise.

As the two men sat there the conversation roamed idly from topic to topic. Brendan was now revealing that earlier in the day, under the strict rule of obedience between slave and owner, he had been commanded by Siobhan to go with her and help collect a sample from a horse called Rollickin' Roger. Siobhan made it clear they were not talking about a sample of blood. They had to collect a sample that would determine the state of Rollickin' Roger's fertility.

'I tell you, Padraig,' Brendan said now, 'you have never seen anything like the size of it. Whatever you thought before, forget it.' He shook his head at the memory.

'You were the man for the job,' Padraig assured him.

At that moment Peter stepped out of the confessional and saw them sitting there. 'I'm sorry, I didn't think anyone was left.'

'No, no, Father,' Brendan said, 'we wanted a word.'

'Not that kind of word,' Padraig added, nodding at the confessional.

They put their proposition to Peter, and as they had expected, he rejected it out of hand. On the way down the hill from the church, Padraig restated the case.

'The long and the short of it is, there's only one man for the job of leading man.'

'Me,' Peter said, making a face. 'I told you, don't be ridiculous, I can't act.'

'You're a priest,' Padraig said, 'the role is a priest. You know the script. And besides, she won't have anyone else.'

Peter looked surprised. 'She's said that?'

'By elimination.'

'What?'

'She's blanked everybody else,' Padraig said.

'And you think she'll have me?'

'She hasn't said no.'

'Because you haven't asked her.'

'You're the director . . . '

Peter shook his head. 'No chance.'

They stopped outside Fitzgerald's.

'Look, Father, it's like this,' Brendan said. 'Unless you do it, there's no play.'

Peter spent a minute looking at it from that point of view. He accepted they were up against a wall. He decided, grumpily, that he had little option but to suggest to Assumpta that he play the male lead.

He tackled her in the back kitchen at the pub. She listened to the proposal as she swept up, and when he had finished, she paused and asked him if he had been at the altar wine.

'You,' she said incredulously, 'and me?'

'Do I look hot for this or something?' Peter asked her. 'Do you think I want to do this? You've turned everyone else down. It's this or no play.'

'Fine by me.'

'Fine. Then you explain to Brian Quigley, who's already spent over a grand on costumes and scenery, to Kathleen Hendley, who's already stocking up for the catering, to everyone else who's given hours of their free time – '

'They have free time to give,' Assumpta said. 'This is costing me a fortune.'

Peter waited.

Assumpta stared at him.

He continued to wait.

'All right,' she snapped, 'all right!'

'It's nice of you to be so gracious, Assumpta.'

'I said I'll do it, OK? God! Is moral blackmail in season in this town or what?'

The bell at reception rang. Assumpta stormed through to the reception hall. Three middle-aged men were waiting politely by the desk. They wore casual clothes and sunglasses, and had suitcases and golf bags at their feet.

'We're full up, I'm sorry,' Assumpta said curtly.

'We have reservations,' one of them said.

Assumpta hauled out her big book. 'What names?'

'Father Clohessy. Father Brady. Bishop Costello.'

Assumpta took a deep breath. She turned the ledger and pushed it forward. 'Sign here, would you?'

Peter had tiptoed through from the back room. He watched the heavy-duty clergy sign in, and decided this was no place for him. He turned and slipped out the back way.

FOUR

AT THAT EVENING's rehearsal Assumpta spoke her lines with more confidence than before and showed every sign of mastering her role. Peter was nervous in the part of Matthew, but because he knew the script so well his delivery was fluent, and between them they put together an encouraging performance.

It was only at the point where they had to kiss that Assumpta lost her involvement in the part. Her lips came to within an inch of Peter's, then she turned sharply aside.

'I can't do this,' she said. 'Not with all you people there.' She pointed to the back of the hall, where Brian Quigley was standing. 'And what is he doing there?'

'Protecting my investment,' Quigley said.

Brendan stood up. 'Assumpta, all we're asking you to do is kiss him.'

'Then you do it.'

'What?'

'All I'm asking is a little privacy.' Assumpta turned and began walking off the stage. 'No, all I'm demanding is a little privacy.'

'She's right,' Peter said. 'I don't feel very comfortable about this, either.'

'And what are you going to do on the night?' Brendan enquired. 'Ask the audience to wait outside?'

'A performance is different,' Assumpta said, striding towards Brendan and Padraig. 'Go on, get out, the lot of you.'

With some grumbling they left the hall. Quigley's parting shot was that he had paid for a rock star, not a priest.

Assumpta and Peter were alone now.

'Right,' Assumpta said, 'let's get to it.' As she climbed back on to the stage and stood near Peter she sensed his nervousness. 'It'll be all right,' she told him, 'it's acting.'

Peter nodded and swallowed hard.

'Right, so . . . ' Assumpta glanced at her script. 'Take it from "I did what I had to do", OK?'

Peter nodded again.

'I did what I had to do,' Assumpta said. 'I'm not proud of it.'

'It's all right. No one can blame you for falling in love.'

'I didn't fall in love. Not with him.'

'Mary . . . '

Peter looked away. Assumpta, caught up fully in the part, put her hand on his cheek and turned his head back to look at her.

'We have one night, maybe less, maybe just an hour.' Her voice became low and passionate. 'If it's a sin, there'll be no repeating it.'

Their heads moved close, their lips almost touching.

'Assumpta,' Peter whispered, drawing away.

'Don't,' she said, 'we have to finish it.'

'I don't think so.'

'Why not?'

'Because standing at the back of the hall is Father Mac, two parish priests and a bishop.'

Assumpta looked. There they were, four frowning members of the clergy, with Brendan and Padraig alongside. Assumpta let out a shocked yelp and ran into the wings. A moment later a door slammed.

Father Mac said, 'Don't take this as a compliment, Father – that was a very convincing performance.'

'Incendiary!' said Brendan,

'You promised us privacy,' Peter said.

Padraig shook his head. 'You can't bar a bishop. They were looking for Assumpta.'

Five minutes later, in the bar at Fitzgerald's, a flustered Assumpta learned from Niamh that the two priests and the bishop had checked out.

'What do you mean, checked out? They haven't spent a night here yet.'

'I know,' Niamh said, 'but they changed their minds. They were hoping to catch you at the hall.'

'Why?'

Niamh gestured awkwardly, unwilling to give offence.

'Niamh?'

'The rooms weren't up to scratch.'

'What?'

'The bishop likes a TV and a mini bar . . . '

'What?'

' . . . according to one of the parish priests.'

'Really.'

'They thought the bar below might be a bit noisy.'

'Did they?' Assumpta's teeth were scarcely parting now.

'They thought it was a bit expensive, too.'

Assumpta waited. 'Anything else?'

'Well,' Niamh said, 'I think Father Mac was a bit embarrassed.'

'How embarrassed?'

'Very embarrassed.'

'Well there you are then,' Assumpta said with a grim little smile. 'Every cloud.'

†

On the evening of the one and only performance of *Ryan's Mother* at the village hall, Assumpta called time in the bar at seven o'clock. Liam demanded to know what she was playing at.

'The theatre really runs in your blood, doesn't it, Liam?' Assumpta said.

He stared blankly at her.

'Showtime.'

The door opened and Finn trotted in with Kevin. Assumpta held up a warning finger to the crowd. 'Don't say it! Any of you.'

'Sure, what do you expect,' Siobhan said, 'when you feed a dog cabbages and Brussels sprouts. A dog needs meat. It's a carnivore.'

'I don't feed it cabbages and Brussels sprouts,' Assumpta said.

Siobhan winked. 'Someone does.' She glanced at Kevin, who suddenly had a guilty look.

'Kevin?' Assumpta said, waiting.

'What?'

'Tell the truth now,' Padraig warned the lad.

Kevin sighed. 'I haven't done anything wrong.'

'No one's saying you have.'

'He likes to eat with the goat,' Kevin said. 'They're friends.'

Assumpta groaned softly.

'It's only a bit of cabbage,' Kevin assured her.

'Kevin,' she said, 'no offence, but will you keep your greens for the goat?'

'OK.'

'Good man,' said his father.

Kevin looked at Assumpta. 'What about beans?'

†

At eight o'clock Peter was dressed in rough period costume, sitting in a hard-backed chair in front of a mirror backstage at the village hall, reluctantly having make-up applied to his face by Niamh. Beside him in another chair, also in period costume, was Assumpta.

'Don't be such a baby,' Niamh told Peter. 'Anyone would think I was pulling out a tooth.'

'I don't need make-up.'

Brian Quigley stepped into the room. 'Is he being a temperamental artiste?' he asked Niamh.

'You'd think he was a rock star,' she said. 'Hold still.'

'Brian,' Peter said, 'the way it works is, you receive visitors after the show.'

'If you're in it you do,' Quigley grinned. 'You're off the case.'

Peter stared at him. A moment later Enda Sullivan limped into the room, beaming at everyone.

'I'm back,' he said.

Assumpta frowned.

'Not quite as agile,' Quigley said, 'but he's mobile.'

Peter asked him if he was the producer now.

'I told you,' Quigley reminded him, 'I have an investment to protect. You couldn't act your way out of a bubble bath.'

Enda raised his knee carefully and slapped his ankle. 'Doc Ryan gave me a blast of anaesthetic spray. Enough to get me through a performance.'

'Good,' Peter said, trying to sound pleased.

'He's the one they've come to see,' Quigley said.

Peter nodded. 'You're right. Well done, Enda.' He gave Assumpta an embarrassed smile. 'Well, I better get changed.'

Later, Peter sat in the audience and watched the play. It was an excellent performance. Assumpta was splendid, and so was Enda. The audience was captivated. Peter was gripped, too, but when the passionate scene came, and their lips moved so close that a kiss was inevitable, he slipped from his seat and went outside.

He stood in the cool night air, taking deep breaths and gazing at the darkening sky. After a minute, Father Mac came out of the hall and stood beside him. They inspected the stars for a while.

Eventually Father Mac said, 'Not my cup of tea.'

'No . . . '

'They make a strong pair, though, I'll say that for them. He could be just what she needs. Is he a religious man, do you know?'

'No idea, Father.'

Father Mac looked along the deserted street. 'Musician,' he murmured, and sniffed. 'I suppose it would be expecting too much. Still.' He looked sharply at Peter. 'We can always hope, can't we?'

FIVE

ENDA SULLIVAN did not use his small triumph in *Ryan's Mother* to catapult himself socially, as might have been expected of a pro too long away from the limelight. He continued to live quietly at his farmhouse in the hills, working at his music for all anyone knew, and following quiet leisure pursuits, like panning for gold.

'You never know,' Liam said.

He and Donal stood on the riverbank, watching Enda squatting in the shallows beyond the bridge, dipping his pan in the water, swirling it, pouring the water away, over and over, a mesmeric ritual.

'You think there's gold in there, do you?' Brian Quigley said, coming down the bank beside them.

'There was a gold rush here in the last century,' Liam said.

'Is that right? Your wages are in the river then. Listen to me the both of you, if that fella panned every river in the county for the next hundred years, he wouldn't find enough gold to make a tooth.'

Donal shrugged, prepared to go with the dominant opinion. Liam looked unconvinced.

'The end of the rainbow's that way,' Quigley said, pointing to the fence they were erecting.

Liam went on staring at Enda a while longer, then followed Donal to the edge of the field. He picked up a couple of fenceposts and a sledgehammer, then glanced along the river at Enda again. Donal was watching, too.

'You fellas thinking of claim jumping or something?' Quigley said.

'Dreams cost nothing,' Liam said.

'They do on my time.'

At that moment, up in the Ballykissangel National School, Brendan Kearney was addressing a class of brightly attentive boys and girls. It was Brendan's gift that when he spoke to a class, the children were held by what he said.

'Try to find a way of remembering it,' he was telling them, referring to the date when the Irish Constitution was introduced. 'I know it was 1937, because that's the year that Sunderland won the FA Cup, and my grandmother comes from there.'

A hand went up.

'Yes, Kevin?'

'It's easy for you sir, but we all support Man United, and they win all the time.'

'Oh, is that right? Well then try it this way. The year that Manchester United didn't win the FA Cup, that's when De Valera introduced the constitution.'

A girl put up her hand this time. She asked Brendan if he was a Protestant.

'No. Why do you ask, Eileen?'

'My mammy says you don't go to Mass.'

'Well, the freedom of religion is also the freedom not to have to practise it. Now does that make sense, Eileen?'

Kevin asked if that meant they didn't have to go to Mass. Brendan told him not to push his luck. He looked again at little Eileen, who appeared to have trouble with the answer he gave to her question.

'Eileen, do you understand what I said?'

She shook her head.

'OK, no problem.' Brendan thought a moment before continuing. 'I do go to Mass. Not always, but when I do go it's by choice, not because someone tells me I have to. That's my right under the constitution. When you grow up, you can go to Mass as often as you like, or not at all. The law says you can do either, it's up to you. Now, Eileen, any better?'

She nodded solemnly. The bell sounded for the end of the class. The children began trooping out of the classroom. Kevin stopped beside Brendan and said, 'Is it true we're going to lose a teacher?'

'It looks like it, yes.'

'Is it going to be you?'

'That's not up to me,' Brendan said, then with a wink he added, 'They wouldn't dare.'

'They'd better not,' Kevin said, and followed the others out of the room.

Brendan was touched. And he was troubled. That morning he had received a letter, by hand, summoning him to a meeting of the School Board that evening at the school. The only specification in the letter was that he should attend. It told him nothing else, and that made it more ominous.

There was already speculation in Fitzgerald's.

'Of course it won't be Brendan,' Padraig said. 'Would they get rid of the best man they've got?'

'Well, I think it's a scandal anyway,' Siobhan said.

Padraig nodded. 'This country is run by accountants. At least you knew where you were when the clergy were in charge.'

'Damn,' Peter said. 'When was that?'

The door opened and Niamh stuck her head round the edge.

'Ambrose,' she said sharply. 'Come on.'

Ambrose, standing by the bar, turned deep pink. 'Niamh . . . '

'No buts. Come on.'

Ambrose put down his glass and did as he was told with as much dignity as he could. The instant the door closed behind him Padraig, Siobhan and Assumpta burst out laughing.

Peter stared at them. 'What?"

'They're trying for a baby,' Padraig said. 'These things go in cycles, Father.'

The mirth died away and the talk got back to the possibility of Brendan losing his job. They all said it was unlikely, in fact it was ridiculous even to think such a thing. The possibility worried them nevertheless, even though none of them said so.

At seven o'clock that evening Brendan presented himself before the four members of the Ballykissangel School Board: Father Mac, Brian Quigley, Dr Michael Ryan and Mr Deasey, the school principal.

Without lengthy preamble, Father Mac told Brendan it was the decision of the School Board that he would be dismissed from his current post at the end of the month.

Brendan was stunned. 'Why me?'

'Our hands are tied,' Father Mac said coldly.

'Brian?'

Quigley sighed. 'It wasn't an easy decision.'

Brendan looked at the doctor. 'Michael?'

Dr Ryan chewed his lip for a moment. 'They all know how I feel about this.'

'Michael,' Quigley said sharply, 'you know as well as I do that in order to sustain three teachers we have to have fifty-eight pupils on the roll. And since Mr and Mrs Graw decided to send little Courtney off to Rathnew we only have fifty-seven. Now – '

'That's enough, Brian,' Father Mac said. He looked at Brendan. 'It's done. I'm sorry.'

The news travelled fast. When Peter heard he went straight to Brendan's house and knocked on the door. He knocked several times, but there was no reply. Brendan wasn't at the pub, either. No one had seen him. Peter decided to drive out to Quigley's house. He found Quigley on the patio relaxing with a drink.

'Are you mad?' Peter demanded.

Quigley stared at him. 'Ah, how are you, Brian? Not so bad. Yourself, Father?'

'He's the best teacher in the whole school.'

'How would you know?'

'Why him?' Peter demanded.

'Because it had to be someone.'

Quigley's mobile phone warbled. He snatched it up. 'Brian Quigley.'

It was Liam. He wanted to know if Quigley needed him and Donal tomorrow.

'I don't know,' Quigley said. 'Why?'

'We have things to do.'

'What things?'

'What difference does it make, what things?'

Quigley sighed quietly. 'Liam, I think you misunderstand the master-slave relationship.' He sighed again. 'Go on. And watch out for the sharks.'

'What?'

'You'll find them in the river before you find gold.'

Quigley broke the connection and looked at Peter. 'You were saying.'

'Brendan Kearney?'

'The Chairman of the School Board deals with enquiries about the staff. Talk to Father Mac.'

'Oh, I will,' Peter promised. 'I warn you, Brian, this community's not going to let go of its best teacher without a fight.'

'Talk to Father Mac!'

Later, in Fitzgerald's, Peter told Assumpta and Siobhan that he would be broaching the matter of Brendan's dismissal with Father Mac first thing in the morning.

'And don't just talk to him,' Assumpta said, 'shove it up him, you know what I'm saying?'

'Yeah,' Peter nodded, 'that should help, Assumpta. What shall I use, a pike?'

'You show him too much respect.'

'He's the parish priest, for God's sake,' said Siobhan.

'He's the parish priest for his own sake,' Assumpta snapped. She jabbed a finger at Peter. 'Let's see what you're made of.'

Next day Father Mac received Peter in the study at his house in Cilldargan.

He listened dispassionately as Peter outlined the strength of public reaction to Brendan Kearney's dismissal. When Peter had finished, Father Mac spread his hands in a small gesture of helplessness.

'The Ministry makes the rules, Father, not the Board. Last in, first out. He was the last in.'

'I understand that, Father, but Mrs Riordan, you know, from Donegal, I heard she can't wait to retire. I mean, if anyone has to go . . .'

Father Mac looked shocked. 'Father, did you think we pulled straws out of a hat?'

'No, but Brendan Kearney is the best teacher we've got.'

Father Mac stared at Peter. 'Is he?'

'So everyone says.'

'Eileen O'Connor's mother doesn't think so.'

'Sorry?'

'What would you think now, Father, about a teacher in a national school who instructed a ten-year-old child she could make up her own mind about going to Mass?'

Peter was caught off balance. 'He wouldn't do that.'

'Ask him.'

†

That afternoon as Assumpta crossed the bridge with her dog she looked down and saw Enda crouched by the side of the river, swirling water in his shallow pan. She crossed the bridge and clambered down the bank, Finn bounding ahead of her.

'How're you?' she called to Enda.

He looked up and nodded.

'What are you really looking for?' she said.

'Lost City of the Incas.'

'They'd have to have mislaid it in a big way.'

Enda laughed softly as he stood and emptied his pan back into the river. 'Peace and quiet, Assumpta, that's all it is.'

'Hey, rock and roll.'

He looked at her. 'Have you got something against me?'

'Excuse me?'

'I said I'd do you a gig for nothing, I meant it.'

Assumpta bent and ruffled Finn's coat, using him as an excuse not to answer.

'I didn't mean to be familiar,' Enda said. 'Onstage, that is.'

She looked at him candidly, trying to read him. 'Why do you want to live here?'

'Are you serious?' Enda looked around, spreading his arms appreciatively. 'When we were kids, my Da used to bring us down from Dublin.'

'Yeah?'

'Yeah. But we'd always find our way back home.'

Assumpta smiled. As she walked away again up the riverbank, she was still smiling. She liked Enda Sullivan.

Later, as Peter was passing Kathleen's general store, a middle-aged woman came out and put her shopping into her wheeled basket by the door. As she moved off, one of the wheels detached itself from the axle and rolled into the gutter. Peter caught it and brought it to her.

She wore a headscarf and even when she raised her head momentarily to thank him, he took a moment to recognise her. It was Mairie Kilfeather. What distracted him as much as the headgear was a bruise over her eye.

'That looks nasty,' he said.

Mairie smiled nervously and slapped the wheel back on her basket.

'What happened?'

'I fell over the cat.'

Peter had worked in Manchester long enough to know a punched face when he saw one. He watched Mairie scurry away. 'Watch out for that cat,' he called after her.

He decided to call on the doctor. As soon as he was inside the consulting room, Ryan insisted that he remove his jacket and shirt.

'I want to listen to your heart. It's important.'

Peter complained that there was nothing wrong with him, but Ryan insisted. Peter took off his shirt and submitted to the examination. He asked Ryan if he knew Mairie Kilfeather.

'Yes, I know her. And him. I thought all this had stopped. Even while it was happening she wouldn't hear a word against him. Ask Guard Egan. If she'd a bruised rib or a black eye it was her own fault. A broken toe, she'd tripped up. Fractured jaw, she walked into a door. She could fall over for Ireland.'

'Can't Ambrose do anything?'

'He can now, yes.' Ryan tut-tutted. He sat back and unhooked the stethoscope from his ears.

'What's up?'

'It's what I was afraid of.' Ryan held up the stethoscope. 'Blockage in one of the tubes.' He tossed it into a cardboard box. 'Thanks, Father.'

'Any time.'

As Peter put his shirt on again he said he wished there was something he could do to help Mairie Kilfeather.

'I know how you feel,' Ryan said. 'But she could help herself.'

Peter went straight to see Ambrose, who was preparing for a meeting with his superiors in Wicklow. Peter told him what he suspected had happened to Mairie, and asked if it was true that something could now be done to help her.

'Yes, the law's been changed,' Ambrose said. 'I don't need her corroboration. Are you sure about this?'

'Well no, I'm not sure, but given her history . . . '

'I thought he'd calmed down.' Ambrose dug both hands deep into a filing cabinet. 'Is she badly hurt?'

'See for yourself.'

Peter followed Ambrose outside.

'He only stays home till his money runs out,' Ambrose said, dropping a stack of files in the boot of the police car. 'Then he's back to England.'

'What a prince.'

'I'll catch up with him,' Ambrose promised.

He got in the car and drove off. Ten minutes later he was at the smallholding that Mairie Kilfeather ran practically single-handed. As soon as she saw Ambrose she assured him that the bruise on her face was the result of an accident.

'Mairie,' Ambrose said, nearly pleading, 'listen to me, please. This doesn't have to keep happening. We can do things . . . '

Her husband Jimmy appeared from the house. He was a thin, seedy man with oily hair and a grubby suit. He came and stood beside Mairie. Between them they reinforced the story. Her bruise, according to the yarn, was the result of an entirely accidental collision of Jimmy's elbow with Mairie's face while he was banging nails into the skirting board and she, handing him the nails, got too close when he turned round.

'You're a liar and a bully,' Ambrose told Jimmy, 'and those are your good points. If I have to come out here again . . . '

Jimmy threw Ambrose an unconvincing look of disdain, then turned away. Mairie went indoors behind her husband.

Ambrose drove off to his meeting, certain that his business with Jimmy and Mairie Kilfeather still had some distance to run.

six

EARLY THE FOLLOWING morning, a Saturday, Peter went down to the bridge, rested his elbows on the parapet and gazed at the River Angel, as he did most mornings, letting the sound of it soothe him as he took these few minutes to gather his thoughts.

In common with most other people in the village, he was still worried about Brendan Kearney, who hadn't been seen in Ballykissangel since his dismissal by the School Board. And there was the matter of Enda. That was something harder to deal with, because there was only apprehension, and no perceptible wrong to put right. The young woman Peter and Padraig had seen slipping out of Enda's house was Enda's baby-sitter. Peter knew that now because she had come to confession and he recognised her. She had confessed that her love for this man was wrong, because he didn't truly love her in return. Peter believed she was a fine young woman with a faithful spirit, and Enda did not seem now to be quite such a straight and decent man as he would have people believe. There was also the worrying fact that Assumpta appeared to be drawn to him.

Peter's thoughts were interrupted by a movement down on the river-bank. Through the trees he saw what looked like shoulders in a pale blue robe, moving through the dappling shadows. As the figure moved to where the trees thinned he saw it was a statue of the Blessed Virgin, life size and crudely executed in polystyrene. A grey metal pan had been stuck to one of her hands. The statue was being carried by Liam and Donal.

Peter took the path from the end of the bridge down to the riverbank. He approached Liam and Donal as they set the effigy down on a concrete plinth near the water.

'I'm going to regret asking this,' Peter said.

'It's all bought and paid for,' Liam assured him.

'No, not that. Why is the Blessed Virgin – '

'Our Lady of Bonanza,' said Donal.

'Our Lady of what?'

'Our Lady of Bonanza, that's what she is.'

Peter paused to take that in. 'Why is Our Lady of Bonanza holding a wok?'

'What are you talking about, a wok? It's one of them yokes prospectors use.'

'A colander,' Donal said.

Liam shook his head. 'A sieve.' He smiled brightly at Peter. 'Was there something else, Father?'

'Ah, no, no.'

Liam turned to Donal. 'OK, switch it on.'

Donal pressed a switch on the back of the statue. The Blessed Virgin's heart began to glow red through her robes, on and off, on and off, like a beacon.

'Liam,' Peter groaned.

'I know.' Liam grinned proudly. 'What can you say?'

†

Later in the day Brian Quigley came down to view the enterprise on the riverbank. Donal was lounging at the foot of the statue, smoking a cigarette. On a table nearby were sieves and pans in various colours and materials, and beside the table was a free-standing brass multi-candle holder.

'Show a bit of respect, Donal, will you?' Quigley said.

Donal shot to his feet, touching his cap. 'Sorry, Mr Quigley.'

'Not to me. To her.'

Liam ambled out of the bushes, zipping up his fly.

'Oh, very nice,' Quigley drawled. 'You won't mind if I don't shake hands.'

'Do you want to light a candle?'

'Can I afford it?'

Liam shrugged. 'No obligation.'

'What's going on?'

Liam said they were setting up in business to take advantage of opportunities provided by tourism.

'And where are you going to get the tourists from?'

'Timmy Joe drives a tourist bus.'

'Oh right,' Quigley said. 'And you'll rent the tourists all the gear, will you?'

'We will,' said Donal.

'Which you've paid for.'

'Of course which we've paid for,' Liam said.

'Along with the statue.'

Liam nodded firmly. 'So?'

'So by the time you've cleared all that,' Quigley said, 'and paid off Timmy Joe, and looked after Father Mac – '

'Father Mac?'

'I think he'll insist.'

'What's your point?' Liam said

'When are you going to go into profit?' Quigley asked. 'Judgement Day?'

Liam and Donal looked at each other and tried, as they often did, not to look sheepish in front of Quigley.

†

That afternoon Siobhan made her weekly shopping trip to the supermarket in Cilldargan. When she had finished she lugged all the bags into a pub and took a stool at the bar. She ordered coffee and a ham sandwich. As the barman poured her coffee she turned and saw Brendan Kearney sitting alone at a table in the corner. He had a pint and a short in front of him.

Siobhan took her cup of coffee over to his table. 'Can I join you?'

Brendan looked up. 'It's a free country.' He looked away again.

Siobhan nodded at his lager and the whiskey chaser. 'Are you going for it?'

'Oh . . . ' He looked at her blearily. 'Should I be teaching?'

'It doesn't become you, self-pity.'

'Well maybe that's why I came down here to indulge it in peace.'

The barman brought Siobhan's ham sandwich. She handed him a tenner and he went for change. 'Here.' She pushed the sandwich in front of Brendan. 'At least line your stomach.'

'Siobhan, I – '

'I know, you and Greta Garbo.' She stood up, then sat down again. 'I'm going,' she promised. 'I just wanted to say this one thing. There are people at home that look up to you . . . and not all of them are children.'

She stood, picked up her coffee cup and went back to the bar.

At six o'clock that evening, Peter, Siobhan and Padraig sat on the bench opposite the bus stop in Ballykissangel. To pass the time, Peter had been telling the other two about the prospecting scam down by the river.

'Our Lady of Bonanza?' Padraig said.

Peter nodded. 'Apparently for centuries she's been standing down there by the river, just waiting for any passing prospector to make his pitch.'

Siobhan grinned. 'Is that right?'

'So the professor tells the tourists. You know the professor as Donal, of course.'

Padraig was thoughtful for a second. 'Where'd they get the batteries from?'

Peter frowned. 'Sorry?'

'In the seventeenth century, for her glowing heart, where did they get the batteries from?'

'They hooked her up to the mains,' Peter said.

'Ah, right.'

Siobhan pointed. 'Here it comes.'

The bus from Cilldargan came over the bridge and rounded the corner to the bus stop.

They sat calmly and waited. The bus pulled up and disgorged its passengers. Then Brendan, the last one, appeared at the top of the steps and stood there for a moment.

'He looks fine,' Peter said. 'Thank God for that.'

Brendan's knees gave way suddenly and he collapsed, falling down the steps and into the street.

They got him on his feet again and walked him back to his house. Peter stayed with him, plying him with hot coffee. By gradual stages a seething hangover pushed aside Brendan's intoxication. He began to talk. He began to argue. Peter believed that was a good sign, and saw it as an opportunity to raise the matter of young Eileen O'Connor.

Brendan wandered out through the French windows into the garden, clutching another mug of coffee.

'Of course I didn't tell her she didn't have to go to Mass,' he said.

Peter came out carrying a garden chair in one hand and a glass of fizzing Alka Seltzer in the other.

'Chaser.' He put the glass on the little garden table and sat down.

'I told her that when she grew up, the constitution allowed her to make a free choice.'

'Bit young to grasp the distinction, isn't she?'

'I didn't think so,' Brendan said. 'You might be right, but I didn't think so. The point is she asked, and where it won't hurt or confuse I try to give an honest answer.'

'I'd say it confused.'

'Ah, well . . . ' Brendan sniffed his coffee. 'You know everything, Father.'

'Have you talked to her mum?'

'I have.'

'And?'

'She doesn't agree with me.'

Hours later, down in Fitzgerald's, Brendan's value to the local educational system was once again the topic of conversation.

'I have three grandchildren there,' said Eamonn, 'and I think 'tis a disgrace.'

'The kids love him,' Padraig said.

Niamh was pulling on her coat. 'How's he taking all this? I heard he'd been hitting the jar.'

'What rubbish.' Siobhan looked incensed. 'Where did you hear that?'

'I saw him getting off the bus, and don't take it out on me, Siobhan.' Niamh turned to Peter and Padraig. 'If Ambrose comes in – '

'We'll tell him,' they said in unison.

Self-consciously Niamh slipped out, returning each greeting with brief nods of mounting mortification.

'Good luck there, Niamh,' called Timmy Joe Galvin, the tourist bus driver.

'Yeah . . . ' Assumpta waved. 'Good luck.'

Eamonn wished her all the best. By the time she got out through the door her face was scarlet.

'So,' Assumpta looked at her customers, 'this is how it's going to be, is it? Great man Brendan, we're all going to miss him?'

Padraig asked her what she meant.

'Are we going to talk about it all night,' she said, 'or are we going to do something?'

Ambrose came in. Siobhan, Peter, Padraig and Assumpta said, 'Go home!'

Ambrose turned and went out again.

Peter looked at Assumpta. 'Like what?' he said.

'Like a bit of direct action. Like taking our protest to the one man responsible for all this.'

'Father Mac,' Peter said.

'Exactly. And you're going to have to decide whose side you're on.'

With a fair amount of dignity, Peter turned and walked out.

'Bit strong there, Assumpta,' Padraig said.

'With the clergy?' she nodded. 'Every time.'

A moment after the door closed behind Peter, it opened again and Brendan walked in.

The place fell silent. Nobody was sure what to say. Brendan looked grim.

'Did somebody die in here?' he said. 'Assumpta, have you stopped serving?'

'Oh no,' she said, flustered, 'no.'

'Club orange, so,' Brendan said, 'and whatever anybody else wants.'

Siobhan closed her eyes with relief.

'I'll have a fizzy water with you, Brendan,' Padraig said.

'A Diet Coke would go down well,' said Siobhan.

Brendan looked at his friends and smiled shyly, glad to be back amongst them, back from the brink.

Next morning Padraig pulled up outside St Joseph's in a yellow minibus. Assumpta was beside him in the passenger seat. Peter stood at the church door in his green and white Mass vestments, shaking hands with the departing congregation, one eye unavoidably on the bus.

Padraig and Assumpta got out and opened the side doors. They began shepherding a little group on board – Siobhan, Eamonn, a clutch of children and their mothers – who carried with them a rolled-up banner.

Assumpta pulled the door shut behind the last one and stood staring at Peter as he continued to shake hands. He turned to look at her and saw the glare of contempt. She turned and got back in the bus.

Padraig drove down the main street and turned right across the bridge. At the far end of the bridge he passed Timmy Joe Galvin's tourist coach, parked at the top of the path leading down to the riverbank. Four tourists with cameras dangling from their necks were making their way back up to the coach from the riverside. They looked wearily contemptuous. Timmy Joe, standing by the front of the coach, looked down to where Donal and Liam were standing. He shrugged, which was his way of conveying that he had done what he could. Any flaws in the enterprise had nothing to do with him.

Donal, wearing the suit of dark tweed and the glasses that were supposed to bolster his credentials as a professor, shrugged back at Timmy Joe and blew out the few candles that had been lit. Liam switched off the Blessed Virgin's glowing heart and scooped the few coppers from the coin box. He looked round at the sound of crunching footsteps on the gravel. It was Quigley.

'Will I get Securicor for that?' he said brightly.

Donal and Liam tried, again, not to look sheepish.

'Nice suit, Donal.'

'What do you want?' Liam asked testily.

'That's not very polite now, is it? I've come to bail you out. If you're interested.'

Liam still looked surly. 'What do you mean, bail us out?'

'Your equipment,' Quigley said. 'Those pans and sieves and stuff, I'll buy 'em off you.'

Donal's face lit with hope.

'Why would you do that?' Liam said.

'I have a heart of gold. What do you say?'

'You'll give us what we paid for them?'

'I didn't say I had a brain of sponge. I'll give you half.'

'Half?'

'It's a better return than you'll ever get.'

'And what'll you do with the stuff?'

'Not your problem.'

Liam shook his head. 'No way.'

Quigley shrugged easily. He turned and walked back up the path. Donal looked as though he might cry.

A short time later the yellow minibus drew up outside Father Mac's presbytery, which stood beside the parish church in Cilldargan. As soon as the vehicle braked the passengers piled out.

Moments later Father Mac looked out of his study window and saw a group of demonstrators, orderly, silent and implacable, holding up a large banner which read

'Parents for Brendan Kearney:
the Best Man for the Job.'

Father Mac was furious. His anger went up another notch as Father Peter's ancient, elegant Jowett Javelin drew up and Peter got out and stood behind the banner.

Father Mac came storming out. 'What is the meaning of this? Father Clifford, are you with these people?'

Peter nodded. 'I am, Father. It's nothing personal.'

'Oh yes it is,' Assumpta shouted.

Peter looked embarrassed. 'Assumpta . . . '

Father Mac glared at her. 'I'll have your respect, Assumpta Fitzgerald.'

'In a parallel universe,' she said.

'You don't even have children!'

'I do,' Padraig said, and his cry was echoed by several others.

'And,' Padraig added, 'we want them taught by Brendan Kearney.'

That drew a roar of approval from the others. Father Mac flinched at the noise. He turned to Peter. 'When you have finished flaunting your liberation theology, I'll see you in my study.'

Peter stayed with the protesters a few minutes longer, just long enough to get Assumpta's silent acknowledgement that she approved of his action, then he decided to go in and face the music.

When the housekeeper showed him into the study he could see Father Mac's anger hadn't cooled. If anything it was worse than before, because he had been kept waiting. He stood by his desk, ashen faced, glaring.

'I have never,' he said, 'in all my years as a parish priest, encountered such insolence.'

'I'm sure she didn't – '

'I didn't mean Miss Fitzgerald. In the name of God, on a Sunday . . . to take the side of those gurriers against me!'

'It was a dignified protest,' Peter said.

'Don't talk to me about dignity. Where's the dignity in that?'

'Father, all they're saying – '

'They?'

'All right, we. All we're asking is please reconsider. Don't sack him.'

'He has not been sacked, he's been transferred.'

'And we'll lose him. Father – '

There was a loud knock at the study door. Brian Quigley's beaming face poked into the room, puffing on a fat cigar.

'God bless this house.'

He came into the room, brandishing a bottle of champagne.

'Brian,' Father Mac said, 'it's not – '

'Listen,' Quigley said, 'which one of you wants to do the christening?'

Father Mac frowned. 'What?'

'I'm going to be a grand-daddy!'

'Ambrose?' Peter said. 'He's done it? I mean, Niamh's pregnant?'

'Got it in one,' Quigley laughed, 'or in his case . . . '

'Brian . . . ' Peter slapped his shoulder, 'that's wonderful news. Congratulations.'

'I'm very happy for you, Brian,' Father Mac said, more coolly than Peter. 'Give my regards to them both.'

'Will we have a drink?'

'Probably not,' Peter said, glancing at Father Mac.

'Ah, go on,' Quigley said. 'Father Mac?'

'Yes,' Father Mac said, 'I'd say I'm entitled.'

'Absolutely,' Peter said, moving to the door. 'I'll be off then.'

Father Mac ignored him. Peter left.

SEVEN

AMBROSE AMBLED through the village instead of proceeding at the measured pace laid down in regulations. His face, for once, was a picture of happiness. As he passed a double-parked car the anxious-looking driver wound down the window.

'Can I park here just for a moment?'

'Of course you can,' Ambrose told him. 'Would you like me to look after it while you're away?'

'Uh, no, thank you.'

The driver smiled nervously, steeling himself for a volley of sarcasm. Ambrose simply smiled and walked away.

Peter, just back from the demo at Cilldargan, saw Ambrose and crossed the road to greet him.

'So it's true. A man really can walk on air.'

'How're you, Father?'

'Congratulations, mate, I'm made up for you. How's Niamh?'

'Looking through a book of names.'

Peter slapped him on the shoulder and hurried on into the church. He went straight to the sacristy, put on his black vestments and picked up his Bible. In the church he genuflected and crossed himself before the altar, then went to the confessional to wait for penitents.

While he waited he read from his Bible, turning to the Psalms, as he often did, to enjoy the rhythm of the words as much as their meaning. He whispered a favourite passage to himself, 'Keep me as the apple of thine eye, hide me under the shadow of thy wings.'

Someone stepped into the other side of the confessional. Peter heard agitated breathing, then a woman spoke.

'Bless me Father, it's been a week since my last confession. My name is Mairie Kilfeather.'

'You don't have to tell me that.'

'I think I do.'

Peter caught the hesitancy, the familiar false-starting of someone anxious to speak but unsure how to begin.

'No rush,' he said.

She began to talk about her husband, Jimmy. He had come home from the pub drunk that lunchtime. A taxi had brought him from Wicklow. He'd been grumbling about them throwing him out of the pub, just because he'd spent enough money with them to get merry.

'He wanted chips,' Mairie said, 'and I went to the cupboard and there was no oil. What could I do, only melt some fat. I did that, but he didn't want chips made with fat. I tried to explain, and he started hitting me.'

She stopped. Peter heard her take a deep breath, calming herself.

'I'll tell you Father, I could have put up with the beating, but it was when the hot fat from the pan fell on to my hand – and I swear to you Father, as God is my witness, until that moment I never meant him any harm.

'I struck him with the pan. I mean really struck him. And he fell and I hit him again . . . and he got up and I hit him again. And he got up on his knees and he said. "Mairie, for pity's sake", only I had no pity.

'I went to the door, and I opened the door and I said he was no longer welcome in the house.'

'And he left?'

'After I struck him again.'

'Where did he go?'

'I don't know, Father.' Her voice started to break. 'I think I might have killed him.'

They were both silent for a minute.

Finally Mairie spoke. 'Father, will you come with me to the Guards?'

Peter took her to the police office, which formed one side of the house where Ambrose and Niamh lived. As they walked in, Ambrose was putting down the telephone. He appeared startled to see Mairie there.

'Mairie! Are you OK?'

'Never mind me . . . '

'She thinks she might have killed her husband,' Peter said.

'She might have done, too,' Ambrose said, 'if I hadn't found him.'

Mairie took a sharp breath.

'I got a call from the Wicklow police to tell me he'd been kicked out of a pub there and put in a taxi home. I thought I'd best go out to the house and make sure everything was all right.'

'Where did you find him?' Peter said.

'In the river. He was a bit of a mess, and I noticed that gold tooth of his was missing. The ambulance is taking him to hospital now.' Ambrose looked at Mairie. 'What did you use, the skillet?'

Mairie nodded. Ambrose winced. Then he smiled. 'Will I put on the kettle?' he said.

†

That night Enda Sullivan did a gig at Fitzgerald's. To his own guitar accompaniment and a taped orchestral backing he sang song after song, sweet contemporary numbers that held the regulars spellbound for over an hour. Peter found the performance enchanting, but his stomach did an involuntary twitch when he noticed the intense way Assumpta was staring at Enda.

At the end of the evening Peter learned from an inebriated Brian Quigley that Father Mac, having overdone the celebration champagne that afternoon, and then again later in Fitzgerald's, was now asleep in Peter's house. Peter asked how he got in.

Quigley grinned drunkenly at him. 'I have a key. I own the place.'

'Oh, cheers, Brian. Next thing you'll be telling me is he's in my bed.'

Quigley nodded. 'Better you know now.'

Brendan, meanwhile, had driven Enda home, and when they reached the house Enda suggested coffee. Brendan said it would make a nice change from orange juice.

They went into the house and as they entered the living-room the baby-sitter, Aileen Hegarty, stood up from the settee, where she had been reading a book.

'Aileen,' Enda said, 'sorry I'm a bit late . . . '

'No problem,' she said. 'He was good as gold.'

'Great stuff,' Enda said. 'You're all right to get home?'

For a moment she was unable to hide her disappointment, and Brendan couldn't help noticing. She recovered quickly and brought back her fading smile.

'I'm fine,' she said.

'You're sure?'

'Really.'

She and Enda went to the front door.

'Aileen,' he whispered, facing her, 'I'm sorry, he gave me a lift home, I had to ask him in.'

'I know.'

Enda brushed the side of her face with the back of his hand and smiled. He did not kiss her but he kept his face close to hers. Systematically, with a light brush of her hair, a touch on the side of her neck, he manipulated

Aileen's mood until she was smiling with apparent gratitude. Still smiling, she backed out of the house, bathed in the warmth radiating from Enda.

When he returned to the living-room Brendan was studying his CD collection. He turned.

'Enda, can I ask you something?'

'Baby-sitter,' Enda said. 'Daughter of a friend.'

'No, the child upstairs . . . is he your child?'

'He is.'

Enda wandered through to the kitchen and Brendan followed him.

'How old would he be?'

'He would be nine,' Enda said, filling the kettle.

'You must think I'm very nosy.'

'Not at all.' Enda plugged in the kettle and spooned coffee into mugs. 'His mother lives in America but she'd like him to go to school here.'

Brendan looked stunned.

Enda pointed to the spirits bottles in the corner of the worktop. 'Are you sure you wouldn't like anything stronger?'

'Which school, exactly?'

'Well,' Enda said, 'I hope you won't be offended, Brendan, but the local school, of course. Why, is it full?'

Brendan smiled tightly. 'Not exactly. You really don't know?'

'Well, I know they're giving you the elbow. Are you telling me there's no place for the boy either?'

Brendan smiled. 'Do you know, I think I will have something stronger.'

Peter slept on the couch that night, with Father Mac snoring in the bed upstairs. At four o'clock in the morning Peter had dropped into his fifth or sixth fitful sleep of the night when there was a loud hammering on the front door.

'Oh great!'

He sat on the edge of the couch for a minute, letting the thumping in his chest settle, then he pulled on his dressing-gown and shuffled to the door. He opened it and blinked a couple of times.

'Brendan?'

'I know it's late. I thought you'd want to know.'

They went indoors, sat down and talked. After a few minutes Peter forgot how tired he was. As the sun began to rise, he and Brendan went out for a bracing walk across the fields behind the church. When they got back, Peter made a telephone call, then he and Brendan took turns to freshen up in the bathroom.

At nine o'clock, just as Peter had arranged four mugs on a tray and had spooned instant coffee into each, there was a knock at the front door. Peter opened it to find Brian Quigley on the step, hung-over and looking angry.

'Well?'

'Come in, Brian,' Peter said smoothly, 'how are you feeling this morning?'

Quigley followed him inside. 'Save it for the punters, Father.' He pointed at the ceiling. 'Is he up?'

'Well, I don't know about Homo erectus, but he's on his feet.'

As Peter spoke Father Mac came downstairs in trousers and vest, dabbing his face with a towel and looking dreadful. He glowered at Quigley. 'What is it, Brian? Couldn't it wait until I had a cup of tea?'

Quigley looked puzzled. 'You wanted to see me.'

Brendan appeared from the kitchen.

'What's he doing here?' Quigley said.

Brendan smiled and spread his arms. 'Brian, Father Mac . . . oh, happy day.'

They all sat down with coffee. Peter explained that Enda's son would shortly be enrolling at the local school.

'Which brings the numbers up to fifty-eight, thus entitling the Board of Management to take on – sorry, take back, a third teacher.' Peter threw a hard-eyed look at Father Mac. 'You must be delighted, Father.'

Father Mac was seething. He looked at Quigley, who simply shrugged and stood up. He looked casually around the room.

'About due for a rent review, aren't we?' He went to the door and opened it. 'I'll be in touch, Father. Well played, Brendan.'

Ten minutes later, as Donal and Liam stood morosely in the midst of their unused pile of sieves and pans, Brian Quigley came crunching down the path to the riverbank.

'Great,' Liam grunted.

As Quigley approached he pointed to the statue of the Blessed Virgin on its plinth. 'Maybe she disapproves. Did you ever think of that?'

'What do you want now?' Liam demanded.

'I have a job for you. If you can spare the time.'

Donal threw a small hopeful look at Liam, who was sagging with defeat, in spite of himself.

'It wasn't a bad idea,' Liam said. 'It could have worked, you know.'

'Oh, I know,' Quigley agreed.

Liam said, 'Is that offer still open?'

'What offer?'

'To buy our stuff.'

Quigley laughed. 'I don't know about that.'

'What difference does a day make?'

'What difference?' Quigley thought about it. 'Twenty-five per cent.'

Donal stared at him. 'You said you'd give us half.'

'Exactly,' Quigley said. 'It's a better return than you'll ever get.'

Donal looked at Liam. He shrugged, caving in.

'OK,' Donal said, 'what's the job?'

'Gather up all that stuff and take it down to Farrell's – '

'The tour operator?' Liam said.

'Yeah, in Wicklow, he'll take it off your hands.'

Liam's eyes narrowed a fraction. 'He's expecting it?'

'He's expecting it, yes.'

'You've already sold it to him?'

Quigley smiled faintly. 'It's just business, Liam. Nothing personal.'

'How much?' Liam said.

Quigley shook his head. 'Don't do this to yourself.'

'I have to know,' Liam insisted.

Quigley leaned forward and whispered in his ear.

'What?' Liam was appalled.

'I know,' Quigley said. 'It's a miracle, isn't it?'

Later, when Liam and Donal had removed all the tackle from the riverbank, Enda took up his usual position down-river of the bridge and started panning. Assumpta, out walking Finn, saw him there and came down the path to the side of the river.

Enda was examining something he had trapped in his sieve. He picked it up and turned it. He realised suddenly what it was. A gold tooth.

'Got your claim back then?' Assumpta said.

'Yup.'

'Enda, you could prospect in this river for the next hundred years and not find enough gold to make a tooth.'

'I think I have.' He held up the tooth.

'Let it grow.'

Enda flipped the tooth back into the river.

'Don't you feel better for that?' Assumpta said.

'Not really.'

Enda came to the edge. Assumpta held out a hand and helped him onto the bank.

'Thanks for last night,' she said, as he fell into step beside her. 'It was good.'

'If I'd a pound for every time a woman said that to me . . . '

'Yeah, yeah.'

'Do you do breakfast?' he said.

Assumpta stopped. 'I don't give it away.'

She walked on. Enda stayed where he was for a moment. 'That's the challenge, then,' he said.

He put down his sieve on a stone in front of the abandoned statue of the Blessed Virgin, then hurried along the bank to catch up with Assumpta.

EIGHT

AT TEN TO NINE on Monday morning the traffic along Ballykissangel's main street was blocked by Liam and Donal setting out traffic cones. They worked under the direction of Brian Quigley, who shouted instructions at them through an electric megaphone. At one side of the street was a canvas chair with 'Quigley' printed on the back; in the middle of the road a video camera had been set up on a tripod. Responding to Quigley's barrage of orders, Liam and Donal finished off blocking the road and took up their positions – Liam behind the camera, Donal with a headset and a stick microphone

Brendan Kearney was at the head of the queue of traffic on his bike. He watched the activity of Quigley and his crew for a couple of minutes, then decided it was time to complain on behalf of himself and the cars and vans backed up behind him.

'Brian! What are you doing?'

'I won't be a minute.' Quigley put the megaphone to his mouth and shouted, 'You know what to do, Eamonn?'

Eamonn's head appeared round the corner of a house up the street, wearing a green leprechaun-style hat. He gave Quigley a thumbs-up sign.

'I'll cue you when we're ready,' Quigley told him.

Eamonn disappeared again behind the building.

Siobhan leaned out of the Land Rover behind Brendan. 'What's going on?'

Brendan shrugged. 'Ask the director.'

Quigley heard that and addressed them over his shoulder. 'A cousin of mine in America gave me the idea. He said a video about the town and its people would attract tourists to the area. And you know what tourists mean.'

'Traffic jams?' Siobhan said.

The line of vehicles was getting longer and horns were tooting impatiently. One driver banged on his horn five times, issuing a longer note at each thump.

Quigley waved his clipboard at him. 'Just wait a minute, will you?'

'Will you get on with it, Brian?' Brendan said. 'Some of us have got work to do.'

'You can't rush these things.' Quigley closed on Brendan and his bike. 'Move back a bit now, will you?'

Peter came down the road from the church, carrying a small bag of coins.

'Ah, Father.' Quigley beamed at him. 'You're just in time for the opening shot.'

'What's going on?'

'It's a promotional film.'

'What's it promoting?'

'Brian Quigley,' Brendan said.

'Ballykissangel,' Quigley said, glaring at Brendan. 'Watch, Father. Liam, are you ready?'

'Ready, Mr Quigley.'

'Sound?'

There was no response from Donal, who was still fiddling with the microphone and his cans, oblivious to everything.

'Sound?'

Still no response from Donal. Quigley stepped forward and yelled into the microphone with his megaphone. 'Sound?'

Donal leapt in the air. 'Ready, Mr Quigley.'

'OK. Quiet, everyone . . . '

Silence descended on the main street.

Quigley raised his hand with the clipboard and pressed the megaphone close to his mouth. 'And . . . action!'

Everyone looked up the street. Nothing.

'Action!'

Suddenly from behind the building Eamonn appeared astride a donkey. Now his whole ensemble could be seen, a comic-book 'Irish' costume of hat, wellington boots, tweed trousers, hairy shirt and wide braces.

Siobhan blinked. 'What on earth? . . .'

'Traditional rural Ireland,' Quigley said with some pride. 'It's what the Americans want. My cousin in Boston told me.'

Siobhan and Brendan exchanged a look. Eamonn seemed very unstable as he attempted to steer the donkey down the middle of the main street. The creature paid no attention to what Eamonn wanted. It veered off in completely the wrong direction.

'This way, Eamonn!' Quigley yelled into the megaphone.

'I'm trying,' Eamonn piped desperately.

As he tugged on the reins the donkey stopped, backed up a couple of yards and jerked forward again, making Eamonn sway dangerously on its back.

'Has he ever ridden a donkey before?' Peter said.

Quigley nodded. 'He told me he had.'

'People will say anything on a casting couch,' Brendan muttered.

The donkey now looked as if it was fed up with Eamonn. It trotted a few yards one way, turned and trotted the other way, then stopped abruptly and pitched him into the gutter.

'Cut!' Quigley yelled. 'Cut! Cut!'

He turned away in frustration, just in time to see Ambrose striding purposefully towards him.

'Oh wonderful.'

Peter crossed the road to Fitzgerald's where Assumpta was unloading boxes from the back of her van.

She pointed to the film crew. 'Are you not involved in this then, Peter?'

They watched Ambrose remonstrating with Quigley while Liam and Donal scurried around gathering up the camera equipment.

'No thanks.' Peter held up the bag of coins and shook it. 'Do you think you could change this for me?'

'I think I can manage. Just.'

As they turned from the van to go into the pub Enda Sullivan appeared, walking down the road with his son, Feargal, and Aileen, the baby-sitter.

'Morning, Father,' Enda called. 'Assumpta.'

The look Enda gave Assumpta was not pitched to disguise his interest in her. No one missed it, and it appeared to offend Aileen.

Peter smiled and dutifully asked after the health of Enda and Aileen. They both said that they were fine, and Aileen struggled to make a little smile.

'What about you, Feargal?' Peter said. 'How are you settling down in your new school?'

'OK,' the boy said sullenly.

'He loves it,' Enda said, 'don't you, son?'

Feargal shrugged.

'I went there when I was your age,' Assumpta told him. 'I was always getting into trouble for being late even though I lived the closest.'

Feargal avoided looking at Assumpta.

'That explains a lot,' Enda quipped.

Assumpta told him to behave or he would be barred.

'Promises, promises,' Enda laughed.

Aileen looked uncomfortable at this jousting. Feargal tugged her arm.

'Come on,' he said. 'We're late.'

Aileen touched Enda's arm, making an awkward show of intimacy for Assumpta's benefit. 'See you later,' she said to Enda.

As Aileen and Feargal moved off Assumpta turned to Peter. 'I'll sort that change out for you.'

Peter gave her the bag of coins. She weighed it in her hand. 'You'll not be heading for Rio just yet.'

'No, I think Cilldargan is about as far as I'm going today.'

'Oh, if you're heading that way, Father,' Enda said, 'can I cadge a lift off you? My car's in having a physical.'

'Sure.'

†

On the way into Cilldargan Enda explained that he was going to look at a guitar he had seen in a shop there. It was an extravagance, he admitted, but he had yet to make a final decision about the instrument, and it didn't hurt to keep in touch with it while he was making up his mind.

Peter's errand was more serious. He had come to talk to Father Mac about the dwindling attendances at St Joseph's.

In the parish priest's study they sat facing each other across the desk, sipping weak tea made by the housekeeper.

'There aren't enough new young people in the congregation,' Peter said. 'Frankly, all the regulars are knocking on a bit.'

Father Mac nodded. 'Aren't we all?'

'Trouble is, I'm not quite sure what to do about it. Moving the time of the Mass might help but I don't think it'll be enough.'

'Well, Father Clifford, it's your responsibility to make sure your church is full of the faithful whatever time of day it is.'

'Any suggestions will be gratefully received.'

'I'm sure you'll find a way,' Father Mac said. 'After all, there is an incentive for you to increase the size of your congregation.'

'What's that?'

'Your electricity bill. Unless you want to be responsible for Ireland's first disconnected church.'

The problem hung over Peter like a dense cloud as he drove back through Cilldargan. Stopping at a red light, he heard gospel music on the radio and turned up the volume. After a moment he realised two significant things had happened, both of them in spite of his gloom. One, he had instinctively turned up the music when he heard its insistent, uplifting beat, and two, in spite of feeling so rotten, he had been sitting there tapping his foot in time to the tune.

One thought led to another. He switched off his left indicator and turned on the right. When the traffic light changed to green he drove back into the centre of Cilldargan and parked at McNeill's Music Shop.

Mr McNeill asked how he could help.

'Do you have any gospel sheet music – you know, real upbeat Christian songs?'

'Certainly, Father. If you wait a moment, I'll find a selection for you.'

McNeill disappeared to a back room. Peter wandered through to the rear of the shop, following the pleasant sound of guitar music. As he thought, Enda Sullivan was sitting there, engrossed in his sound, his head low over the body of the guitar as he played. When he finished Peter applauded.

'Very good, Enda,' he said, as yet another idea formed. 'Very good indeed.'

'Well, it helps when you have an instrument like this.'

'What are you doing Sunday morning?'

Enda thought for a moment. 'Going to Mass?'

Peter grinned. 'I was hoping you'd say that.'

†

Quigley was making slow progress with his film. The second item on the shooting list for that morning was a visit to the general store of Kathleen Hendley. Kathleen, who was also the organist at St Joseph's, was a sour-faced widow in her sixties who never smiled much, and who was inclined to judge people by their worst characteristics. She had agreed to appear in Quigley's film only because she believed that her own presence in promotional material for Ballykissangel could only help sway the balance in the direction of rectitude and decent values.

The camera was set up opposite the counter, Donal was on his knees below frame level with the microphone, and Quigley was beside Liam at the camera, holding up a wad of large prompt cards. Kathleen was behind the counter, wetting her dry lips with the tip of her tongue, her knuckles white with tension.

'Action.' Quigley held up the cards.

Grim-faced, Kathleen cleared her throat before speaking. 'Hello. My name is Kathleen Hendley and I own the village shop in Ballykissangel.'

Quigley made an exaggerated smile and pointed to his mouth, trying to get Kathleen to relax and look halfway pleasant. Her response was to force a tight smile that made her expression slightly worse.

'Every day,' she read stiffly, 'I get fish deliveries to the shop and . . . '

'Cut!'

Kathleen looked mystified. 'What's the matter now?'

Quigley pointed to the prompt card. 'It's fresh deliveries, not fish.'

Kathleen scowled at him. 'It's your writing,' she said.

'No wonder they're called idiot boards,' Quigley mumbled.

They did the scene again, and this time Quigley dropped a card. On the third take everything went well, although Liam quietly observed that he thought Kathleen looked a bit stiff and unreal.

'A true-to-life performance, then,' Quigley muttered. 'Come on, get this stuff outside.'

They set up on the steps in front of the window display and Kathleen, holding a packet of potato cakes, faced a new set of prompt cards.

'Action!'

'As you can see,' Kathleen said, peering slightly to see the words, 'I sell many things in here but the most pop-ular item, of course, is – ' she held up the prop; 'potato bread . . . ' Her tight smile suddenly went back to a scowl. 'Stop!' she shouted.

'Cut!' Quigley stared at her. 'What's up now?'

'The most popular item in my shop is not potato bread. It's Pot Noodle.'

'Potato bread is more traditional, Kathleen.'

'I don't care. I refuse to tell blatant lies to anyone, especially on film.'

Quigley took a deep breath. 'Do you want to be in this or don't you?'

'I'm beginning to wonder.'

'So am I!'

Kathleen turned and stomped off into the shop.

'God preserve me from amateurs,' Quigley groaned, going after her.

That afternoon, a bunch of flowers was delivered to Assumpta from a florist's in Cilldargan. The card simply said, 'Affectionately, Enda'. Assumpta put the flowers in a vase of water behind the bar.

Later, when Peter dropped him off in the main street, Enda went into the pub. Padraig was in his usual place at the end of the bar, talking to Assumpta. She broke off to pull Enda a pint. The conversation changed direction to take account of Enda's presence. Assumpta asked him if he'd done much shopping in Cilldargan that morning, and she made a sidelong glance at the flowers. He told her and Padraig that he had lost his heart to an item in Mr McNeill's music shop.

'You should see this guitar,' he said. 'It's the work of angels.'

'So why don't you buy it?' Padraig asked him.

'I'd have to make too many sacrifices.'

Assumpta raised her eyebrows. 'Such as?'

'Well, for a start, I couldn't afford to take you out to dinner tonight.'

Assumpta chose to look amused, for the sake of appearances. A slight flush at the line of her jaw suggested she had been seriously affected by the remark.

Enda was staring at her. 'What do you say?'

Before she had a chance to say anything, young Feargal Sullivan came into the pub, followed by Kevin O'Kelly.

'Your son's here,' Assumpta said, as Enda continued to stare at her.

Enda turned to the boy. 'What are you up to?'

Feargal was looking at Assumpta with obvious disdain.

'We're going to walk the dog,' Kevin said.

Padraig introduced his son to Enda.

'How d'you do, Kevin?'

Kevin smiled and blushed. 'OK,' he said.

'You know where the dog is,' Assumpta said.

'Come on,' Kevin said to Feargal.

Feargal said he would wait with his dad. Kevin went round the bar and disappeared into the kitchen.

Enda looked at Assumpta again. 'So do we have a date?'

'Only if you let me take you out.'

'All right,' Enda said. 'I'll get Aileen to baby-sit.'

Feargal was frowning. He asked his father where he was going.

'Mind your own business.'

'I suppose Niamh wouldn't mind,' Assumpta said. 'I'd have to check with her.'

'Sort it out,' Enda said, 'and I'll come round in a taxi about eight.'

'No, we'll use my van.'

'OK.'

Now Feargal was scowling at Assumpta.

NINE

AILEEN HAD STAYED late at the cottage to play a game of Snap with Feargal. For once he didn't appear to enjoy the play and kept missing opportunities to snatch cards. When Aileen asked him what was wrong he said it was nothing, but something was obviously troubling him.

As Aileen won the fourth game in a row Enda came halfway down the stairs. He smiled hesitantly. 'Aileen, I know it's short notice, but do you think you could baby-sit tonight?'

'Sure. Have you got a gig?'

'Well, not as such, no . . . '

Feargal stared at his father accusingly. 'He's going out with Assumpta Fitzgerald.'

Aileen could never help letting her face betray her feelings. At that moment she looked shocked and hurt.

'Is that right?' she asked Enda.

'Yeah, well, I, you know – yes.'

'Really.'

Enda watched Aileen withdraw into herself. 'It's OK then?' he said.

She shook her head. 'Sorry, I've just remembered. I can't do tonight, I have to go out.'

'Where?'

'I have my own social life, too, you know.' It wasn't convincing, but Aileen's tone made it clear that she wouldn't change her mind. 'You'll just have to find someone else instead.'

Later, when she had gone, Enda shaved and got changed. He put on a red shirt and his best black jacket. Feargal watched sullenly as he checked his hair at the mirror in the living room.

'Right, young fella, let's be having you.'

'Where are we going?' Feargal said.

'I'm going to dinner. You're going to spend the evening with a friend.'

Ten minutes later they were down at Padraig's house at the lower end of Ballykissangel. Enda explained to Padraig that the baby-sitter had let him down at the last minute. He said he knew it was short notice, and a bit of a cheek, but did Padraig think Feargal could spend the evening with

Kevin? Padraig said that would be fine.

'You're a saviour,' Enda told him.

'No problem. Go inside, Feargal, he's in there somewhere.'

Feargal went into the house, but not before he had thrown his father a look of deepest contempt.

Meanwhile, at Fitzgerald's, Eamonn was sitting at the bar, still wearing his bright green hat and lighting up a cigar with a certain amount of flourish.

'So what's your next film, Eamonn?' Siobhan asked him.

'I don't know yet,' he said, blowing out the match. 'I'm waiting for the call.'

'You don't understand, Eamonn,' Brendan said. '"Don't phone us" means "keep your day job".'

'You wait,' Eamonn blew a plume of smoke into the air above his head, 'the offers'll come flooding in once I get myself an agent.'

Assumpta appeared from the room behind the bar. She wore a matching mustard jacket and long skirt with a white top.

'You going like that?' Niamh said.

Assumpta nodded. 'What's wrong with it?'

Niamh grinned. 'It depends how you want the evening to go.'

Assumpta made a face and went back to the parlour to touch up her lipstick.

As usually happened around nine o'clock, the pub started to get busy. Ambrose came in and ordered a pint of lager and a packet of crisps. A couple of minutes later Brian Quigley appeared with Liam and Donal. Quigley, in surly mood, ordered the drinks and sat down with his employees at a table by the door.

When Peter came in he was greeted by several people at once. Niamh took the opportunity of the diversion to lean across the bar and take a handful of crisps from Ambrose's packet. Ambrose saw her do it. He was a bit annoyed but said nothing, since his wife's recent food cravings were something he believed he must learn to live with until they had run their course.

'A glass, is it, Father?' Niamh asked through a mouthful of crisps.

'Thanks.'

Ambrose said, 'You wouldn't order some crisps, too, would you, Father? I seem to have lost mine.'

Peter asked where Assumpta was.

'She's going out tonight, on a date,' Niamh said. 'Enda.' She pointed to the flowers. 'They're from him.'

'Oh. Right.' Peter smiled uncertainly.

'Father,' Quigley called, 'do you know anyone who might like to front our film? Preferably someone famous.'

'I don't know about famous. Shouldn't it be someone local? Give it authenticity?'

'My point exactly,' said Eamonn, but Quigley was ignoring him now, after the fiasco with the donkey.

'Are you volunteering, Father?' Quigley said.

'No, thanks all the same. I'm busy arranging a new kind of Mass for Sunday.'

'What's the idea?' Ambrose asked.

'To get more people in.'

Siobhan asked if Peter was offering good money.

'No, but I am offering a new sound. A folk Mass. Enda's playing his guitar for me.'

'What about the gorgon on the organ?' asked Brendan.

'If you mean Kathleen, I haven't told her yet, but I'm sure she'd like a break from her duties.'

Brendan nodded. 'I know we would.'

Peter turned to Quigley. 'What about you, Brian? Why don't you be in the film yourself? Lots of directors work in front as well as behind the camera.'

'You mean like an actor-director?' Quigley said.

'Why not?'

Quigley looked thoughtful for a moment. He smiled, warming to the idea. 'Why not, indeed?'

Liam and Donal threw each other worried looks.

Enda came in and went to the bar.

'Is she ready?' he asked Niamh.

At that moment Assumpta appeared. She smiled awkwardly at Enda as she came around the bar.

'I won't be late,' she told Niamh.

'Take your time,' Niamh said, and winked.

†

They went to La Perla, an Italian restaurant in Cilldargan. The place was pleasantly busy, with just enough buzzing conversation to eliminate the possibility of awkward silences. Assumpta went for the pasta starter, which was spaghetti in a garlic and butter sauce. Enda ordered the same, and ended up struggling with the mechanics of getting the stuff into his mouth.

'I've never been very good at this,' he apologised.

'I suppose you're more used to the hoops,' Assumpta said.

He put on a wounded look. 'Not all single parents live on tinned food.'

Assumpta smiled. 'So what's this I hear about you doing a gig in St Joseph's on Sunday?'

'Father Clifford asked me.'

'Not really your scene, is it?'

Enda managed to get a coil of spaghetti to hold around his fork. He stuck it in his mouth quickly. 'I note a hint of disapproval,' he mumbled.

'It'll take more than gimmicks to get me into a church.'

'Well, for an atheist, you seem to get on OK with the priest.'

'I'm not an atheist,' Assumpta said, 'and even if I was, it wouldn't stop me being friends with Peter. He's a good man.'

'Yeah, well anyway, we didn't come here to talk about Peter.'

'I know. Who shall we talk about then?'

'Anyone you like.'

'OK.' Assumpta rolled several strands of spaghetti expertly on her fork. 'How about Aileen?'

Enda immediately looked evasive. 'What can I tell you?'

'How well do you "know" her?'

'Reasonably.'

'What about biblically?'

Enda narrowed one eye. 'I thought we were keeping off religion?'

Assumpta abandoned the questioning. For a minute they ate in silence.

Finally Enda said, 'My relationship with Aileen is purely professional. One of mutual convenience. She needs the money, I need a baby-sitter.'

'Sounds very clinical.'

'That's the way it is.'

Assumpta smiled at him over her glass.

As the evening wore on, the wine and the good food had a mellowing effect. Enda proved to be amusing company. He bantered with the waiter between telling Assumpta tales of his days on the road with the band. Before they knew it, the time had come to leave.

The waiter banged down a plate with the bill in front of Enda.

'Thanks,' he said, carefully displaying the kind of smile designed to turn away wrath.

Assumpta was smiling, too, with amusement. 'He is not happy,' she said.

Enda shrugged. 'I was only trying to explain why Ireland beat Italy in the World Cup.'

He reached for his wallet.

'I'll get this,' Assumpta said.

'You will not.'

Assumpta pulled the plate towards her and looked at the bill. 'Well OK,' she said, 'we'll split it.'

'Whatever.' Enda spread his hands in a gesture of submission, smiling. 'Let's do it and get out of here – there's something I want to show you.'

When they left the restaurant Enda led Assumpta round a corner to the left, then round another to the right. They stopped in front of McNeill's Music Shop. The guitar with which Enda had become mildly obsessed was displayed in the centre of the window, its blue-green finish glowing like a cool beacon on the darkened street.

'This is it, then,' Assumpta said.

'This is it,' Enda nodded. 'Isn't it magnificent? And it plays like a dream.'

Assumpta looked at him. 'I could buy it and you could pay me back in gigs.'

Enda frowned, staring at the guitar.

'It's good business,' Assumpta said.

He nodded slowly. 'I'll think about it.'

'Better be quick. I'll probably take it all back tomorrow.'

Assumpta walked off to where she had parked the van. Enda followed her.

†

Late that evening Peter stood in the sacristy at St Joseph's and completed his rough draft of the poster to advertise the folk Mass. When he was finished, he went into the church to lock up. He blew out the few burning candles and as he turned at the altar he noticed a woman sitting in a pew near the back of the church. Moving closer, he saw it was Aileen Hegarty. Getting closer still, he could see she had been crying.

'Hello, Father.'

'May I join you?'

She nodded and Peter sat next to her.

'Sorry,' she said. 'I know it's late. I just had to go somewhere.'

'In my opinion,' Peter said, 'there's no better somewhere.'

He sat quietly and waited, letting Aileen take her time to say what she clearly needed to say.

'I thought the man I love didn't love me. Now I know for sure.'

'You seem very certain.'

'He's seeing another woman, Father. He's gone out with her tonight.'

Peter tried to remain impassive but it was hard.

'I love him, Father. I'm jealous, but what's the point if he doesn't love me?'

'Maybe he does, but he's just not very good at showing it. You know what some men are like.'

She sighed. 'I know what Enda's like.'

'Then ask him what he really wants.'

Aileen shook her head: she couldn't. She turned in the pew and looked at Peter.

'You want me to have a word with him?'

'Would you, Father?'

It was the last thing he wanted to do. 'I'll try,' he said.

As Peter agonised over how he would approach Enda with this difficulty, elsewhere Padraig was also worried about what he would tell Enda. The problem was, young Feargal had disappeared. The boys had been playing hide and seek, and on Feargal's turn to hide, he vanished.

Padraig and Kevin looked high and low, calling for the boy, widening the search to take in the streets beyond Padraig's house and around his filling station. After half an hour they gave up.

'God in heaven, what's happened to him?'

As Padraig stood in the road in front of his house, bewildered and worried sick, Assumpta and Enda were drawing up in her van outside Enda's farmhouse.

Enda got out and walked round to the driver's door. Assumpta got out and looked up at him.

'So,' she said, 'have you thought about it?'

He nodded. 'All right.'

Suddenly the front door of the house was flung open. Bright light flooded out into the dark. Feargal was standing in the doorway, staring at his father.

'What the – what are you doing here?'

Feargal said nothing. He was staring at Assumpta now.

'Did Mr O'Kelly bring you home?'

'No,' Feargal said. 'I walked.'

Enda grabbed him by the arm. 'You did what?'

'Enda, please,' Assumpta whispered.

Enda released the boy. 'You have some explaining to do, young man.'

'I should go.' Assumpta turned back to the van.

'No, please . . . ' Enda turned to Feargal. 'Go to bed this minute. I'll speak to you in the morning.'

Feargal was fighting back tears. He ran inside.

Assumpta noticed headlights approaching along the lane.

'I'm sorry about this,' Enda said. 'I'd better call Padraig.'

'No need.'

Padraig's car drew up in front of the house. Enda went forward as Padraig wound down his window. When he spoke he sounded frantic.

'Enda, I'm so sorry, so terribly sorry, but I don't know where Feargal – '

'It's OK, Padraig, he's here. He's fine.'

'What?'

'He's home, in the house. He's safe and sound.'

'Oh, thank God.'

'I was going to walk down later and pick him up,' Enda said. 'Sorry.'

'No, no.' Padraig shook his head, hugely relieved. 'As long as he's OK.'

'He is now,' Enda said. 'I can't promise how he'll be after I've finished with him.'

'Don't be too hard on him,' Assumpta said.

'I'll be off then,' Padraig called.

Enda thanked him again.

'No problem. Goodnight, Assumpta.'

As Padraig drove off Assumpta got back in the van and started the engine.

'I'm off, too,' she said.

'Come in for a coffee.' Enda put his face down at the open van window. 'We could both use one.'

Assumpta shook her head. 'Talk to Feargal,' she said.

Enda stood back and waved, trying to hold onto his smile as she drove away.

TEN

ONE OF EAMONN'S cows was about to calf, and Quigley thought that would be a perfect opportunity to film an event in the average working day of Ballykissangel's vet. A few minutes before nine in the morning Liam and Donal had the video equipment set up in Eamonn's barn. Siobhan was already in her parturition gown, ready to go to work. Eamonn stood by, ready for any opportunity to appear in shot, while Quigley made last-minute adjustments to his script.

'I'm going to have to deliver this calf soon,' Siobhan warned him.

'OK, we're all set,' he said. 'Now first of all, I'm going to introduce you as Ballykay's resident vet, then we get a shot of you here delivering Eamonn's cow. You got that?'

'I think so.'

'Good.'

Eamonn stepped forward. 'Where do I stand?'

'I don't need you for this,' Quigley said.

'What d'you mean? It's my cow!'

'And it's my film.'

Siobhan pointed out that she needed Eamonn to hold aside the tail.

'Right.' Quigley gestured impatiently at the pregnant cow. 'Take up your position, Eamonn. Quickly!'

Donal had sidled over to Siobhan, clutching his microphone on a pole. 'This isn't going to be too gory, is it?' he whispered.

Siobhan coated her hands vigorously with lubricant. 'Sure don't all good films have a bit of blood and guts in them?'

Donal stepped back. He looked queasy.

'And, action!'

Quigley stepped forward and addressed the camera, at approximately the same moment that Siobhan slid her arm inside the cow to palpate the calf's head.

'Ballykissangel is of course mainly a rural community,' Quigley said. 'Siobhan Mehigan is the local vet. Here she is about to deliver a new calf.'

'Any minute now,' Siobhan said as the camera turned towards her. As she repositioned her hand within the animal there were a number of squelching sounds and some nervous mooing from the cow. Suddenly it was all too much for Donal. As the blood drained from his face he pitched forward and landed on the barn floor in a dead faint, right in front of the camera.

'Cut!' Quigley roared.

Elsewhere, Peter was feeling no more cheerful than Brian Quigley. His first job of the morning had been to explain to Kathleen, the regular organist at St Joseph's, that she was being supplanted by a folk guitar this coming Sunday. Her response had been to flounce out of the church, after telling Peter that she might not be available for Sunday organ playing at St Joseph's ever again.

He was on his way now to the second job, which was to confront Enda about Aileen, his lovelorn baby-sitter. As Peter braked the car outside Enda's house, he could hear the guitar playing.

He got out of the car and crept up to the open front door. He could see Enda in a chair by the fireplace, strumming and singing a blues ballad. He appeared to be naked. Peter knocked on the door jamb. Enda looked up and immediately stopped playing. A split second later he started again, this time setting up a strident beat on the guitar as he sang the first line of 'Michael Row the Boat Ashore'.

He stood up, laughing, and revealed to Peter's relief that he was wearing an open shirt and jockey shorts.

'Father. Come in.' He gestured to his apparel. 'Sorry, I'm not up long.'

Peter, his nervousness mounting, forced a smile and gestured at the guitar. 'How's it going?'

'Oh great. Would you like to hear some?'

'No, it's OK. As long as you're ready for Sunday.'

'No sweat. Would you like a cuppa?'

'Thanks.'

They went to the kitchen. Enda made tea while Peter steeled himself. He hated this, yet it was an inescapable part of what he did and was expected to do.

'So.' He cleared his throat. 'Did you have a good time last night?'

'It was great, apart from a rather abrupt ending.'

'Oh?'

'Feargal was playing up.'

'That's a pity.'

'Yes, it's not like him.'

'Well, it must be hard for him in a new place,' Peter said, trying to steer himself to an appropriate opening; 'with new faces . . . '

'He's used to that.'

'Maybe it's something else.'

Enda frowned. 'Like what?'

Peter shrugged.

'Perhaps he needs a bit more stability in his life for a while.'

'Has Aileen said something to you?'

'He seems to be very close to her,' Peter said.

Enda gave Peter a hard look. 'So?'

It was a tense moment. Peter said nothing.

'Father, I love my son, but, with all due respect, I'm not going to let him or anyone else for that matter tell me who I should or shouldn't go out with.'

Peter got the message. He nodded and sipped his tea.

†

Next morning was Saturday. When Assumpta took Finn for his early walk Feargal went with her. It was no carefree trek across the fields, however. While Assumpta threw sticks for Finn to fetch, Feargal trailed behind, petulant, making it perfectly clear he would rather be anywhere else.

'It was nice of you to join me,' Assumpta told him. 'When I was at school, I used to spend my Saturday mornings asleep in bed.'

'I had to come,' Feargal said. 'Dad made me.'

'Oh.'

They walked on again in silence for a few more yards, the dog running ahead, impatient for another stick to be thrown.

'You know, Feargal,' Assumpta said finally, 'I like your dad a lot, but I'd never try and come between the two of you.'

'You're not,' Feargal said.

Assumpta smiled. 'I'm glad to hear it.'

'You're coming between Dad and Aileen.'

Assumpta stopped dead in her tracks, genuinely shocked. Feargal carried on walking.

They said no more on the subject. On the way back, walking down the main street, Assumpta offered Feargal the leash.

'Would you like to take him?'

Feargal shook his head.

'Go on,' Assumpta coaxed him. 'He's trained only to bite priests.'

After a moment Feargal reluctantly took the leash. They walked on. As they drew nearer the pub Finn began to pull hard on the leash.

Feargal looked at Assumpta. 'What do I do?'

'Just say heel.'

'Heel,' Feargal said. 'Heel, Finn!'

The dog obeyed, falling back and walking alongside, letting the leash hang loose.

Assumpta grinned. 'There y'are!'

Feargal almost looked as though he was enjoying himself. Assumpta asked him if he wanted to come to the bar for a Coke. He said he would.

As they turned in at the front door of Fitzgerald's Aileen called to Feargal from the bus stop across the road.

For a moment Assumpta was at a loss. She did not feel inclined to talk to Aileen just yet, in the light of what Feargal had said. She had to straighten out her thinking. On the other hand, it would have been churlish to avoid the girl, who had done Assumpta no wrong at all. Finally Assumpta decided to follow Feargal and Finn across the road to talk to Aileen.

Aileen reached down and stroked the dog's head.

'We've just taken him for a walk,' Feargal told her.

'That's nice.'

'Hi,' Assumpta said awkwardly.

'Hi.' Aileen continued to stroke the dog. 'He's lovely, isn't he?'

'Yeah,' Assumpta said, then caught the cutting stare as the double meaning sank in. 'Look, Aileen . . . '

'It's OK. You don't have to say anything.'

'Where are you going?' Feargal asked Aileen.

'Cilldargan. Do you want to come?'

Feargal looked at Assumpta.

'It's up to you,' Aileen told him.

As the bus came round the corner Assumpta took the leash from Feargal. The bus stopped and its doors opened. Aileen went ahead. Feargal turned to Assumpta.

'Thanks,' he said.

'Any time.'

With immaculate timing, Enda telephoned Assumpta two minutes after she got back to the pub and asked her if she would like to go out that evening. She said she would talk to him later and confirm.

She put down the phone and turned to the kitchen table, where Niamh was adding slices of banana to a cheese and onion sandwich.

'Niamh! That's horrible!'

Niamh continued to pile on the banana. 'Was that your new bit of trouser?'

'You mean Enda.'

'Has he asked you out again?'

'Tonight.'

'I'll cover for you.'

'I haven't agreed to go out yet.'

Niamh wrinkled her nose. 'What's wrong with you? Don't you like him?'

'Yeah,' Assumpta nodded, 'I like him. So does Aileen.'

Niamh put the top on the sandwich. 'I thought you said there was nothing between them?'

'That's what Enda told me. Feargal thinks otherwise.'

'Sure he's only a child. What would he know?'

Assumpta turned aside as Niamh bit into the sandwich.

†

That afternoon Peter gave his living-room carpet its weekly going-over with the vacuum cleaner. He moved the noisy old upright machine back and forth over the threadbare pattern to the rhythm of 'Michael Row the Boat Ashore', and accompanied it with his own off-key singing. His back was to the door so he didn't see Father Mac let himself in, and because of the racket he didn't hear when Father Mac called to him three times, the third time at the top of his voice. When finally Father Mac pulled the plug and the machine died, Peter stood staring at it, bewildered. He turned sharply as Father Mac cleared his throat.

'Father! How long have you been standing there?'

'Long enough to know Pavarotti has nothing to worry about.'

Peter pushed the vacuum cleaner into a corner. 'I'm in training for Sunday.'

Father Mac nodded glumly. 'I want to speak to you about this singalong Mass.'

'It's a folk Mass,' Peter corrected. 'Enda Sullivan is leading the music on his guitar.'

'What's wrong with the organ?'

'Nothing is wrong with the organ as such, it's just that I thought a folk Mass might be more relevant to the young people in the parish. Let me try it for just this Sunday, see how it goes. If it works, we could do it maybe once a month.'

'And if it doesn't?'

'Then we'll go back to the usual routine,' Peter said. 'What have we to lose?'

'Sounds like you've already lost an organist.'

Peter sighed. Whenever anything upset Kathleen, she went running to Father Mac with her complaint. 'I'm sure Kathleen will come round to it eventually. If it proves to be popular, we might even see an increase in attendance and that, of course, would do no harm to the collection.'

'All right.' The prospect of bigger collections appeared to mollify Father Mac, at least enough to make him stop scowling. 'You can go ahead for this Sunday, but on one condition.'

'What's that?'

'You don't sing "Michael Row the Boat Ashore". I can't stand it.'

A couple of miles away, still keen to imbue his movie with the essence of Ballykissangel, Quigley and his two assistants were preparing to film Enda Sullivan singing to his own guitar accompaniment. The filming was to take place outside with the farmhouse as a backdrop, but for the moment Quigley and Enda were inside, while Liam and Donal set up the equipment.

Enda had tried a few numbers on Quigley, who wasn't sure that any of them conveyed the essential flavour of the town and its setting.

'Have you anything a little more "Irish"?'

'What about "She Moved Through the Fair"?' Enda suggested. 'That's always popular.'

'Perfect. The Americans'll love it.' Quigley patted Enda's shoulder. 'I'll call you when we're ready.'

'Fine.'

Quigley went outside to harangue his men and Enda practised a few bars of "She Moved Through the Fair". As he finished he looked up and saw Aileen leaning in the doorway. She was half smiling, half frowning, standing with her arms folded and ankles crossed.

'What is it?' Enda said.

'Can we talk?'

Enda made a helpless gesture. 'I'm a bit busy.'

She stood away from the door frame, unfolding her arms. 'I want to know where we stand, Enda. You and me.'

'Not now, Aileen . . . '

She remained where she was, staring at him. 'Are you going to see her again?'

'Who?'

'Assumpta.'

'I don't know.' He fussed with the tension of the guitar strings. 'Maybe. Look, Aileen – '

'Feargal?' Aileen called.

'Leave him out of it,' Enda said.

Feargal appeared. He had obviously been standing outside the door waiting for his cue. He carried a guitar case. Enda looked puzzled. Feargal came across and handed the case to him.

'What's this?'

'It's a present,' Feargal said. 'From Aileen and me.'

They watched as Enda opened the case. Inside lay his dream guitar, the one from McNeill's Music Shop in Cilldargan. He was astonished. He looked up.

'How did you? . . .'

'We both raided our piggy-banks for the deposit,' Aileen said. 'The rest I got on credit.'

Enda was flushing with gratitude. 'Aileen, you shouldn't. You can't afford it.'

'I wanted to do it,' she said. 'We both did.'

Enda drew Aileen close and kissed her. Feargal stood watching, wearing the biggest smile he had managed all week.

Ten minutes later, Liam and Donal were ready to shoot. Enda took up his position on a straight-backed chair in front of the camera. He carefully tuned his new guitar, watched by Aileen and Feargal.

Liam stuck up a thumb. 'All set, Mr Quigley.'

'OK.' Quigley looked at Enda. 'Ready?'

Enda nodded.

'And action!'

Enda went into 'She Moved Through the Fair'. He had sung only a few bars when the sound was drowned out by the racket of a tractor nearby. Quigley turned, wild-eyed. He looked over Liam's shoulder. In the background, wearing his bright green hat, Eamonn was driving his tractor across the field adjacent to the farmhouse. As he passed he waved at the camera.

'Hold it!' Quigley yelled. 'Just excuse me a moment.'

He marched off to the fence, ducked under it and strode up to where Eamonn had stopped the tractor. Eamonn stared out of the cab, his face all innocence.

'What d'you think you're doing?' Quigley demanded.

'Authenticity,' Eamonn said.

'What?'

'I'm adding authenticity to your film. And you can't get more authentic than a farmer on a tractor.'

'There'll be a farmer under a tractor in a minute if you don't clear off!'

Liam and Donal had meanwhile stopped for a smoke. The camera was running unattended. Enda was still in his chair, strumming lovingly on his new guitar.

Aileen came up beside him. 'Is it all right?'

'It's wonderful,' he said.

'Here . . . ' She brushed the hair off his face. 'That's better.'

Enda held her hand as she made to take it away. He pulled her gently towards him and kissed her lightly on the mouth. It almost became a lingering kiss but Quigley came striding back and they separated. As Quigley got back in the director's chair Eamonn's tractor could be heard retreating into the distance.

'Right. Positions, everyone.'

Liam saw he had left the camera running. He looked to see if Quigley had noticed. 'Still running,' he murmured.

'One thing, Brian,' Enda said.

'Yes?'

'Can I try another song?'

Quigley groaned and closed his eyes.

ELEVEN

AN HOUR AFTER the filming session had finished, Enda agreed with Aileen that he should telephone Assumpta and tell her he wouldn't be available to go out with her that night, or any other night.

When he did call Assumpta, however, it was to ask if she had decided to go out with him as he had proposed. She said no, something had come up. Some other time then, he suggested lamely, and hung up. When Aileen appeared, he told her that he had made everything plain to Assumpta.

At Fitzgerald's, Niamh arrived at half-past six to do stand-in and was surprised to find Assumpta in her work clothes. Change of plan, Assumpta told her, and apologised for not calling to tell her she wouldn't be needed. Niamh said that was all right; given Assumpta's state of preoccupation, it was surprise enough that she had remembered to open the pub.

Back at the police house, with Niamh out of the way, Ambrose was able to organise some conventional food for a change. Since Niamh had been declared pregnant her dietary regime had grown stranger by the day, and she relentlessly expected Ambrose to eat everything she did. This evening, she had left a tripe casserole for Ambrose and her father to have for dinner. It had been despatched into the garbage shortly after she left for the pub.

Now Ambrose and Quigley sat on the couch in the living room, eating delivery pizzas from the boxes. While Ambrose energetically tucked into his, Quigley ate with less relish, watching the amateurish quality of his video on the TV set in the corner.

'Look on the bright side, Brian,' Ambrose said through a bite of pizza. 'You could always send it in to that TV programme – you know, the one that shows all those terrible home videos.'

Such a remark coming from Ambrose was not sarcasm; he meant it, and it was offered as a suggestion to cheer Quigley up. But Quigley did not take it that way. He glared at Ambrose and was about to say something when they heard the back door open.

They stared at each other for a frozen, horrified moment. Ambrose moved first. He stuffed his pizza, box and all, down behind the cushion at his back. Quigley did the same, wiping his mouth with his handkerchief.

Both men then sat back, looking unnaturally relaxed, gazing at the video as the footage of Enda appeared.

Niamh came into the room.

Ambrose looked up with a stiff, bright smile. 'Niamh. You're home.'

'Assumpta decided to stay in.'

Another feature of Niamh's pregnancy was an enhanced awareness of smells. She sniffed the air suspiciously.

'How was dinner?'

'Fine,' Ambrose patted his stomach.

Niamh lunged forward and snatched his pizza box from behind the cushion. She held it out in front of him.

'So what's this?'

Ambrose looked at it. 'Um, dessert.'

Quigley shot to his feet. 'I'll put the kettle on.' He hurried out to the kitchen.

'I'll give you a hand,' Ambrose said, and rushed out behind Quigley.

Niamh smiled to herself. She took a slice of pizza from the box and bit off a chunk. She chewed it with relish, then she noticed what was happening on the television screen. She watched Aileen brush Enda's hair away from his face. Then she watched them kiss. A moment later Enda looked towards the camera and asked if he could try another song. He strummed for a moment, then launched into a heartfelt rendition of 'When a Man Loves a Woman', glancing all the while off camera to where Aileen was obviously standing.

'Well, well,' Niamh murmured, nearly forgetting to chew.

†

At five to ten on Sunday morning Assumpta was still in bed. Niamh's voice from outside penetrated the darkened bedroom.

'Assumpta?'

There was a groan from under the duvet. Niamh burst in, dressed for church.

'Assumpta?'

'We're closed,' Assumpta grunted.

Niamh shook her. 'I have to talk to you.'

'Go away,' the voice ordered from under the duvet.

'I've been awake all night worrying,' Niamh said.

'What about?'

'There is something going on between Enda and Aileen.'

Assumpta slowly appeared from beneath the duvet, her hair tousled.

Niamh took a video from her shoulder bag and held it up. 'It's all on here,' she said. 'You see, Dad was filming Enda and – '

'Stop!'

'But I – '

'I don't want to hear about it, Niamh. I'm fed up with people interfering all the time. If I want advice, I'll ask for it.'

Niamh waggled the tape. 'But I have proof!'

'Go to Mass and leave me alone.'

Assumpta pulled the duvet back up over her head.

'Very well.' Niamh put the tape on the bedside table. 'I'll leave it here in case you change your mind.'

Niamh left, closing the door softly. After a minute Assumpta surfaced again and propped herself on her elbows. She stared at the video tape and sighed. There was no chance of her falling asleep again.

She got up, bathed and dressed. She made herself a cup of tea, then took it with her into the lounge and put the tape into her video player. She curled up in a chair in the corner to watch. Niamh had wound the tape to the point where Aileen brushed aside Enda's hair, and he kissed her.

As he began to sing 'When a Man loves a Woman', Assumpta continued to stare impassively. Then a smile spread across her face as she noticed the guitar he was playing.

†

St Joseph's was packed to the door. Up in the gallery at the back Brian Quigley, Liam and Donal were at the ready with the camera and sound equipment. Quigley had warned his assistants that they would get only one shot at this, so they had better get it right. He signalled Liam to start rolling as Peter, in his Mass vestments, began to address the congregation.

'Welcome, my dear brothers and sisters in Christ, and a particular welcome to those of you who are new to St Joseph's, or are just revisiting. This morning I've asked Enda Sullivan, formerly of the band Dark Rosaleen, to lead the music for us. Enda.'

Everyone stood and watched in total silence as Enda picked up his guitar. In the centre of the congregation Kathleen Hendley stood beside Father Mac, her expression midway between disapproval and disdain. Enda touched a switch somewhere in the array of instruments behind him and a loud organ chord reverberated through the church. The note was sustained, then suddenly a drumbeat cut in, sharp and insistent, as Enda joined in with his guitar and began to sing 'For the Life of the World'.

The words were as reverent as always, but now they had a beat, and feet began to tap. Father Mac and Kathleen looked at each other. Kathleen, by a tiny fraction, was the more astonished.

Up in the gallery, Liam filmed and Donal stood with his microphone held high to catch the glorious rush of sound. Quigley stood swaying, his foot tapping, already too close to the plug on the sound unit on the floor. As the first hymn reached its closing crescendo, his foot did a series of drumstick taps, the third one completely dislodging the sound cable. Donal said nothing, but he began to look puzzled.

By the time Enda struck up with 'Michael Row the Boat Ashore', at which Father Mac and Peter exchanged glances, the congregation were fully won over to the folk Mass. The single exception was Kathleen, who had now gone huffy, having noticed during the previous number that Father Mac was moving his foot like everybody else.

When the number came to its resounding close Quigley turned to Liam and said, 'Now did you get that?'

'I did,' Liam said, 'but he didn't.' He jerked his thumb at Donal. 'You pulled his cable out.'

Quigley looked down and saw the cable lying by the side of his foot.

'That's it!' Quigley slammed down his clipboard. 'I give up. If my cousin wants a film, he can come over and make it himself.'

He marched out through the balcony door, leaving Liam and Donal staring after him.

The Mass was a huge success. As the congregation filed out at the end they all wanted to tell Peter how much they liked it.

'Great, Father,' Brendan said. 'I really enjoyed it.'

'Put a bit of life in the place,' Siobhan said.

When Father Mac emerged Peter said, 'It seems to have worked, Father. It certainly brought in new blood.'

'Even if it drives the faithful out,' Kathleen snapped as she swept past.

The two priests watched her stomp away through the gates.

'It'll be all right now and again, perhaps,' Father Mac said grudgingly.

'Thank you.'

'As long as you can hang on to that one.' He pointed to Enda, who was walking away from the church with Aileen and Feargal, acknowledging the congratulations of everyone they passed.

At the foot of the hill, Assumpta was leaning in the open doorway of Fitzgerald's, watching the people come away from St Joseph's. She waved when she saw Enda, Aileen and Feargal arrive at the bus stop across the road.

'Have you got a minute?' she called to Enda.

He came over, watched by the other two.

'How are you?' He spoke softly, giving Assumpta his best intimate smile.

She looked down at the new guitar case. Enda did too.

'Did you win the lottery?' she said.

She held up the video tape, taking care that it was shielded from the sight of Aileen and Feargal. She began to sing, 'When a man loves a woman, can't keep his mind on nothing else . . . '

'I don't get it,' said Enda, frowning.

She handed him the tape.

He looked at the box, still frowning. 'What is it?'

'A tender moment captured on tape.'

Suddenly he realised what she meant. 'I can explain that.'

'Don't worry, Enda. It's no big deal.'

She turned to go into the pub but he stopped her with a touch on the arm.

'Look, Assumpta, we can sort this out. We can have a lot of fun together.'

'It's not working, Enda.' Assumpta nodded towards Aileen, who was still watching from across the road.

'Tell me what to do,' he said.

'Well, you could try growing up.'

'What about the gigs?'

Assumpta shook her head. 'I can't afford you.'

Peter, out of his vestments, came running down the road.

'Enda . . . ' He stopped by the door and slapped Enda's shoulder. 'I didn't get a chance to thank you properly. Are you coming in?'

Enda pointed across the road to Aileen and Feargal. 'They're waiting for me.'

'Well, thanks a lot,' Peter said. 'For everything. I owe you one.'

As Enda went back across the road Peter turned to Assumpta.

'You missed something great,' he said.

She smiled. 'You reckon?'

She went into the bar. Peter followed her.

TWELVE

LATE ON MONDAY night it began to rain, a drenching downpour which even by Irish standards of rainfall was considered in Ballykissangel to be severe. At a little after half-past ten, a car drew up opposite the church. The engine was switched off, then the lights, but the windshield wipers kept going. Inside the car were two teenagers, a boy of seventeen at the wheel, and beside him a sixteen-year-old girl. They sat for ten minutes, gazing through the rain-smeared windscreen at Peter's neat cottage with its red door and lion knocker.

Then Peter's bedroom light went out.

'OK,' the girl said. 'Let's do it.'

The boy was suddenly nervous. 'I don't think we should – '

'Do it,' she said firmly.

A few seconds later, up in his bedroom, sinking into a soothing sleep, Peter was awakened sharply by the banging of the door knocker. He threw himself out of bed. As he struggled into his dressing-gown it rattled again. He ran downstairs and out onto the step, just in time to see the car drive off.

'Very funny,' he muttered, and turned back to the house. As he lowered his head against the rain he saw a box at the side of the step. He picked it up. Inside was a sheet of black polythene tucked around something – something warm, from the feel of the bottom of the box.

Peter hurried indoors and put the box on the hearth rug. He carefully lifted away the polythene. Nestled in a soft blanket underneath was a new-born baby, asleep with its thumb in its mouth.

Peter lifted the child out carefully and held it in his arms, staring at it, his mind racing. He couldn't think of any recently pregnant woman in Ballykissangel who would want to abandon her child. On the other hand there were people in the hills – small farmers, the occasional itinerant New Wave commune – where the domestic situations were completely unknown to Peter, or to anyone else on the outside.

The baby moved and made a small soft sound. Peter stood up, holding it carefully, and went to the telephone.

Dr Ryan arrived within ten minutes, during which time the baby had awakened and lay gazing up at Peter in a way that did odd things to his submerged sense of parenthood.

Dr Ryan gave the baby a thorough medical check-up. It went on much longer than Peter had expected, but finally the doctor stepped back, unhooking his stethoscope and nodding.

'How is he, Michael?'

'The umbilical cord looks like it was cut with a pair of blunt scissors,' Ryan said, 'but otherwise he's in pretty good shape.'

'When was he born?'

Ryan shrugged. 'A few hours ago, probably.'

There was a sharp knock at the door. Peter looked anxiously at the doctor. 'Let's hope it wasn't twins.'

Peter opened the door. Assumpta was there, holding Finn by his leash. The rain, Peter noted, had stopped.

'Oh, you're OK,' Assumpta said. 'I was just passing and saw Dr Ryan's car. Thought you might've had a . . . ' She stopped at a tiny cry from inside; ' . . . baby?'

'You'd better come in.'

Assumpta was as startled as Peter had been to see how small the baby was. Ryan let her stand there for a minute, expressing her wonderment, then he intervened to say he would have to set the machinery in motion to get the social services involved. Peter cradled the baby in his arms while Ryan telephoned from the next room.

'I suppose he's kind of cute, if you're into that sort of thing,' Assumpta said.

'Don't listen to her,' Peter told the baby, 'she's a big softie really.'

Assumpta asked if he had noticed the number of the car.

'No, it was too dark. But I reckon whoever it was must've come from somewhere outside Ballykay.'

'How'd you work that out, Columbo?'

'Well, I didn't recognise the car and I don't know of anyone round here who was expecting a baby so soon. Do you?'

'Not officially anyway.'

'What does that mean?'

'It wouldn't be the first time in Ireland that a girl gave birth to a baby in secret. It comes with living in a country where some people think family planning means getting the kids to Mass on time.'

'Don't tell me, it's the church's fault again.'

'Well you don't exactly make things easy,' Assumpta said, 'do you?'

Peter was considering his reply when Dr Ryan hung up and came back to the kitchen.

'I've spoken to the social worker in Cilldargan,' he said. 'She'll be round as soon as possible to collect the wee fella.'

'Thanks, Michael.'

'Do you mind looking after him till she gets here? He's better off staying in the warm.'

'I'll do my best,' Peter said.

'It could be overnight, mind.'

'I'll give you a hand if you like,' Assumpta said. 'See if I can discover any mothering instincts.'

Peter said he would appreciate that. He handed the baby to Assumpta. She took it in her arms with the exaggerated care of one unused to handling infants.

Peter grinned. 'He's in safe hands now.'

'That's debatable,' Assumpta said.

At the other end of town, Ambrose Egan was having his bedtime bath while Niamh sat on the closed toilet seat in her nightie and dressing-gown, reading to him from a book of children's names.

'Deborah,' she said.

'No.'

'Delia.'

'No.'

'Delilah . . . Doreen . . . Dymphna! We'll call her Dymphna!'

Ambrose shook his head. 'What if it's a boy?'

'Then we won't call her Dymphna.'

'If it's a girl,' Ambrose said, 'we should call her Ann, Bernice, Denise, Colleen, Linda, Maureen Egan.'

'We are not naming our daughter after the Nolan Sisters.'

'Just Bernice then,' Ambrose said, pretending to plead. 'She was my favourite.' He held up the shower head like a microphone and sang into it, 'I'm in the mood for dancing, romancing . . . '

'Sinead,' Niamh said.

Ambrose stared at her. 'No way.'

'Why not? It has a certain mystery about it.'

'Talking of mysteries . . . ' Ambrose was searching about in the water. 'Where's the soap gone?'

'Search me.'

'OK, I will!' Ambrose grinned and snatched the book from Niamh's hand. He stood up in the bath, reaching for her with both hands. 'You're not leaving this bathroom until you agree on Bernice.'

'Sinead!' Niamh squealed.

'Bernice!'

Niamh ran from the bathroom howling with laughter. Ambrose leapt from the bath in full pursuit. As Niamh pulled the door shut she heard a crash, then Ambrose let out a roar.

She put her face to the door, scared to open it. 'Ambrose?'

She heard him groan with pain. 'I've just found the soap,' he said.

†

The next morning at nine o'clock Niamh stood by the bed of her pain-racked husband and explained to Superintendent Foley, over from Cilldargan, just what had happened to put Ambrose in his present incapacitated condition.

'You see, Mr Foley, my husband was lifting a big box of police files, he often works late, you know, and then I heard this terrible cry and I came running in and found him crashed out on the floor.'

Foley nodded. 'I see. Where did it happen?'

Niamh said upstairs. Ambrose said downstairs.

'Ah, on the stairs,' Niamh said hastily. 'We thought at first he might have slipped a disc but the doctor said it's just a bad strain. He suggested a few days' rest.'

'Well, Guard Egan,' Foley said, 'you're lucky you didn't do yourself any permanent damage, and that you've got such a lovely wife to look after you.'

Niamh forced a smile.

'Yes, sir,' Ambrose said.

At that moment Brian Quigley walked into the room.

'Good morning, Sergeant Foley,' he said brightly.

Niamh rolled her eyes. Foley and her father were long-time enemies.

'I am Superintendent Foley, as you well know, Mr Quigley.'

'Of course. How could I forget?' Quigley ran his eye up and down Foley's uniform. 'It certainly suits you.'

'Dad,' Niamh said through gritted teeth.

Quigley turned to the bed. 'And how's the patient?'

'I think I'll be out of action for a couple of days,' Ambrose said.

Quigley laughed. 'When was the last time you saw any action round here?'

'Action or not,' Foley said, 'I've arranged a temporary replacement to keep an eye on things while you're convalescing. We wouldn't want anyone taking advantage of the situation . . . ' He looked straight at Quigley. 'Would we, now?'

'Heaven forbid,' Quigley said.

'If it's OK with you, Mrs Egan, I'd be most grateful if you would put him up here.'

'Certainly.'

'Do I know this Guard?' Ambrose said.

'I shouldn't think so. He's fresh out of police college. Name's McMullen.'

Quigley looked interested. 'So Ballykay is his first assignment, is it?'

'He's a very capable Guard,' Foley said.

Quigley nodded. 'That'll be a first,' he muttered.

†

At ten o'clock, Peter, Dr Ryan and Father Mac stood outside Peter's house and watched two social workers leave with the baby.

'What'll happen to him now?' Peter asked Ryan.

'They'll just take him to the hospital for a final check-up.'

'And then?'

'If they don't find the mother,' Father Mac said, 'he'll be adopted.' He turned to the doctor. 'Keep me informed, won't you?'

'It's not much of a start in life, is it?' Peter said.

Ryan shrugged. 'We all have to start somewhere.'

As Ryan went off to get in his car Peter had a thought. He followed Ryan.

'There must be something we can do to help prevent this sort of thing, Michael.'

'Prevention is always better than cure. What did you have in mind?'

'Well, what about some sort of sex education for the young people round here? It might help.'

Ryan considered it for a moment and nodded. 'Good idea. Perhaps you should give a talk to the youth club.'

'Me?'

'Why not? You get on well with youngsters. And besides, there's the novelty value.'

'What's that?'

'A priest talking about sex.'

†

Quigley drove straight from visiting Ambrose to a field he owned a mile north of Ballykissangel. It was two acres on a breezy slope at the heart of lush agricultural land. When Quigley arrived Liam and Donal were already there. He led them to the middle of the field and told Donal to dig out a sod with his shovel. Quigley took the chunk of sward in his hand and let the earth trickle through his fingers.

'Top-soil,' he said, as if he were addressing a meeting. 'Irish top-soil. God's own earth. Worth a small fortune, at least it would be if it wasn't here.'

Liam and Donal glanced at each other, puzzled.

'Gardeners,' Quigley said. 'They love good soil but they can't get it. I've got it but it's in the wrong place.'

Liam caught on. 'You mean you want to take the top-soil from here and sell it?'

'Precisely. I'm going to sell a little bit of Ireland to the Irish. And anyone else who'll pay for it.'

'But sure it wouldn't be worth it, Mr Quigley,' Donal said. 'You know the size of our truck, it'd take weeks to shift all this.'

'He's right,' Liam said. 'You'd need one of those trucks the size of County Wicklow to make it worth your while, and they're not allowed on the roads round here. They're too big. Ambrose would never let . . . '

Liam stopped as something else dawned on him.

'You . . . are a genius, Mr Quigley.'

'It has been said,' Quigley grinned. 'Put simply, lads, I want you to go out and hire the biggest truck in Ireland. And don't worry about the new rookie Guard. Leave him to me.'

As the morning wore on, Peter's plans for a talk to the teenagers began to take shape. Over coffee he explained to Assumpta what he was trying to achieve, and while she found the idea laudable, she shared his biggest misgiving; holding the attention of a roomful of teenagers would be nearly impossible. Peter decided the answer might be to use a movie. Kids, he reasoned, could always be relied on to gawp at a film.

Now all he had to do was try to find some way of using a popular film as the vehicle for his message. The means, he decided, would depend on the film he chose. With that in mind, he paid a visit to the video section in Kathleen Hendley's shop.

He hadn't been looking long before he attracted Kathleen's curiosity. She approached as he was rooting through the section headed 'Romance'.

'Were you looking for any particular title, Father?'

'I'm looking for a film that deals with love and relationships.'

'Love and relationships?'

'Can you suggest anything?'

Kathleen put a finger to her temple, trying to think. 'How about *Gone with the Wind?*'

'Have you anything more recent?'

Kathleen thought again. '*Brief Encounter?*'

'I think what I need is something more modern.'

Now Kathleen was suspicious. 'What exactly do you mean by modern?'

'You know, the kind of thing that would appeal to a younger audience.'

'Really, Father! I'd have you know, I do not keep that sort of film!'

Kathleen stomped back behind the counter.

'No,' Peter soothed, 'nothing like that, Kathleen, I didn't mean a – '

'Having problems, Father?'

Peter turned. Brian Quigley was standing behind him.

'Brian. I think we're talking at cross-purposes here.'

Quigley lowered his voice. 'This is the last place on earth you'd find that sort of special interest video.'

Peter sighed. 'I'm looking for a film to help me with my talk at the youth club.'

'Oh,' said Quigley, 'the sex talk. I heard about that.'

Kathleen was still behind the counter, but her ears always picked up certain key words. 'The what?'

'I'm giving a talk to the youth club but it's not about sex,' Peter said, 'it's about responsible relationships.'

'Is it now?' Kathleen was clearly unconvinced.

'You think Father Mac sees it that way?' Quigley said.

Peter said he was trying to prevent more unwanted babies.

Quigley shrugged. 'There's always somebody who'll adopt them.'

There was no doubt, Peter thought, that Brian Quigley found that point of view perfectly reasonable.

THIRTEEN

SHORTLY AFTER the visit of Superintendent Foley that morning, Niamh began to feel strange. As the morning went on the feeling got no better. Then, quite suddenly, as she made Ambrose a cup of tea, she was aware that something profound was happening to her. A few minutes after that, she knew she had lost the baby.

She said nothing to Ambrose. Instead, she went straight to the surgery. Dr Ryan saw her at once. He examined her thoroughly, and while she was behind the screen dressing again he sat down at his desk and wrote up her notes, enforcing an air of calm.

'You were very early in the pregnancy,' he said, trying to find some way of mitigating what had happened.

'So, that's it?'

'I'm sorry, Niamh. I know how much it meant to you.'

Niamh came from behind the screen and sat at the desk.

'You must realise,' Ryan said, 'that just because you've miscarried this time, doesn't mean it'll necessarily happen again. I know it's little comfort for you now but there'll be other times.'

Niamh suddenly sat up straight in the chair. 'Time,' she said.

'Sorry?'

'What time is it, Doctor?'

He looked at his watch. 'Half-eleven. Why?'

Niamh stood up. 'I've got to get some things in for the new Guard. He'll be here soon and we've nothing in the house and Ambrose can't – '

'Niamh.' Ryan spoke calmly. 'Try not to overdo things for a while. OK?'

'OK.'

When she got home, she sat on the bed beside Ambrose and told him. He couldn't find anything to say in response. They lay on the bed with their arms about each other, silent and sad.

After several minutes, Ambrose spoke. 'It's my fault. If I hadn't fallen over and caused all this trouble.'

'Don't be daft. These things happen. Don't ask me why, but they do.'

'There'll be other times,' Ambrose whispered against Niamh's hair.

'That's what the doctor said. It doesn't make me feel any better.'

'Would it make you feel better if I told you I loved you?'

'It might.'

'I love you.'

Niamh smiled and stroked Ambrose's cheek. 'I love you, too.'

She kissed him gently. At that moment, a man standing by the open bedroom door cleared his throat loudly.

Niamh leapt off the bed with shock. The man was tall, barrel-chested and stern looking. He held a suitcase.

'Sorry,' Niamh said. 'Excuse us.'

For the moment the man ignored Niamh. He stared at the prostrate figure of Ambrose on the bed. 'Guard Egan, I presume?'

'Yes?'

The man clicked his heels and saluted. 'McMullen, P., reporting for duty.'

Ambrose and Niamh looked at each other.

'I'll show you to your quarters,' Niamh said.

She led him to the little room along the hall and watched as McMullen put his neatly folded clothes into the drawers. She noticed a lot of books and videos in the suitcase on the bed.

'Is this going to be OK for you, Mr McMullen?'

'It's fine, thank you, Mrs Egan.'

'Niamh, please.'

McMullen made no return gesture. Informality was probably not something that sat easily with such a man, Niamh thought.

'If you don't mind me saying,' she said, 'you seem a little mature to have just graduated from police college.'

McMullen nodded. 'I was a prison officer for many years before I had my calling to the Guards.'

'A prison officer? Well, then you'll be used to this small room.'

McMullen did not get the connection. Niamh lost her smile. 'This was going to be the nursery,' she said.

'We all have a responsibility to the children of tomorrow, Mrs Egan.' McMullen took a book from the suitcase and handed it to Niamh. 'If we get to them before the criminals do, then there's hope for the future.'

Niamh glanced at the cover. It was called *Beginner's Guide to the Criminal Mind*.

'I have made it my mission in life,' McMullen said, a touch zealously, 'to guide the young people of Ireland towards a decent, law-abiding life.' He picked up his uniform cap and stepped to the door. 'And by the way, I don't eat anything with peanuts in it.'

'Um . . . fine,' Niamh said.

'Now if you'll excuse me, I have a beat to patrol.'

McMullen bowed before he left. Niamh stood by the door, nonplussed.

†

The police had located a red Ford saloon answering the description of the car Peter saw moving off from his house the night before. The car was stolen and had been abandoned on the Springville council estate in Cilldargan. People living in the vicinity had been questioned, but no one knew anything.

That afternoon, Peter decided to visit the estate himself. For a while he simply walked around, getting the feel of the place, then he watched some young lads playing football on waste ground at the south end of the estate.

He spoke to them, and they were happy to talk, but they went noticeably stiff when he mentioned the abandoned car. They knew nothing about it, they said. Peter noticed that a couple of them kept glancing at one particular little boy, the only one wearing a Liverpool shirt.

Later, still walking about the estate, Peter made a point of keeping himself within range of the football game, able to see it and hear the shouts of the boys as he wandered the same tight network of snaking streets.

When the game broke up, Peter followed the lad with the Liverpool shirt. He kept a discreet distance, hanging back as far as he could without losing sight of the quarry. When the boy went indoors Peter waited a few minutes, then went up to the door of the flat and knocked.

The door was opened by a lad of seventeen. Peter introduced himself, and the lad began to look very nervous.

'I'm Father Peter Clifford, the curate at St Joseph's in Ballykissangel. I'm in the area visiting,' Peter said. 'Have you got a moment?'

The boy hesitated, then he stepped aside and nodded Peter in.

The flat was small and untidy. Washing, most of it bed linen, was hanging to dry on the stair rails, and over radiators and chairs. Peter asked the boy what his name was.

'Roy Quinn.' He led the way into the living-room. 'It's a bit of a mess in here.'

'Don't worry,' Peter said. 'You should see my place.'

The youngster wearing the Liverpool shirt was watching TV and pointedly ignoring Peter.

'That's my brother Sean,' Roy said.

'We've met.'

Without a word, Sean got up and left the room.

'Excuse me, Father, I have to get the dinner on.' Roy headed for the kitchen.

'Sure.'

Left alone, Peter took the opportunity to do a little snooping. The only thing he learned for sure, from all the Roman Catholic iconography in the form of statues and pictures, was that this was a Catholic family.

He wandered into the kitchen, where Roy was opening a tin of baked beans.

'Do you ever go to Ballykissangel yourself?' Peter said.

The question appeared to make Roy anxious.

'Why would I want to go there?'

'You tell me.'

Roy turned his back and fussed with a pan. 'I haven't been there in ages,' he muttered.

'Are your parents around?'

'Dad's away at work.'

'Where's that?'

'Dublin.'

Peter was surprised. 'Dublin? What time does he get home in the evening?'

'He doesn't. Stays with a cousin. He gets home weekends if he can. When he was working in London, we didn't see him for weeks at a time.'

'That must be hard for your mother.'

'She's left,' Roy said.

'Where's she gone?'

'I don't know and I don't care.' Roy glanced to the side and saw Peter's troubled frown. 'Sorry, Father. I have to get on with the dinner.'

'Of course.' Peter felt he should take the hint. He went back to the living-room and Roy saw him to the door.

'Maybe I'll drop by at a more convenient time.'

'If you like.'

Roy was about to close the door when Peter turned.

'In the meantime, if there's anything you want to talk to me about, you know where to find me.'

Roy nodded.

'Goodbye, then.'

Roy closed the door behind Peter. Immediately the bedroom door at the top of the stairs opened and his sixteen-year-old sister stuck her face out. She was tired and pale. And she looked angry.

'What did you let him in for?' she demanded.

'I had to, didn't I, or he would've got suspicious.'

Roy went back to the kitchen, leaving his sister at the top of the stairs. She took a deep breath, fighting back tears.

That evening Assumpta told the regulars in the pub that since they would learn about it eventually, she might as well tell them now – Niamh had suffered a miscarriage.

The news saddened everyone. Dr Ryan, who was in the bar at the time, told those present that Niamh would need plenty of support from her friends. They all swore she would have that, and while they sat in baleful silence, accommodating the sadness of the news, the floor began to tremble, then the bar, then all the bottles and glasses in the pub.

'It's an earthquake!' Eamonn shouted and dived to the floor. The others, blessed with a better sense of hearing than Eamonn, turned their heads in the direction of the river bridge.

As the trembling got worse, they all hurried outside. In the dusk, the lights of some monstrosity, a mechanical device as yet ill defined, glowed and flashed like the beacons of an extra-terrestrial craft.

'It's an enormous dumper truck!' Peter shouted above the din.

The thing came round the corner off the bridge, Donal walking in front, shouting directions to Liam, who was up in the cab driving, doing his best to avoid hitting the cars parked on the lower main street.

Kathleen Hendley was at the door of her shop, shouting, complaining, but nobody could hear her for the rumbling and roaring of the truck. The regulars from Fitzgerald's talked to one another without hearing or being heard. They bawled in each other's faces and had to try lip-reading to make any sense of what was being said to them. They finally stood in stunned, deafened awe and watched the thing go rumbling up the main street, with Donal running and scrambling to get back up into the cab beside Liam.

As the noise died Peter said, 'What was that all about?'

'That,' said Assumpta, 'was Brian Quigley taking advantage of a change in the law.'

Eighteen minutes later the massive truck wended its way past the driveway leading to Brian Quigley's house, heading for the top-soil digging site at his field on the outskirts of town. Watching the vehicle from the high western veranda of the house were Brian Quigley and Guard McMullen, in his civilian clothes.

'There it goes.' Quigley put a large glass of whiskey into McMullen's hand. 'Like they say, big is beautiful.'

He raised his glass. 'To co-operation.'

McMullen raised his, too, and sipped the whiskey.

They walked to chairs at the other end of the veranda and sat opposite each other, a low table between them.

'It must make a nice change for you, being out of the city,' Quigley said.

McMullen sipped again. 'Very pleasant.'

'And you'll need to get to know the lie of the land . . . '

'I think I'm beginning to.'

'Enjoy the countryside,' Quigley said, 'at your leisure.' He pushed a set of car keys across the table.

'Little runabout. Feel free to use it whenever you like.'

'In the line of duty?'

'Sure, it would only be sitting there rusting away otherwise.'

McMullen looked at the keys, then at Quigley. He grinned.

†

The next morning Niamh was busy washing the floor with a mop, slopping water everywhere, trying to work her way clear of the depression that was encroaching like a fog on the edge of her sanity. She stopped mopping as the back door opened and her father came in. He looked sombre and awkward. At last, she thought, somebody had told him.

'Hello, Niamh.'

They looked at each other for a moment, then Niamh started mopping again. Quigley took a step towards her.

'Mind the floor, Dad. I'm trying to clean up round here.'

'So I see.' He looked at the puddles she had made. Then he looked at her again. 'Why didn't you call me?'

Niamh put the mop in the bucket. 'Sorry, Daddy. I should have – I just couldn't . . . '

Ambrose called from upstairs.

'Wait a minute!' Niamh called.

'How is he?'

'He's worse than a baby.'

Father and daughter looked at one another as she said that. Niamh, embarrassed, feeling incredibly uncoordinated, made to grab the mop again.

'You're making a terrible mess.'

'I know,' she snapped. 'I can't clean, I'm a terrible cook and I'd probably make a terrible mother, too.'

'You're right about the cooking.'

Despite herself Niamh smiled, but her eyes were filling with tears.

'Come here,' said Quigley.

Niamh dropped the mop and embraced her father, burying her head in his chest.

'Oh, Dad.'

'I'm sorry, love,' he whispered, stroking her hair.

'No, I'm sorry.'

'What for?'

'I know this baby meant a lot to you, too.'

'Not nearly as much as you mean to me.'

Niamh made a little shuddery sigh. 'I'm just watching for number three.'

'What do you mean?'

'First Ambrose, now this. What else can go wrong?'

The doorbell rang.

'Not the doorbell anyway,' Quigley said.

Niamh smiled and went to answer the door.

'I better be going myself,' Quigley said, coming with her. 'I've got the earth to move.'

'The what?'

'Nothing for you to worry about.'

As they approached the front door a voice came from the other side. 'Mrs Egan. It's Superintendent Foley.'

Quigley stopped abruptly.

'Actually I think I'll slip out the back instead. See you later, love.'

'OK. And Dad? Thanks.'

Quigley smiled at her as he slipped back out through the kitchen. Niamh wiped the tears from her face before she opened the door.

'Mr Foley.'

'Mrs Egan. I was wondering if I could have a word with your husband?'

They went upstairs. Foley stood at the end of the bed where Ambrose still lay. On an impulse, a deep twinge of anxiety, Niamh went and sat next to him.

Foley asked stiffly how Ambrose was feeling. 'Are you still in pain?'

'Not too bad,' he said. 'I'll be getting up later, perhaps.'

'Let's wait and see, shall we?' Niamh put in quickly.

'There's no rush,' Foley said. 'Guard McMullen seems to have every-

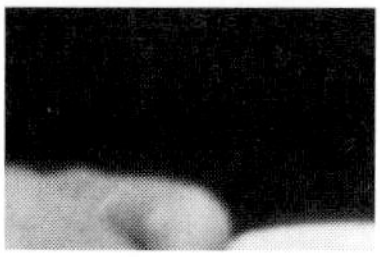

on the hills *of ballykay*

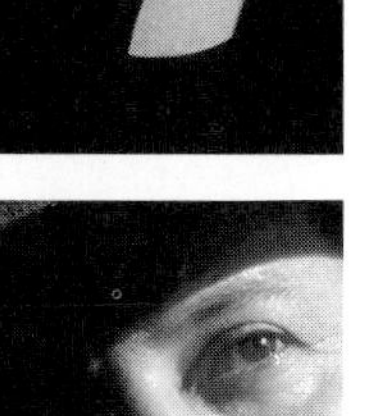

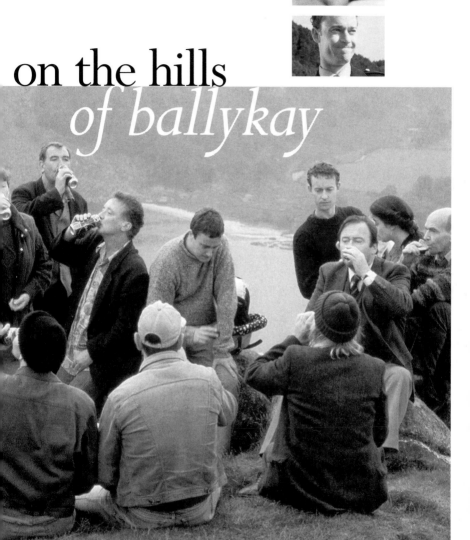

father *peter clifford*

enda *sullivan*

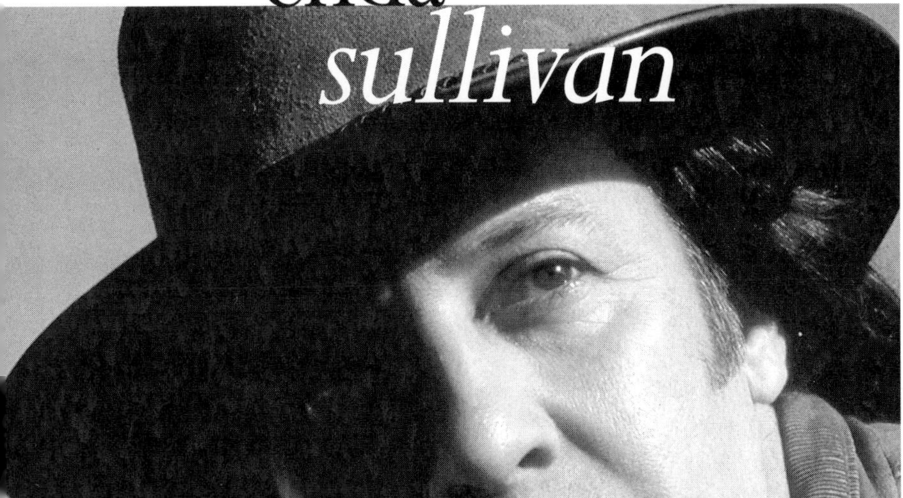

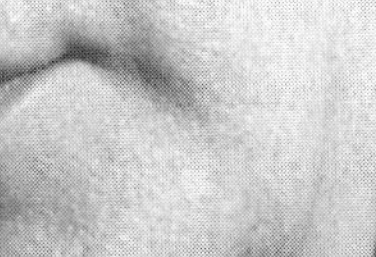

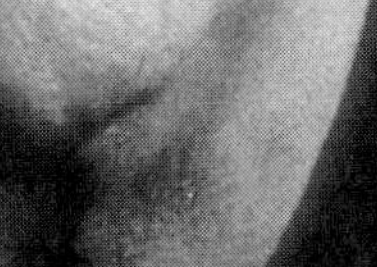

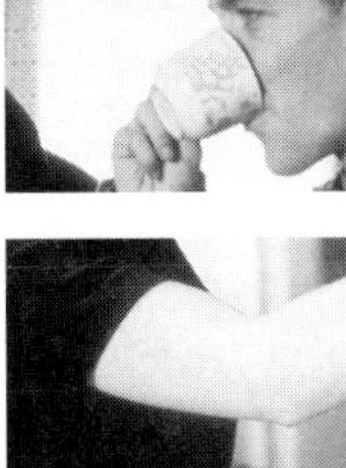

tea and sympathy

assumpta *fitzgerald*

fitzgerald's

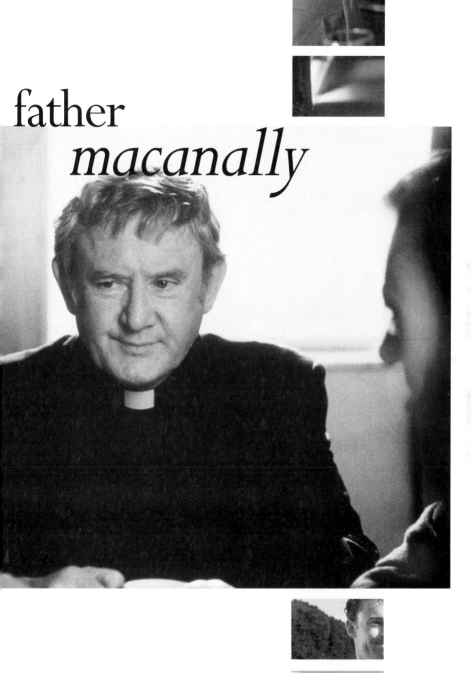

father *macanally*

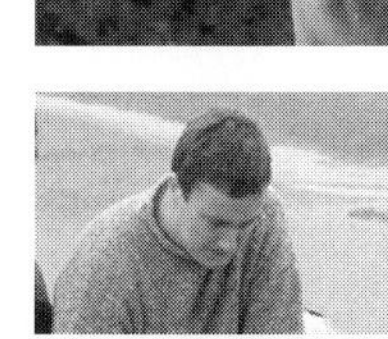

ambrose *egan*

thing in hand. He says he's really starting to like it round here.'

Ambrose struggled to muster a smile. 'Great.'

'Perhaps,' Foley went on, 'it's no bad thing having an outsider in this place.'

'Why's that, sir?'

'Well, for instance, now the two of you are married, that makes Brian Quigley your father-in-law.'

The implication hung between them like a pointer of guilt aimed right at Ambrose's chest.

'Let me assure you, sir, I would never show favour to anyone just because they're family.'

'That's as may be. But we must be seen to be totally impartial. In fact I am giving serious consideration to keeping Guard McMullen on in Ballykay.'

'But . . . ' Ambrose frowned. 'Sure there's not enough going on here for two Guards.'

'Precisely,' said Foley. 'That's why we'd have to find you a new posting.'

'What?'

'Perhaps a move to an inner-city beat might be good for you.'

Ambrose looked horrified.

Under her breath Niamh said, 'Number three.'

FOURTEEN

A FEW MINUTES after the visit of Superintendent Foley, Ambrose was propped up in bed, trying to make himself eat from a bowl of cereal on a tray across his knees, when he became aware that the bed was shaking. He looked down and saw ripples on the milk in his bowl. Glancing up, he saw that the lamp on the ceiling had begun to swing.

Elsewhere in the town bottles fell off shelves, loose slates hurtled from roofs, cats ran for cover and startled babies screamed as Quigley's monster truck lumbered its way down the main street, laden with top-soil. At the wheel, Liam sang a catchy trucker's song while Donal beat time with his hands on the dash. The unusual height of the cab meant that Donal's line of vision was nearly at streetlamp level, so when Guard McMullen walked up the centre of the road with his arm outstretched in front of him, the truck was nearly on top of him before Liam saw him and braked.

The truck screeched and shuddered to a stop. Guard McMullen took out his notebook. When Liam got out to ask what the trouble might be, McMullen told him the truck was being used illegally and that appropriate action was therefore being taken.

Twenty minutes later Brian Quigley was at the police house, standing in the office at the front, demanding to know why his truck was outside with a large 'Vehicle Impounded' notice stuck on it.

'You can't do this!' he told McMullen.

'Oh yes I can.'

'I demand you release my truck immediately!'

McMullen walked to the window and looked out, as if someone might have sneaked the truck away when he wasn't looking. He turned to face Quigley again. 'Impossible,' he said.

'Why?'

'It's too big for these roads. You're breaking the law.'

Quigley paused to get a hold on his temper. 'You know what I think, Guard?'

'What?'

'I think you're overdoing things a little. You need to relax more. Take a walk, or perhaps a long drive in the country.'

McMullen could hardly have missed the implication, but he was clearly not playing along. 'Perhaps instead of arguing,' he said, 'we should sit down like a couple of gentlemen and talk this thing through. I'm sure we could come to some agreement.'

Quigley glared at him. 'I thought we had an agreement.'

'You thought wrong.'

At the same time as Quigley found himself speechless in the teeth of Guard McMullen's stubborn adherence to the law, Peter was sitting in Father Mac's study, suppressing a fleeting fantasy about grabbing the parish priest by the lapels and shaking him.

'What's got into you?' Father Mac demanded. 'A priest teaching sex to children!'

'I believe the Church has a moral responsibility to do something,' Peter said.

'Do you really?'

'We need to talk to these young people now if we don't want more babies dumped on our doorstep in the future.'

'Any news on that front?'

'I believe the police are still investigating the case.'

Peter thought it best to say nothing of his own tentative investigations.

'I've several parishioners struggling to have a child of their own,' Father Mac said. 'Whoever that mother is, she clearly has no interest in raising him.'

Peter found Father Mac's line incredibly harsh. 'We have no proof of that,' he said.

'I would say abandoning her baby on your doorstep was proof enough. I will be making suggestions for suitable adoptive parents to the appropriate authorities – and I expect your full support.'

'Have I got yours?' Peter said. 'Can I give this talk?'

'Only if it corresponds with the teachings of the church.'

'Don't worry, Father. I won't be handing out condoms at the door.'

Father Mac made a sour face. 'This is not a flippant matter.'

'No. I'm sorry. It will all be done in the best possible taste.'

'Very well.'

Peter was surprised. 'You agree?'

'Yes,' Father Mac said dismissively, 'yes.'

'Thank you, Father. You won't regret it.'

'I hope you won't.'

A couple of minutes later, as Peter got into his car, he noticed Roy Quinn walking on the other side of the street with his little brother Sean.

Seeing them gave Peter an idea. He got in the car and drove directly to the Springville Estate. With the two brothers out of the house, he was interested to see who would answer the door.

He parked near the house, got out and hurried up the path. He knocked on the door sharply and waited. After a moment it was opened by a young girl, fair-haired and pretty, wrapped in a thick dressing-gown.

'Hello, I'm Father Clifford from Ballykissangel. And you are?'

'Grainne Quinn.'

'Roy's sister?'

She nodded. Peter noticed how desperately tired she looked. Then it clicked, and all at once he knew a lot more than he had known a minute ago.

'Of course . . . ' he murmured.

'What?' She was frowning and looking very uneasy.

'May I come in?'

'No.'

'I want to help, Grainne.'

'I don't need any help.'

Before he could say anything else she had slammed the door in his face.

He went back to the car, got in and waited. Five minutes later Roy and Sean appeared. Peter got out of the car and waited for them to approach. As soon as they saw him they began to look shifty.

'Hi, Roy,' Peter said brightly. 'Sean.' He waited until they were beside him. 'Can I have a word with you, Roy?' He glanced at Sean. 'Alone.'

Roy told Sean to go on home, he would be there in a minute. The boy sullenly did as he was told. Peter and Roy got in the car. Roy sat in the passenger seat staring ahead, avoiding eye contact with Peter.

'I know about the baby,' Peter said.

'What baby?'

'Come on, Roy, it wasn't me that was born yesterday.'

Roy sighed and bit down on his lip.

'You helped Grainne with the birth, didn't you?'

Roy nodded.

'Who's the father?'

'Some fella Grainne met.' Roy's voice was husky. ''Course he scampered as soon as he found out she was pregnant. Dad doesn't know. She kept it hidden from him. It wasn't hard. He's hardly ever around.' He turned his head and looked at Peter. 'She really misses the baby. She pretends she doesn't but I know. She cries herself to sleep at night.'

'I want to help, Roy. But I need your help first.'

Roy hesitated for a moment. Finally he nodded.

†

Grainne was still in her dressing-gown, doing the ironing, when she heard the front door open, then close again. She looked over to the hall door. Sean, in front of the TV set, sank further into his chair.

Roy came in, followed by Peter.

'What's he doing here?' Grainne said.

'He wants to talk to you.'

'Roy!'

'It's my fault, Grainne,' Peter said. 'Anyway, I'd already worked most of it out for myself.'

Grainne still looked upset, but some of her tension had gone. She told Sean to go to his room. He stayed where he was, silently staring at the television.

'Sean!'

Reluctantly, the boy pulled himself out of the chair and left the room.

Grainne looked at Peter. 'Is the baby OK?'

'He's fine. He's still in the hospital while they try and arrange adoption.'

Grainne nodded. 'He's better off having someone who can take proper care of him.'

'You could care for him, Grainne,' Peter said. 'You've cared for this whole family virtually on your own. But you're not alone. Not any more. There's help, if you want it.'

Grainne was hesitant. She looked at Roy. He shrugged.

'I couldn't do it to Dad,' Grainne said. 'It's hard enough for him.'

'I can talk to your father,' Peter said, 'if you want me to.'

Again Grainne hesitated, considering it.

'At least see a doctor,' Peter said. 'You're not well.'

'No.' Grainne shook her head, looking angry again. 'If I go to a doctor, the Social Services will get involved. They could split us all up.'

'They could help you,' Peter said.

'I can't take the chance,' Grainne said, picking up the iron again. 'What's done is done.'

†

Assumpta was tidying in the kitchen behind the bar when Niamh appeared in the doorway.

'Hello,' she said, and smiled wanly.

Assumpta wiped her hands on a towel. 'How are you?'

'Exhausted. I've been walking for miles.'

Niamh sat down at the table. Assumpta turned to the fridge in the corner and took out a bottle of champagne. She started opening it with her back to Niamh.

'It's a nice day,' Niamh said vaguely. She had found that tiring herself was a way of dulling the edge of her unhappiness, but getting tired was easier now than it had been before.

'Fancy a drop?' Assumpta said, turning. She held out the bottle in front of her and pulled out the cork the last fraction of an inch, making an agreeable pop.

'What's that for?'

'I put it aside for you.'

'To wet the baby's head, you mean?'

'Yeah. Still want some?'

Assumpta poured two glasses.

'Give it here,' Niamh said, grinning.

Assumpta raised her glass. 'To the next time.'

They clinked glasses and sipped.

'If there is a next time,' Niamh said.

Assumpta smiled. 'There will be. Trust me.'

Back at home, Ambrose was now out of bed and sitting in an armchair in the living-room, though he still had on his pyjamas and a dressing-gown. He had hoped for a quiet hour or two of meditation on his future, grim though that might have been. Instead, he had Brian Quigley for company, and all Quigley could do was complain.

'Do something!' he snapped, pointing out at the street. 'That thing there's costing me a fortune in hire charges!'

Ambrose sighed. 'If McMullen catches me not acting impartially, he'll tell Foley and that'll be it. I'll be packed off to the inner-city and you'll probably never hear of me again.'

'Every cloud has a silver lining.'

'And where I go,' Ambrose added, 'Niamh goes, too.'

'You're not going anywhere,' Quigley assured him. 'It's that monster McMullen who has to go.'

'It's your fault,' Ambrose said, and winced as the effort of raising his voice put a twinge across his back. 'You created that monster. Giving him the use of your car! Now he's talking about settling here. He's even started looking for a house!'

'Has he?' Quigley looked thoughtful.

'I suppose he could always use your car to move his things in.'

'Where is he now?'

Ambrose pointed to the office. 'He's in there, typing up his report.'

Quigley headed for the door.

'What's the plan?' Ambrose said.

Quigley paused at the door. 'The plan is to keep my daughter in Ballykay, which means keeping you here. Capisce?'

'Capisci,' Ambrose replied.

Twenty minutes later Ambrose decided he'd had enough and got out of the chair. He hobbled through to the bedroom and rolled onto the quilt. He was getting under the covers when Guard McMullen appeared in the doorway.

'I've completed my report on your father-in-law.'

'Good for you,' Ambrose grunted, pulling up the clothes. 'Now if you'll excuse me . . . '

'There's something else. I'm giving a lecture this evening at the youth club.'

Ambrose stared at him. 'What lecture?'

'The curate is giving a talk to the young people, so I've decided to address them afterwards on the subject of road safety.'

'You'll have to clear it with the Super first.'

'I already have.' McMullen was almost gloating. 'He's coming along to hear me.'

He allowed himself a smug grin before he left the room.

Ambrose pulled the duvet over his head, hoping everything that hurt him and annoyed him would simply go away.

Later that afternoon McMullen visited Brian Quigley at home. He waited while Quigley poured himself a whiskey.

'I don't see why I had to come all the way over here to talk.'

'It's a delicate matter,' Quigley said. 'I didn't want my son-in-law overhearing. Drink?'

'If you could get to the point.'

'As you wish.' Quigley sniffed his whiskey and took a delicate sip. 'I hear you may be looking for a place of your own here in Ballykay?'

'I might.'

'Well, it's just possible I might be able to help you.'

McMullen's eyelids dropped a quarter inch. 'Oh yes?'

Quigley picked up a brochure from the sideboard and dropped it in McMullen's lap.

McMullen read the cover aloud. 'Holiday homes by Quigley Developments.'

'I have one particularly nice property standing empty at the moment,' Quigley said smoothly.

McMullen was trying to look neutral, but his interest was visible.

'I could do with someone living there,' Quigley said, 'just to keep an eye on the place.'

McMullen appeared to have caught the subtext. He smiled tightly. 'Perhaps I will have a small one.'

FIFTEEN

AT TWENTY TO six the seats in the youth club hall were filling up. Peter stood at the door to the hall with Dr Ryan, greeting the young people as they came in. Nearby, Guard McMullen was bullying a few lads through the door he wanted them to use, as distinct from the one they were going to use on their own initiative.

'No, no,' he shouted at them, 'further that way!'

'How did he muscle in on this?' Ryan asked Peter.

'I think it's thematic – safety first in all things.'

Ryan shook his head. 'By the way,' he said, 'Father Mac phoned me earlier. Wanted to find out what time you were giving your talk.'

'Why didn't he call me?'

'I think he wanted to surprise you.'

'I bet he did.'

'The thing is,' Ryan said, 'I may have accidentally got mixed up. I thought you were speaking after McMullen so I'm afraid he may get here too late.'

He gave Peter a wry look.

'Good man, Michael.'

The time came for the talk to begin. Ryan wished Peter luck as he marched to the front of the little hall and faced the teenagers.

'OK, everyone, if I could have your attention, please?'

The response was slow. A few stopped talking, but several did not.

'Quiet!' McMullen shouted from the back of the hall. Silence fell.

'Um . . . thank you, Guard McMullen,' Peter said.

McMullen nodded and took his seat beside Ambrose, who had turned up in full uniform, in spite of his pain, to show Superintendent Foley that he was still the right stuff for the job.

'Right.' Peter rubbed his hands together. 'Hello, everyone. As you know, I'm here to talk about one thing and one thing only . . . '

Someone wolf-whistled and there was laughter. McMullen stood angrily to see who was the guilty party. Peter smiled.

'I think what I mean is we're all here to talk about love and what it means to us. We all, each one of us, have the desire to be loved, but we also have a responsibility towards those we love, and to ourselves . . . '

Brian Quigley was listening through a small partition between the foyer and the hall. As he stood with his face poked halfway through the opening, Donal came and whispered in his ear.

'All set, Mr Quigley.'

Quigley nodded, his face grimly satisfied.

Donal left.

As Peter continued there was some bored fidgeting amongst the members of his audience. From time to time as he talked, he glanced uncertainly at the doctor.

'Of course the love between any two people is a precious gift and like any gift it should be treasured. But it may also raise difficult questions and dilemmas which need answers . . . '

'Get on with it, Father!' a boy shouted.

McMullen was on his feet like a shot. 'Who said that?'

'As I was about to say,' Peter continued, 'these difficulties arise particularly when we come to express our love in a physical way.'

The fidgeting stopped. Quigley raised his eyebrows with amusement.

The talk lasted another ten minutes. Peter covered the topics of self-control, mutual respect and the virtue of deferred gratification. He managed to do it without mystifying, shocking, frightening or boring any of his audience.

'So, in conclusion, let me say that if you have any questions, please don't hesitate to come and talk to either me or Dr Ryan. Our doors are always open. Thank you.'

There was a loud surge of applause as Peter gathered his notes and stepped down from the platform.

Guard McMullen promptly took his place.

'Well done,' Dr Ryan said as Peter reached the back of the hall.

'Thanks, Michael. It's a start anyway.'

At that moment Father Mac appeared. He looked puzzled by the applause.

'Ah, Father,' Peter said.

'Did I miss it?'

Peter nodded. 'I'm afraid so.'

'My fault, Father,' Ryan said. 'I got mixed up.'

'And you a doctor,' Father Mac said, his eyes hardening for an instant.

'Of course if you'd told us you were coming,' Peter said, 'I could have – '

'Yes well, never mind,' Father Mac said, looking guilty.

Dr Ryan assured him it had gone well.

'Time will tell,' Father Mac grunted. 'Good night.'

He turned and left.

'That was close,' Peter muttered.

Dr Ryan's mobile phone rang. He went to a corner to answer it.

McMullen was meanwhile telling his audience that he had come to talk to them about road safety.

'Boring!' somebody yelled.

McMullen raised the long pointer he was holding. 'Any more of that and you're out!' he yelled, thereby setting the mood of his relationship with his listeners.

Ryan turned off his mobile. He looked concerned. 'Father, do you want to come to the hospital with me?'

'What for?'

'The baby's mother's just been admitted as an emergency.'

They left at once.

McMullen used the pointer to tap a flip-chart showing a plan of a road with various signs, traffic-lights, cars and pedestrians dotted across it.

'Now as you can see from the diagram, boys and girls, in this situation, there are a number of potential hazards for pedestrians. In particular, here, here and here. It is vital when crossing the road that you stay well clear of these areas; that is if you want to stay alive. So what should we be doing when we're standing on the kerb?

'Well it's really very simple. We should be observing the traffic . . . '

As McMullen droned on, Ambrose glanced anxiously at Superintendent Foley who was sitting beside him, listening intently to the lecture, seemingly unaware of a number of young people who were filing out of the hall shaking their heads.

Suddenly Liam appeared. He leaned in front of Foley, who looked put out, and held out a packet to Ambrose.

'Excuse me,' he said to Foley, without actually looking at him. 'Ambrose? Here are the keys to the cottage for Guard McMullen.'

Ambrose took the packet. He looked puzzled. So did Foley.

'What cottage?' Ambrose said.

'It's one of Mr Quigley's holiday homes,' Liam told him. 'He's lending it to the Guard until he gets fixed up with somewhere.'

Foley was wide-eyed. 'He's doing what?'

Foley's raised voice caused McMullen to stop speaking for a moment. He threw Foley a puzzled look before he continued.

'Of course it's essential that you remember to look left, look right and look left again. But don't forget to use your ears, too. You must look and listen as you cross the road. But don't hurry in case you trip and fall over. Next, let's take a look at pedestrian crossings . . . '

Liam, meanwhile, explained in hushed tones to Ambrose and Superintendent Foley just what the arrangement was between Quigley and Guard McMullen.

'It's OK, it's all fixed. Mr Quigley said to tell him that he'll leave the car for him in the driveway. So if you'll give him the packet, Ambrose, and Mr Quigley says to tell him he'll drop off the video machine later.'

Liam turned and slipped away.

Foley stared at Ambrose. 'What's going on?'

'Well, I heard the Guard was looking for somewhere to live,' Ambrose said, 'but I would never have thought he'd accept all this.'

'He isn't going to,' Foley said between clenched teeth.

†

In the corridor outside the surgical ward at the hospital, Peter was talking to Mr Quinn, father of Grainne, who had arrived back from Dublin that afternoon. Grainne had been taken ill shortly after he arrived.

As they talked, Dr Ryan joined them. 'They're giving her a blood transfusion. Otherwise she seems OK, physically anyway.'

Mr Quinn crossed himself. 'Thank God. How could I let this happen?'

The social worker from Cilldargan approached them from the top of the stairs. She was holding the baby in her arms. Roy was with her. He nodded to Peter.

'Hello, Father.'

Mr Quinn was on his feet, walking almost on tip-toe towards the social worker. He peered at the baby. 'Is this? . . .'

Roy nodded.

'Grainne wants to see him,' the social worker said.

'She wants to keep him, Dad,' Roy said.

'We all have to do some talking first,' the social worker added.

Peter put his mouth close to Dr Ryan's ear and said, 'So will I – with Father Mac.'

Mr Quinn pulled back the blanket to reveal the baby's face. As he looked at the tiny features tears welled up in his eyes.

'My grandson,' he whispered.

The social worker touched his shoulder. 'Shall we go in?'

Mr Quinn nodded. Roy told them he would be along in a minute. He turned to Peter and held out his hand. 'Thank you, Father.'

Through the window in the door Peter and Dr Ryan watched as Grainne, hooked up to drips, a nasal tube and a monitor, let go young Sean's hand and held out her arms for the baby. She took him and held him close, nestling him against her breast. Dr Ryan put his hand on Peter's shoulder as they watched, from a distance, the unifying of the Quinn family around its newest member.

†

At nine the following morning, as Assumpta crossed the road from Kathleen's shop, Peter came striding down the street to meet her.

'So how did the talk go last night?'

'Very well – I think,' Peter said. 'And I've got some good news.'

'You're taking it on tour.'

'About our baby. It looks hopeful that he'll go back to his mother.'

'That's grand.'

'It is, isn't it?'

'Father Mac will be really thrilled.'

'I can live with that,' Peter said. 'He'll have to.'

As Peter was about to enter Kathleen's he saw Guard McMullen come out of Ambrose's house carrying a suitcase. He glared sourly in the direction of the gigantic dumper truck, which Liam was revving up.

Inside the police house, Superintendent Foley was just taking his leave. As he pulled on his gloves he said, 'Of course I knew all along you were the right man for the job, Guard Egan.'

'Thank you, sir,' Ambrose said.

'In fact there probably isn't anyone else who could do it. So I'm relying on you to get things back to normal.'

'Certainly, sir.'

As Foley turned he saw Quigley appear and added, 'If normal is possible in this place.'

Foley saluted Ambrose briefly and left. Ambrose held the door for Quigley to enter. They approached the desk, Quigley rubbing his hands after a job well done.

'Right,' he said, 'mission accomplished. Business as usual.'

Ambrose sat down behind the desk. 'I hope you're not thinking of using that truck of yours again, Brian.'

Quigley stared at him.

'Aw, come on now, Ambrose . . . '

Ambrose picked up a green folder from the desk.

'Oh look,' he said with mock surprise. 'Mr Foley's forgotten his report about you. Will you take it out to him or shall I?'

He held it out towards Quigley, who realised at once that he had a choice. He snatched the report.

'You know, Ambrose, you're wasted here,' he said, his eyes slitted for a moment. 'The inner-city wouldn't stand a chance with you in charge.'

Quigley left. On the way out he passed Niamh, just coming in, and he kissed her cheek without breaking his step. She paused and threw a quizzical little smile at Ambrose. He smiled back.

SIXTEEN

IT WAS A FEATURE of Father Mac's nature that when he showed favour to a friend, he could make it look as if he were performing an act of charity for someone else entirely. The case in hand was typical. Kathleen Hendley wanted to find a job for her widowed cousin; Kathleen was a long-time friend and ally of Father Mac, therefore Father Mac took it upon himself to do Father Peter a favour and find him a housekeeper.

Peter and Father Mac argued about it as they walked down the main street towards Kathleen's house, which was round the corner from her shop.

'I don't need a housekeeper,' Peter said. 'I can manage perfectly well on my own.'

'Nonsense! She'll be a godsend. A sensible woman about the place to keep an eye on . . . things.'

'But Kathleen's already convinced I'm a rabid Communist. Her cousin will probably take me for a devil worshipper.'

They stopped at Kathleen's front door. Father Mac looked at Peter sternly as he knocked. 'Kathleen's cousin is a respectable widow who comes highly recommended,' he said. 'I hope you're not going to let superficial impressions affect your judgement.'

Peter choked back further comment. The door was opened by Kathleen. She beamed delightedly at Father Mac, as she always did.

'Father, hello.'

'Kathleen! Lovely day.'

'It is, thanks be to God.'

Kathleen's smile of welcome died almost entirely as she acknowledged Peter. 'Hello, Father . . . ' She touched Father Mac's elbow. 'Please, go on through.'

They went along the narrow passage to the sitting-room. A woman was sitting by the fireplace with her back to the door. She stood up as they came in, spilling a few biscuit crumbs from her plate.

'Nora,' Kathleen said, 'this is Father MacAnally, the parish priest, and Father Clifford.'

'Hello,' Nora said. 'Oh – excuse me.'

She bent briefly to brush the crumbs from her skirt, which clung to the shapely contours of her legs. Her bosom, too, was displayed to some effect by the bending. As she straightened again she smiled at the two priests, displaying perfect teeth and long lashes that fluttered gently over big brown eyes.

'Nora,' said Father Mac, trying not to look stricken. 'Delighted. How are you?' He offered her his hand. The instant her fingers touched his he snatched his hand back.

'I'm very well, thank you, Father.'

'So, you're looking for a post as a housekeeper.'

'That's right, Father.'

'Very good, very good. Well, we had a position on offer ourselves, right up till this morning, but we've had to re-appraise the situation.'

Peter, Kathleen and Nora were all staring at Father Mac with some surprise. He turned casually to Peter.

'Isn't that right, Father?'

Peter realised he had been dropped in at the deep end. He put on a regretful smile, desperately framing a reason for the turnaround.

'What Father MacAnally means is . . . given the current state of the parish finances, well, the resources just aren't there.'

Father Mac shook his head sadly. 'The collection was down again last week,' he said.

Kathleen tutted and glared at Peter. 'Typical. People today have lost all respect for the Church.'

'And Father MacAnally felt we should tell you in person,' Peter said, tidying up the tail-end of the lie.

Father Mac nodded. 'So, there you have it.'

There was a difficult silence in the room. Kathleen hurried to break it.

'Will you have a cup of tea, Father?'

'That'd be grand,' Father Mac said, just as Peter said no, they should be going.

'Maybe not,' Father Mac corrected, at the same time as Peter said maybe they would have one after all.

The muddle was interrupted by the arrival of Brian Quigley. He had let himself into the hall and now he put his head into the sitting-room.

'Kathleen, I just popped round to talk about that wholesale business, but I'll come back.'

'Brian,' Father Mac said cordially, sweeping a hand towards the beautiful woman in their midst. 'Have you met Kathleen's cousin Nora? This is Brian Quigley, Mrs Harrigan, one of our most prominent local businessmen.'

Quigley came into the room with his hand extended. He was staring at Nora so hard he tripped over the carpet. 'How do you do?' he beamed.

Father Mac said, 'Father Clifford had hoped to offer her a job as a housekeeper but circumstances . . . '

'That's a shame,' Quigley said, still beaming. 'But the curate's loss will be somebody else's gain, I'm sure.'

'So,' Nora said, holding Quigley with her steady brown eyes, 'can you think of anybody else who needs a housekeeper?'

No sooner had she said it than Quigley was thinking about it. 'Do you know, it's the oddest coincidence, you'll never believe it . . . '

A few minutes later, as Peter and Father Mac headed back towards the church, Peter made it clear that he didn't like being forced to extemporise like that, especially when it involved wriggling out of something he had believed was fixed in advance. Father Mac pretended not to understand. He had his own high horse to sit up on.

'I just wish you'd told me earlier,' he said.

'Told you what?'

'That the parish couldn't afford to hire a housekeeper. You could have saved me a lot of embarrassment.'

'What?'

Peter started to defend himself, but abandoned the attempt before he started. When Father Mac was entrenched in a position, however wrong-headed or bogus, he stayed there as long as he needed to, and no amount of argument would budge him.

'Still,' Father Mac sighed, 'I suppose it's for the best. Nora was obviously unsuitable.'

'She looked perfectly suitable to me.'

'Yes, I'm sure she did. But trust my judgement on this one.'

'Of course. I just wish you felt you could trust mine.'

'I know, I know, there's no need to tell me, you could resist temptation till hell froze over. But I have a duty not to place temptation in your way. The gossips round here have enough to keep them going as it is.'

'So now they'll gossip about Brian Quigley instead.'

'That's the least of his worries,' said Father Mac, smiling faintly. 'He still has to tell that daughter of his.'

Quigley waited until that evening to break the news. He told Niamh as she served him his dinner at home. She looked furious.

'A housekeeper?'

'Come on. Be realistic. You have Ambrose to look after. And I have you run ragged looking after me as well. It's not fair.'

Niamh folded her arms defensively. 'I don't mind.'

'I know. But you're a married woman now, with a husband of your own. And right now you need each other more than I need you.'

Niamh stared at her father with cold calculation.

'What's she like?'

'Who? Oh. About this tall, with brown hair. This is a lovely bit of steak.'

'Is she good-looking by any chance?'

Quigley shrugged. 'She might be. I didn't really notice.'

'Typical!' Niamh shouted, making Quigley drop his knife. 'All these years I've been waiting on you hand and foot and now I get laid off without even a day's notice!'

'Laid off?'

'Just so you can hire some floozie in a French maid's outfit to flick a duster round the place – '

'She won't be wearing a French maid's outfit – '

'Oh, so you've discussed it?'

'Niamh – '

'God knows what Mammy would have said!'

'She would have said catch yourself on,' Quigley said. 'If you want to nag someone, go home and nag Ambrose, that's what he's there for. And stop hanging round your daddy's house like an overgrown schoolgirl.'

Niamh snatched up her coat and pulled it on. Quigley was already regretting his outburst.

'Niamh – '

She came and leaned over the table. 'So. Does Fifi know how to get gravy stains out of flannel?'

'I would imagine she does, yes.'

'Good.'

Niamh reached across and tipped Quigley's dinner into his lap, then turned and stomped out of the house.

†

Siobhan and Padraig were already seated at the bar when Brendan took a seat between them. He was grinning. Padraig was lost in the evening paper. Assumpta was pulling several pints while the temporary bar help, Peggy, prepared plates of food in the back room.

'Assumpta!' Brendan said. 'God, but you're looking beautiful tonight.'

'What are you after?' Assumpta demanded.

'A drink is all. Whatever my chums here are having as well. And have one yourself.'

'Are you feeling all right?' Padraig asked him.

'Never better. The primary school at Allenstown was closed down today.'

'Huh! And you were nearly out of a job yourself a while back – '

'Sure the place is coming down with asbestos. You can't go near it without one of them NASA suits on.'

'You shouldn't gloat all the same,' Siobhan said. 'That's just, just . . . '

'Schadenfreude,' said Padraig.

Siobhan nodded. 'That's just exactly what it is, schaden-doodah.'

'It's schaden-nothing,' said Brendan. 'They're shipping the teachers off to other schools, but ten of the kids are coming here, to Ballykay. My job will be safe for months yet.'

'Fantastic,' Padraig said. 'Congratulations. Mine's a pint.'

'And I'll have another of these.' Siobhan held up her glass. 'When you're ready, Peggy.'

Peggy was leaning against the bar holding her stomach.

'I'm sorry,' she said, 'I don't feel too well.'

Brendan winked. 'Another patient, Siobhan, get your long gloves on.'

Assumpta came back from delivering pints to a table at the other end of the room. 'Peggy, they're still waiting for their prawns over there – are you all right?'

'I just feel a bit sick is all.'

'Seafood, is it?' Brendan said. 'You haven't been sampling the merchandise, have you?'

Assumpta glared at him. 'You don't mind sampling the merchandise.'

'That's different, Assumpta. The alcohol gets rid of all those nasty bugs.'

'Maybe,' she said. 'I see you're still here, though.'

†

Quigley was up, shaved, dressed and ready to greet his new employee at eight-thirty the next morning. As she hung up her coat and turned to face him, he was struck by her similarity to the late Grace Kelly. Or somebody like that. It was hard to guess Nora's age – early forties somewhere, that was as close as he could estimate – but she had about her the same quality of ageless poise that a few of his favourite screen actresses had possessed.

'Reporting for duty,' she said in her wonderfully soft, deep voice, pulling Quigley from his momentary reverie.

He gave her the tour, showing her first into the sitting room. There were newspapers and articles of clothing littered about the chairs and on the floor. The drinks shelf was well stocked, with several empties jammed in the wastepaper basket.

'In here I mainly watch TV,' Quigley said.

Nora remarked on the size of the television screen.

'Thirty-one inch,' he said. 'Gets all the satellite channels from Europe.'

'Oh yes?' Nora's voice went a little lower. 'I've heard about those.'

'It's the sport I watch, mainly,' he said defensively.

They went to the kitchen.

'It's a bit of a tip, I'm afraid. Needs a woman's touch. Not that I'm one of these men who think a woman's place is in the kitchen.'

Now Nora raised an eyebrow. 'So how many bedrooms do you have?'

Quigley actually felt himself blush. He led her out into the hall. 'Four,' he said. 'Or is it five? Yes, five.'

'You don't spend a lot of time at home.'

'Well,' he put a wistful note in his voice, 'I'm a busy man, and there's not much to come home for.'

He strode to the far end of the hall where a window looked out onto the lawn. In front of the window were bags of cement, piles of sand and a hillock of bricks covered with tarpaulin.

'But I'm going to fix that,' he continued. 'This will be the new snooker-room. The lads are starting on it Monday week. You won't have to worry about cleaning in there, it'll be strictly boys only.'

Nora smiled. 'I thought you didn't believe a woman's place is in the kitchen?'

'I don't. But it's not in the boys' room, either.'

He turned and opened a solid pine door with a small window at eye level.

'A sauna,' Nora said, stepping inside.

'The real thing, all the way from Finland. Father Mac is desperate to have a go. Feel free to use it yourself whenever you like.'

'I couldn't,' Nora said, then added coyly, 'what if you were in there?'

She turned and walked back to the kitchen.

Quigley watched her go, her hips swaying rhythmically. 'I'm sure we could come to some arrangement,' he muttered, closing the sauna door.

SEVENTEEN

AT ELEVEN-THIRTY that morning Niamh walked into her father's kitchen to find Nora up a stepladder, spring-cleaning the cupboards. She wore heavy-duty rubber gloves and was scrubbing vigorously at the inside of the double cupboard above the worktop. She didn't appear to have a hair out of place.

Niamh forced a friendly smile. 'Hi. I'm Niamh. Daddy probably mentioned me.'

Nora smiled back, the same way a receptionist would. 'He did, of course. Hello.' She continued to scrub.

'I only cleared those cupboards out a few weeks ago.'

Nora paused. 'Did you? Well, I always like to make a fresh start.'

She came down the stepladder and took the bowl to the sink.

'Do you need a hand?' Niamh offered.

'You're OK.' The cold smile again, before she tipped away the water and started refilling the bowl. 'I'll have the place spotless in no time.'

Niamh's smile was fading. 'I thought it was spotless. Pretty much.'

'Well, sometimes it takes experience. I mean, look up there.'

'Where?'

Nora pointed to a corner of the ceiling. 'Cobwebs. That's the first thing I look for. Especially where you're preparing food.'

'Is it?' Niamh wasn't smiling at all now.

Nora went back up the ladder with fresh water in the bowl and started rinsing the cupboard. Niamh watched, her mouth setting in a thin line.

'So apart from the place being infested with spiders, you're managing OK?'

'I'm fine, thanks,' Nora said sweetly.

'It's just I'd hate to see Daddy taking advantage.'

Nora paused. 'Brian? Not at all. Nothing's too much trouble. Can I get you a cup of tea?'

'I can manage, thanks.'

Niamh opened a cupboard expecting to find the tea, but it was full of neatly arranged cooking ingredients.

'I thought things needed a bit of rearranging,' Nora murmured, wiping vigorously.

'You might find Daddy liked them the way they were.'

'Well, men . . . ' Nora turned for a second, flashing her flawless teeth. 'When they get to a certain age, they fancy a bit of a change. You'll find that out for yourself, God help you. Now you have a husband of your own.'

She came down off the stepladder and pushed past Niamh to start on another cupboard, forcing Niamh to move away from where she was leaning.

'Did Daddy tell you that? About me being married?'

'I noticed the ring.'

'You have an eye for jewellery.'

'Nice and plain and simple.' Nora nodded at the band on Niamh's finger. 'A lot of people like that sort of thing. Anyway, I must be getting on – shall I give Brian a message?'

Niamh was finding it hard to be civil. 'Just tell Mr Quigley I called. And maybe I'll see him sometime.'

'I'll try to remember. Sorry, I've got so much to do!'

'Yeah,' Niamh said, 'me, too.'

She went to the door, feeling she had been hustled out of her own father's house.

'And any time you want to come round, just give us a call,' Nora said. 'We'll have the place looking lovely for you!'

'Thanks.' Niamh tugged the door open. 'See you.' She was careful to slam it behind her.

Later, in Fitzgerald's, she was still in a slamming mood. 'Bitch!' She banged her glass of orange juice down on the bar.

It was lunchtime and Fitzgerald's was busy. A tourist was leaning over Siobhan's shoulder waving a tenner at Assumpta, who was pulling pints with both hands and taking money in her teeth.

'Her and her cobwebs,' Niamh hissed. 'You'd think it was Dracula's castle the way she went on.'

'Come on . . . ' Assumpta, busy as she was, tried to play down the cataclysmic impact of Quigley's new housekeeper.

'Assumpta, she practically threw me out of the house! As if I was getting in her way!'

'Well, maybe you were.'

The tourist at the end of the bar waved his tenner a bit harder. 'Could I order, please?'

'I'll be right with you,' Assumpta said. She served three drinks, took the money and got change.

Niamh sighed. 'It looks like I'm getting in your way as well.'

'Sorry,' Assumpta said, 'Peggy's gone sick.' She moved along the bar and asked the tourist what he wanted.

'Two bowls of chowder, two pints of stout . . . '

Assumpta made a note on a pad and started pulling the pints.

'How is Peggy?' Siobhan asked. 'Is she over the food poisoning yet?'

Assumpta stared at her. 'Siobhan, she has appendicitis.'

'You have to watch out for the seafood at this time of year.'

'For the hundredth time, Siobhan, Peggy does not have food poisoning!'

The tourist was biting his lip. 'Actually,' he said, 'I think I'll just have two bags of crisps.'

Assumpta grabbed two bags from the back and threw them on the bar. She leaned close to Siobhan and said, 'Why don't you just dump a dead sheep in here and be done with it?'

When Assumpta moved back down to Niamh's end of the bar, she was still moaning about her father and Nora Harrigan. 'He only drops stuff on the floor so he can watch her bend over.'

Assumpta groaned. 'Niamh, what you need is some distraction, and I have just the job.'

'You're right. Why should I sit around fretting myself sick?'

'I need someone behind this bar and I need them right now.'

Niamh was nodding. 'If he wants to fill the house with floozies that's his business.'

'Exactly,' Assumpta said. 'So what about it?'

'Oh, I see,' Niamh snapped. 'You're on his side now.'

The tourist asked if there was any chance of him getting some change. Assumpta apologised and gave it to him. She turned back to Niamh. 'Look, your father's a grown man. We all need someone to look after us once in a while, it's only natural.'

'Huh! Hark at the expert on relationships.'

Assumpta bristled. 'What's that supposed to mean?'

'You've had hordes of men chasing you and none of them were ever good enough. I suppose you only want the ones you can't have.'

Assumpta forced herself to stay calm. 'Niamh, I know things haven't been going great for you recently, but this isn't a good time – '

'I know. You're too busy to listen, but you're not too busy to give lectures.'

'I'm not trying to lecture you, I'm trying to run a bar. If you want someone to talk at go and buy yourself a budgie.' She turned to a man holding two empty glasses. 'Two pints of stout, was it?'

Niamh got off her stool. 'Thrown out of two places in one day. This is getting to be a habit.'

She walked out of the bar.

The day was proving no less stressful for certain other people in Ballykissangel. Brendan's new boys, the temporary influx from the closed-down primary school at Allenstown, turned out to be six loud, snotty, rebellious boys of eleven and twelve, villains all. At their midst they had one especially virulent, foul-mouthed character called Con O'Neill, or Genghis to his mates.

'I don't know what safari park let that lot out,' Brendan confided to the Head at breaktime, 'but I fear the worst.'

Liam and Donal, meantime, had been sent for by Quigley's new housekeeper. When they arrived at the house they were both taken by the woman's comely appearance, but their impression of her as the sunny new presence in Quigley's life swiftly changed.

'You were supposed to be here at ten,' she snapped.

'There was something we had to finish off,' Liam explained.

'A crate of something, by the smell of you. Now get a move on and shift this junk.'

The junk she referred to was the small mountain of building materials Quigley had assembled to make a billiard-room.

Liam was astonished. 'You want it shifted? Where?'

'I don't care.'

'But I thought the boss wanted a snooker-room?'

'I'll be out in one hour,' Nora said, 'and if that stuff isn't gone, you two will be buried underneath it.'

With that she slammed the door in their faces.

'Mother of God,' said Donal. 'You could get tetanus off that tongue of hers. Do you suppose Quigley gets a lashing like that every night?'

'I'm saying nothing.' Liam pointed to the pick-up. 'Just load up the stuff and let's get out of here.'

'But what are we going to do with it?'

'We're going to make ourselves a few hundred quid, thanks to Brian Quigley and the Angel of Death in there. Come on.'

Peter, meanwhile, had just finished taking a penitent's confession at St Joseph's, and had turned to the other side of the confessional. He was sure he had heard someone come in, but when he opened the hatch no one seemed to be there.

Then a boy's voice piped up from below eye level.

'Bless me, Father, for I have sinned, it is two weeks since my last confession and these are my sins. I have been swearing a bit, Father. Well, I think I've been swearing.'

Peter frowned. 'You think you have?'

'Well, is "bloody" swearing, Father?'

'Yes, it is.'

'And "bugger"?'

'Yes . . . '

'And what about "sod"? And "boll – "'

'Yes, those are all swear words.'

'Here's something else,' the lad went on, 'if I ran over a load of teachers with a steam-roller, could I get absolution for all of them at once?'

'Why don't we just stick to the sins you have committed?'

'How much penance would I get? A million "Our Fathers"?'

Peter became aware of a growing racket outside the confessional. 'Have you finished?' he said.

'I can't think of any more right now. But I could come back next week.'

'Why don't you do that? I forgive you in the name of the Father and the Son and the Holy Spirit. Amen.'

As soon as the high-speed absolution was delivered, Peter slammed the hatch shut and got out of the confessional.

A gang of boys were moving away from the confessional laughing, slapping the cheeky penitent on the back.

'Right,' Peter said, 'all of you, get back to school, right now!'

One of them said, 'I thought the Church never closed its doors to sinners, Father?'

'You're all absolved,' Peter said. 'Now go on.'

At that moment Brendan Kearney came pounding into the church. The young ringleader fell on his knees in front of him.

'No! Please, Mr Kearney! Not the electric shocks! I promise I'll be good, I promise!'

'Come on, O'Neill . . . ' Brendan grabbed the lad by the scruff of the neck and lifted him to his feet. 'You're a menace, do you know that? A menace, that's what you are!'

Brendan turned to Peter. 'Sorry about this, Father.'

'Don't let him take us away, Father!' O'Neill wailed. 'He beats us with a big stick full of nails!'

Peter nodded. 'Not big enough, if you ask me.'

†

That evening Fitzgerald's was packed out. Assumpta was a blur behind the bar, running back and forward, promising service at one end while she attended to the other. Brendan had managed to squeeze in at the top end beside Siobhan. He bought her a drink and told her all about his troubles with the new boys from Allenstown Primary.

'I have enough on my plate with the kids who want to come to school, never mind chasing after the ones who don't.'

'Tell you what,' Siobhan said, 'I'll put them down for you.'

'Don't tempt me.'

'It'd be humane. You wouldn't feel a thing.'

Brendan gazed thoughtfully into his empty glass. 'I think we should release them back into the wild, let them feed on the tourists.' He sighed. 'I don't know, I should have jumped when I had the chance. Got myself a nice easy bar job, eh, Assumpta?'

She heard her name and looked round. 'What?'

'Is there any chance of that pint, by the way?'

By the time Brendan said it she had run off again to the other end of the bar, where Peter was putting empties on to the counter.

'Thanks,' she said. 'Do you want a job?'

'Sorry. I've got one. Can't you find anyone to help?'

'Not around here,' Assumpta said. 'They're all too busy feeling sorry for themselves.'

Ambrose pushed his way to the bar. 'A pint please, Assumpta.'

'Try handcuffing her, Ambrose,' Brendan said. 'It's the only way you'll get her to stick around long enough.'

Peter sidled up. 'How are you, Ambrose?'

'Fine, thank you, Father.'

He said it without looking at Peter, which made Peter realise that whatever the reason, Ambrose did not want company. He went back to helping Assumpta with the glasses.

Liam and Donal, in the meantime, had buttonholed Siobhan with a view to selling her a porch. Liam was into his sales pitch, shaping the concept with quick movements of his hands

'A traditional farmhouse porch,' he said, 'built to the highest standards by skilled Irish craftsmen.'

Donal winked. 'That's us.'

'And you'd be buying direct, cutting out the middle man.'

'You don't want Quigley involved,' Donal said. 'Sure he only employs cowboys.'

Siobhan kept a straight face. 'I thought he employed you.'

'That's right,' Liam said, thinking fast, 'but . . . we're tired of compromising ourselves. We want to do first-rate work.'

'I've never stopped you,' Quigley said, behind them.

Liam and Donal whirled to face him. He was smiling faintly, which they took to be the thin edge of wrath. They didn't know he was uncharacteristically mellow.

'Mr Quigley,' Liam said, forcing a smile. 'We were just talking to Siobhan about . . . '

He looked to Donal for help. 'Home improvements,' Donal said.

Quigley nodded. 'Like porches, for instance?'

'About time you had a bit of competition, Brian,' Siobhan said.

Liam and Donal drew back, ready for the explosion.

'I suppose you're right,' Quigley said. He turned to Liam. 'Are you all right for materials?'

'We are, thanks, aye,' Liam nodded, bewildered.

'In fact,' said Donal, 'it's funny you should ask about that, because – '

'Will you have a drink, Mr Quigley?' Liam said quickly, standing on Donal's foot.

'No, no, let me get you one. Assumpta!'

Quigley moved off to get himself into Assumpta's line of vision. Liam glared at Donal.

As Ambrose took his drink to a far corner, watched by Peter, Quigley squeezed in beside Brendan at the bar.

'Assumpta – three pints when you're ready, and whatever these ones are having.'

'Service is a bit slow tonight,' Brendan said.

'That's all right. No hurry.'

Siobhan tapped Brendan on the arm. 'Brian seems very relaxed this evening, doesn't he?'

'He does have a contented glow about him, yes,' Brendan said.

'I've seen that before, you know. In racehorses. When they come back from stud.'

Brendan turned to Quigley. 'So how's this new housekeeper working out, Brian?'

'Has she brought fresh air and sunshine into your lonely bachelor abode?' Siobhan asked.

Brendan grinned. 'Has she been cleaning out those crevices grown dusty from years of disuse?'

'Has she been rummaging through your drawers?'

Quigley looked calmly from one to the other. 'Envy is the vice of the inadequate,' he said. 'I've never suffered from it myself.'

EIGHTEEN

IT WAS THE FOLLOWING morning before Quigley noticed anything amiss. He was walking along the hall, tightening the knot in his tie, when he glanced out of the window. All he saw was the muddy lawn.

'Nora! Nora!'

He ran to the telephone at the end of the hall and snatched up the receiver. He was tapping in a number when Nora came hurrying from the kitchen.

'Where's that moron Ambrose? . . .' he stared at Nora, stark disbelief on his face. 'The materials for the snooker-room – they've been lifted!'

Nora laughed. 'Hold your horses.' She took the phone from him and put it on the hook. 'Liam and Donal tidied them away.'

'Liam and . . . Forget Ambrose! where's my gun?'

He stormed into the sitting-room like a wounded bear. Nora hurried to head him off. 'Will you go easy? You'll give yourself a heart attack.'

'I'll give them a lot worse!'

'Sit down a minute,' she said pleadingly. 'Sit down.'

She took him by the arm and coaxed him onto a chair. As he sank down grunting she began to massage his shoulders.

'A grand's worth of materials!' he snarled. 'Gone to Siobhan's new porch!'

Nora leaned down as she massaged, putting her mouth close to his ear. 'What do you want with a snooker-room anyway? It'd be like an overgrown youth club.'

'I wanted to relax in the evenings with my friends.'

'Your friends,' she snorted. 'I'll relax you. God, the knots in your neck . . . Come on now, think of your blood pressure.'

The kneading of his neck and shoulders grew more delicate, sensual. 'Tidied it up,' he mumbled. 'The cheek of them.'

'Hush now.'

'But my snooker-room . . . '

'Stop talking about it. Stop thinking about it.' Nora's fingers played along the sides of his neck, then squeezed momentarily, making him cry out. He sagged further into the chair.

'Isn't that better?' Nora crooned.

'Yeah,' he grunted. 'I suppose . . . '

He closed his eyes as she continued to stroke his shoulders and his neck.

Down in Ballykissangel, Ambrose was in his uniform and ready to go to work for the day, but all at once he found himself trapped by an outpouring of Niamh's temper.

'All I said, Niamh, was that you could fix up some new curtains – '

'There's nothing wrong with the old ones!'

'I know! You're the one who's always complaining about them!'

'You think I have nothing better to do all day than rearrange the furniture?'

Ambrose sighed. 'I thought that was the problem.'

'It isn't!'

'Well then, for the love of God, what is?'

Niamh glared. 'I'll give you a clue. It's about five foot ten with blue eyes and a gormless expression.'

Ambrose looked at her gormlessly. 'Could you give us another clue?'

There was a knock at the living-room door. It opened and Peter looked in, obviously embarrassed at interrupting.

'Sorry,' he said, 'I think Ambrose is needed up at Kathleen's.'

'What's happened?' Ambrose said.

'Well I'm not quite sure, but it sounds like she's been raided by an armed gang.'

When they got to the shop Kathleen was rearranging her rifled cigarette racks. She was agitated to the point of tears, and Peter stopped offering comfort when he saw it was the last thing she wanted. Kathleen was after justice, nothing less. Ambrose asked how many raiders there were.

'A whole bunch of them!' she howled. 'Vicious, foul-mouthed thugs!'

'Do you think you could give us a description?'

'No. They all had handkerchiefs over their faces. Filthy dirty ones, too.'

'What about their height?'

'There wasn't one of them over four foot six. The scrapings of the Dublin gutter if you ask me.'

Ambrose's pencil froze in the air above his notebook. 'Four foot? . . .'

Peter tutted. 'Brendan's new boys.'

'They tried to distract me while they went for the cigarettes. But I wasn't born yesterday. I bolted the front door and they ran straight out the back.'

Ambrose nodded gravely. 'I suppose they could be anywhere by now.'

Kathleen shook her head. 'I've locked them in the store-room!'

'You mean . . . '

Ambrose was heading for the store-room just as Brendan rushed into the shop.

'You haven't seen six juvenile delinquents around the place by any chance?'

'Follow us,' Peter said.

They went through to the back of the shop. Ambrose undid the top and bottom bolts of the store-room door and gripped the handle.

'Hold on, Ambrose,' Brendan warned.

Ambrose gave him a withering look. 'I can handle a bunch of kids, Brendan. They're probably sitting in the dark scared witless.'

He opened the door and stepped in. He was immediately bombarded with tins, eggs, flour and punctured Coke cans by a whooping mob hidden behind a wall of packing cases. Ambrose ducked, turned and came running out. He slammed the door and leaned on the wall.

'Mother of God,' Kathleen breathed, looking at the mess on Ambrose's uniform and the flour on his cap. 'What have they done?'

'I'm all right,' Ambrose assured her. 'I'm OK.'

'I'm not talking about you,' Kathleen whined. 'Who's going to pay for all this stock?'

'Maybe I'd better go in,' Peter said.

'No, Father,' Ambrose said firmly. 'We don't want a hostage situation.' He turned to the door and cupped a hand to his mouth. 'You boys! Come out now! You're surrounded.'

The clear voice of Con O'Neill penetrated the panels of the door. 'Come in and get us, you big thick!'

Peter stepped forward and tried a wheedling approach. 'Look, fellas, it doesn't have to be this way. No one's been hurt. Just put the tins down and come out, and nothing will happen to you, I promise.'

'We want food sent in!' O'Neill shouted.

'What?'

'Pizzas! Big ones! And we want a bus!'

'A bus?' Ambrose called. 'Where to?'

'Butlin's!'

'This is ridiculous,' Peter said.

Ambrose could see Peter expected him to take the situation in hand. 'I'm not going in there again without body armour, Father.'

Niamh appeared from the shop. She looked at the state of her husband and tried not to laugh. 'Pancake Day was months ago, Ambrose.'

'What are you doing here?' he asked stiffly.

'I couldn't stand the suspense. What's going on?'

'Brendan's new boys have barricaded themselves inside Kathleen's store-room.'

'What? Ah, for God's sake . . . '

Before anyone could stop Niamh she opened the store-room door and went in. She closed the door firmly behind her. Ambrose tried to go in after her, but Peter held him back.

'You'll only make things worse. There's nothing we can do now but wait.'

'And pray,' Brendan added. He saw Kathleen, Ambrose and Peter stare at him. 'Sorry, Father,' he said, 'that's your line.'

They stood in silence, hearing muffled voices on the other side of the door. Abruptly the sound stopped.

The door opened and the six boys shuffled out, looking contrite. Niamh came out after them, calm and unruffled.

'Say sorry to Mrs Hendley,' she said firmly.

'Sorry, Mrs Hendley,' they chorused.

'The school will pay for the damage,' Niamh told Kathleen. She looked at the boys. 'You lot can pay back the school. OK, Brendan? Right then, outside.'

As the boys trooped out Niamh sidled up to Brendan. 'You just have to show them who's boss,' she whispered.

Brendan watched the boys march silently out of the shop. He was amazed. 'I've been trying to do that all week.'

They watched Niamh organise the gang, confiscating the odd can of Coke as she frisked them.

'Look at her,' Brendan said. 'A natural.'

Peter asked him if he could use a volunteer at the school.

'She wouldn't, would she?'

Peter called to Niamh and hurried out to speak to her. As Brendan followed him he paused in the doorway to call back to Ambrose, 'That's some woman you have there!'

Ambrose smiled wanly and picked a couple of fragments of eggshell off his tunic.

†

That evening Peter visited a couple of sick parishioners at the lower end of Ballykissangel and stayed late with one of them, eighty-year-old Tommy Doolan, who liked beating the curate at a game of draughts.

Shortly after eleven-thirty Peter made his way back up the road. As he passed Fitzgerald's he paused to look in through the open door. Assumpta was alone, wearily looking around at the tables and bar piled with dirty glasses and overflowing ashtrays.

'Dear oh dear,' Peter said, stepping inside. 'Looks like you could use a skivvy.'

'It's not a skivvy I need, it's a flame-thrower.'

Assumpta took a sip from a glass of wine on the counter, then started gathering glasses and tipping the contents of ashtrays into a bucket. Peter took off his jacket and rolled up his sleeves. He started at the far end of the bar, stacking empty glasses and putting them on the counter.

'I'm working on this great idea,' Assumpta said. 'A self-service pub. The punters pour their own pints and pay me at the checkout.'

'But how would they get to savour your sparkling wit and repartee?'

Assumpta made a face. 'Would you ever bog off?'

'That's the kind of thing I meant.'

'They can pay extra for it.' She paused and watched Peter for a moment. 'What are you doing?' She had only just noticed that he was clearing glasses.

'I'm training for a second career, Assumpta. In case the bottom drops out of God-bothering.'

'There's more to it than stacking glasses. You have to move about ten times faster. And wiggle your arse a bit.'

'I was wiggling it.'

'Oh. Well,' Assumpta sighed, 'never mind, you make an OK priest, I hear.'

'Finish your drink, please. We're closed.'

'Only if you join me.'

Peter hesitated.

'Go on,' she pressed him. 'It's all the thanks you'll get.'

'All right then,' he said. 'Just a big one.'

In fifteen minutes they had the bar tidied. Peter kept Assumpta entertained throughout the drudgery by telling her about the exploits of Con O'Neill and his gang. As Peter wiped down the top of the bar Assumpta took a gulp from her second glass of wine. It was her favourite tipple, and it was beginning to have an effect.

'And Niamh saved the day?' she said. 'I don't suppose Ambrose liked that.'

'He won't mind. She might go easy on him now she has the teaching job to keep her busy.'

Assumpta looked around the bar. 'Well.' She nodded approvingly. 'Who needs extra staff when you have the intercession of the Church?'

'Don't start depending on me,' Peter said. 'I'm not the reliable type.'

'You're more reliable than most of them,' Assumpta said. 'I could be throwing a fit behind the bar and they'd worry about the head on their pint. No, you're the only one who gives a damn.'

'Oh, I don't know.'

'You are,' Assumpta said earnestly.

'Cheers.' Peter took a drink of his wine and tried to change the subject. 'So what was this terrible thing Niamh said to you?'

'When? Oh, that – it was something about me always wanting what I couldn't have.'

'Ah. The human condition.'

'Yeah, but you're human.'

'Oh, I've been promoted,' Peter said, keeping it light.

Assumpta looked deadly serious. 'Do you ever want what you can't have?'

Peter laughed awkwardly. 'Yeah . . . '

'And what's stopped you?'

Assumpta was looking at him steadily. Her meaning was clear. Peter started to take off his bar apron.

'What stopped you?' she said again.

He shrugged. 'Me.'

'Why? What are you afraid of?'

'Nothing.' Peter sipped his drink. 'Well, I'm afraid I have to say Mass at eight.'

'So that's it? It's that simple?'

'What?'

'Never mind. Go on.' There was no trace of warmth now. 'I'm tired.'

Peter put on his jacket. 'You'll go to bed, yeah?'

'I might do,' Assumpta said airily. 'Some of us have free will.'

'We all have.' Peter opened the door. 'Goodnight, then.'

'Goodnight,' Assumpta called. 'And thanks,' she added coldly.

'You're welcome.'

Peter closed the door gently behind him.

†

The following morning at eight o'clock sharp, Brian Quigley awoke with a moderate hangover to see Nora standing over the bed with a tray.

'Good morning,' she chirped. 'It's a beautiful day.'

He was less than charmed.

The night before she had made him dinner, even though he said he would be out, and sooner than offend her, he sat and ate her meal right on top of one he'd already had. She had now also moved the drinks to a shelf in the kitchen, so that each time he wanted a whiskey, he had to go past her and collect a small disapproving frown for his trouble. Increasingly he had the feeling that the price of a pretty face about the place was a curtailment of his freedom of movement.

'Nora,' he said now, 'you don't have to keep bringing me breakfast in bed . . . '

'It's no trouble. I've laid your clothes out.'

'I wanted to wear my tweed jacket.'

'What?' She looked astonished. 'That old thing? You did not. Anyhow I threw it out.'

She turned and left the bedroom.

Quigley stared at the open door. 'You did what?'

'It was past its best,' Nora said. 'Cluttering up the place. What this house really needs is a good clear-out.'

Quigley emerged from his bedroom tying the belt of his dressing-gown.

'You threw out my Harris jacket?' He could scarcely believe it.

'I'll make a start in here today,' Nora said, indicating the room next to Quigley's. 'It can be my room.'

'But that's Niamh's room.'

'That's a lovely dressing-gown, Brian.' She stroked the material, letting her hand rest on his chest. 'Is it silk?'

'She's keeping all her stuff there. Maybe we should ask.'

'Are you going to be using the sauna this evening?'

'What?' Quigley blinked. 'I don't know, why?'

'I'd like to try it. You wouldn't mind sharing, would you?'

'No, no, not at all . . . '

Nora turned him back towards the bedroom. 'Go on in there and eat,' she said. 'A big man needs a big breakfast.'

Later, when he had bathed and shaved, Quigley put on the striped blazer she had put out instead of his beloved Harris tweed jacket. He studied himself in the mirror as he knotted his tie. It was no good.

'I look like a geriatric gigolo,' he muttered. 'Nora!'

He stamped out into the hall. He could hear her humming softly in Niamh's room. He put his eye to the crack of the door and peeped in.

Nora was pulling Niamh's wedding dress out of the wardrobe. He watched with growing alarm as she held the dress up against herself, stepped in front of the cheval glass and nodded approvingly.

He stepped back from the door. A chill of foreboding passed through him.

NINETEEN

THINGS GOT NO BETTER. Later that morning, as Quigley chose a bottle of wine in Kathleen's as a gift for a business contact, Kathleen appeared to be in one of her occasional moods for conversation. After a mandatory opener about the weather, she got right to the topic of her cousin. She remarked that Nora had always had bad luck with men. 'But I suppose all that's changed now.'

Quigley let her words soak in. He decided they chimed with his general sense of uneasiness about Nora. 'What do you mean, Kathleen?'

She smiled archly. 'With you two getting on so well . . . will there be wedding bells in Ballykay, I wonder?'

Quigley brought his bottle to the counter. 'How do you mean she's had bad luck?'

'Losing two husbands.'

'Two?'

'Fine men they were.' Kathleen sighed. 'Nobody could have looked after them better than Nora. Still, the Lord moves in mysterious ways.' She smiled again. 'I hear Jamaica's a great place.'

She had lost Quigley. 'Jamaica?'

'You know.' Kathleen averted her eyes. 'For a honeymoon.'

Quigley was dumbstruck.

He went straight from the shop to the police house, looking for Niamh. He found her in the sitting-room, preoccupied with cutting figures out of a comic and sticking them on to a large sheet of card. Ambrose, home for his tea break, sat miserably in the corner.

Quigley came straight to the point. He told Niamh he was a fool, he should have listened to her, he should never have allowed that Nora to set foot over his doorstep. Throughout the whole recital Niamh remained engrossed in what she was doing.

'She's throwing your stuff out on the street,' Quigley told her.

'Fine,' Niamh said, without looking up. 'Ambrose can pick it up later.'

'She's given away half my clothes.'

Niamh nodded. 'Maybe she thought you wouldn't need clothes.'

'It's no use asking her anything, she won't listen – '

Niamh pointed to a bottle on the table beside Quigley. 'Would you pass us that glue over there?'

He put the bottle in front of her. 'If I told her you were coming back, she couldn't argue.'

'So tell her,' Niamh said.

Quigley's face lit. 'You'll come back?'

'No.'

'For God's sake, Niamh, I wanted the company of someone my own age. Is that so awful?'

Niamh stared at him.

'All right,' he said, 'I might have been a bit hasty. I'm sorry.'

'I'm sorry, too. But someone else needs me now.'

'Surely to God Ambrose can spare you for a few hours?'

Ambrose opened his mouth, but Niamh spoke first.

'Not Ambrose,' she said, 'the kids. They need me. You're a grown-up, you'll have to sort your problems out for yourself.'

Quigley went to St Joseph's to speak to Peter. They sat side by side on a pew while Quigley poured out his heart. Peter had never seen him so agitated.

'You say she's brainwashing you, Brian – isn't that a bit strong?'

'You don't understand. She's taking over my life. She's like a woman possessed.'

'I'm not sure I can help you. You need special permission for an exorcism.'

'Father, this is not a joking matter.'

Peter shrugged. 'She seems perfectly pleasant to me. Comes to Mass most days, though perhaps that's a bit strange. She does a lovely job on the altar. Have you seen those flowers?'

'Indeed I have.' Quigley glanced sourly at the lavish floral arrangements decorating the altar. 'They're from my garden.'

'A week ago,' Peter said, 'maybe Father Mac would have agreed with you, but now he won't hear a word against Nora Harrigan.'

Quigley lowered his head. 'I'm doomed.'

'Aw come on, Brian. Maybe you should talk to Father Mac anyway. Somebody nearer your own age . . . '

Quigley glared.

'I'm sure he'll tell you you're imagining things.'

'I suppose I could invite him round,' Quigley said morosely. 'He's been looking for an excuse to visit ever since – ' Suddenly he brightened. 'Father, you're a genius. I could kiss you.'

Quigley got out of the pew and practically ran up the aisle to the door. Peter couldn't begin to understand what kind of favour he had done. He hoped it would turn out as terrific as Brian seemed to think it was.

Leaving the church a few minutes later, Peter saw Ambrose go past the railings. He looked miserable, as he did most of the time lately.

'Well, well. Walking the streets again, Ambrose?'

'It's warmer out here than it is at home, Father.'

'I suppose Niamh has buried herself in her work?'

'Buried me in it, more like.'

Peter caught the persistence of the low mood. He stayed determinedly reasonable, anxious to let Ambrose see matters in plain, undramatic terms.

'I shouldn't worry,' he said. 'It's only for a while, until the extra pupils go back to their own school. And it's helping to take her mind off losing her baby.'

Ambrose nodded glumly. 'Right enough. I just wish there was something would take my mind off losing the baby.'

Peter didn't know what to say.

'It wasn't just hers, you know? It was mine, too. Still, no one's worried about that. Good old Ambrose, the turnip in the uniform.'

'Ambrose, I – if you . . . '

'Never mind, Father. You've sorted Niamh out, anyhow. Thanks for that.'

He walked on, leaving Peter feeling like an idiot.

†

That evening Nora came in with a load of wallpaper samples and swatches of fabric. Quigley greeted her in his dressing-gown with a towel round his neck.

'Ah, Nora,' he said cheerfully, 'you're back.'

'Brian! Tell me now, what do you think of these?'

She showed him a few of the samples. He nodded and made little sounds in his throat, feigning enthusiasm for the textures and tints.

'Very nice. Where are they for?'

'In here. They'll brighten the place up a bit. Mind you, that carpet will have to go.'

Quigley kept smiling. 'That's great. Lovely. You must be exhausted traipsing round the shops, aren't you? I was just using the sauna, but I'll be out in ten minutes.'

He moved off up the hall. Nora watched him go. She smiled.

Three minutes later, wearing only a towel, Nora let herself into the sauna. She smiled at the towel-wrapped figure in the corner, sitting stooped forward, his head draped in another towel.

Nora cranked up the temperature a few notches, then sat down on the bench beneath him, her shoulder against his leg. He moved away a little. She looked up, smiled and stroked his bare leg.

'I always wondered what went on in these mixed saunas,' she said huskily.

The door opened. It was Niamh. She looked at the two occupants and blushed. Nora blushed, too.

'Oh, hello,' Niamh said. 'I'm sorry, Daddy, I heard you were looking for me . . . '

The man pulled the towel off his head. It was Father Mac, more red in the face than either of the women.

'Eh, ah, he was here a minute ago,' he mumbled. 'I was just talking to him . . . '

Too late Nora snatched her hand away.

'But there's no sign of him,' Niamh said. 'Sorry to interrupt, Father. I'll leave you to it.'

'No, no, wait, you're all right, I'm just coming out – excuse me . . . '

Father Mac leapt to his feet and scrambled out of the sauna as if his reputation was on fire. He raced past Niamh and disappeared down the hall. She turned and looked coolly at the crimson housekeeper, still sitting on the bench.

'I'll bet you found a few cobwebs up there, Nora.'

Twenty minutes later Quigley rang Father Mac's doorbell. Father Mac himself opened the door, still flustered, his hair wet and his clothes sticking to his damp body.

'What's the panic?' Quigley said. 'And where did you disappear to?'

Father Mac jerked his head towards the study. Once inside, he gave Quigley a triple measure of malt whiskey and explained what had occurred.

'Well . . . ' Quigley shrugged. 'If nothing happened, what's the problem?'

'It's your daughter that's the problem. She's bound to have got the wrong end of the stick.'

'Well, everyone will understand that.'

'I don't want everyone to understand it,' Father Mac said. 'She can't go spreading this all round the parish. Can you not talk to her?'

'I will, of course.'

'Thank God.'

'And we can rely on Nora not to say anything – probably,' Quigley said. He paused, then added, 'Even to Kathleen.'

Father Mac shook his head. 'That's it. We have no choice.'

'Come on now, Father – '

'Brian, it's your Christian duty.'

'But she's the best housekeeper a man could ask for.'

'We're talking about the good name of the Church!'

'But it would be her word against yours,' Quigley said. 'Your position is unassailable.'

'They've said that about bishops before now, and see where some of them finished up, Tierra del Fuego or somewhere.'

Quigley sighed heavily, doing a fine impersonation of a man acting against his own wishes. 'It'd be unfair dismissal.'

'I'll make it up to her. I'll make it up to you, too.'

Quigley finished his whiskey and shuddered pleasurably. 'You've a good taste in malt.'

'Let me get you another.'

As Father Mac went to the sideboard Quigley permitted himself a smirk.

The following morning Donal and Liam completed the porch they had been building for Siobhan. When Liam called her out to have a look, she came hurrying from the kitchen to the front door, unlocked it and opened it. Liam and Donal saw the problem at the same instant. They winced a moment before the outward-opening front door smashed the glass of the porch door.

'Holy God!' Liam shouted as the last of the glass showered to the ground. 'That door opens outwards, Siobhan!'

'I know it does,' she said. 'I told you it did.'

Liam looked at Donal.

'She never,' Donal said. 'Well, maybe she did, I thought she meant – '

'No problem, Siobhan,' Liam called. 'We'll just re-hang the porch door.'

'But there's no room for this one to open.' She fought her way out through the creaking wreckage.

'Well, then we'll re-hang that one, too.'

'There's another alternative,' Siobhan said. 'You can take the whole bloody lot down and give me my money back. Talk about cowboys!'

'Ah now, Siobhan,' Donal said, 'it just needs a bit of a tweak – '

Siobhan reached into her bag in the back of the Land Rover and produced a fearsome looking pair of castrating shears. 'You see these? I'm the one who'll be doing the tweaking if you don't clear that monstrosity out of here.'

'If you're sure that's what you want,' Liam said.

'Today!'

She marched off as Quigley approached, radiant with his newfound sense of freedom.

'Lovely morning, Siobhan,' he called.

She ignored him. He turned to Liam and Donal. 'So how's this job going, lads?'

'Fine.' Liam pointed at the wreckage. 'Siobhan wanted us to demolish this old porch for her.'

'And I see you've made a start already. Pity. There's some nice materials in there.'

Liam and Donal looked at each other, realising they had been rumbled.

'Your woman said you didn't want them,' Donal muttered.

'I don't now, anyway,' Quigley said. 'Don't worry.'

Liam looked enormously relieved. 'Are you sure?'

Quigley nodded. 'You can pay me back out of your wages. Unless you're still in business for yourselves?'

'No, Mr Quigley. Thanks.'

'Think nothing of it.'

A little later that morning Nora Harrigan lugged her suitcase onto the Dublin bus. From the other side of the street, Quigley and Niamh watched it pull away.

'That was close,' Niamh said.

'I suppose it was,' Quigley said, sounding oddly wistful.

'Come on, Dad, don't pretend you're sorry to see her go. You're the one who called me up to the house so I could catch her with Father Mac.'

They walked across the street arm in arm.

'It was nice while it lasted, Niamh, that's all. Having a good-looking woman around the place.'

'You had me round the place.'

'That's not quite the same thing. For a while there, it felt like I could start my life over again. I'm not getting any younger.'

'You're not getting any wiser, either,' Niamh told him. 'You're too set in your ways to change now. You like being single.'

'I suppose I must. Just make sure you don't end up the same way.'

Niamh looked surprised. 'Me?'

'Poor old Ambrose looked like a dog in the rain the last time I called round. Are you two even talking to each other?'

'Of course.'

'Good. Because decent partners don't grow on trees.'

Niamh took her arm out of her father's and stopped walking.

He looked at her. 'Are you not heading up to the school?'

'I've just remembered, there's something I forgot to do at home.'

She hurried back towards her own house. Quigley shrugged and walked on, unaware that Ambrose was walking along the other side of the street, and Niamh was running after him.

As Quigley went into Kathleen's for his newspaper Assumpta was morosely mopping the floor of Fitzgerald's.

Peter put his head round the door. 'Hi. I saw Peggy's mother at Mass. She'll be back next Monday, as long as you promise not to make her laugh.'

Assumpta stared at him. 'I think I can manage that.'

'So if you want me to moonlight in the meantime . . . '

'I don't, thanks,' she said coldly.

'You'll be all right?'

'Not really. It's just easier by myself.'

Peter finally realised she was upset about something. He went in and closed the door.

'Assumpta?'

She was staring at him again, an appraising look with not a trace of approval. 'I don't mind the regulars,' she said. 'I can rely on them to let me down. But you . . . '

'What have I done?'

'We were having a conversation. You walked out.'

'Assumpta, it was past midnight. You'd had a hard day. You were tired.'

'What does that mean?'

Peter hesitated.

'Are you saying I was drunk?'

'You weren't yourself.'

'What did I say?'

Peter started feeling uncomfortable again. 'It wasn't so much what you said – '

'What sort of friend are you?' she said. 'You're there for everybody else, but when I want to talk you run off.'

'I never wanted to upset you.'

'Well, you managed it all the same.'

'Look, this is silly.'

Assumpta, angry suddenly, threw down her mop and strode to the door.

'Assumpta, listen to me . . . '

'Just make up your mind where your priorities lie, OK?' She pulled the door open. 'Until then, please don't come into my bar.'

Peter looked at her for a moment, then walked out. She slammed the door behind him.

Peter stood outside, staring up at the sky in impotent fury.

Quigley came past, crossing the road from Kathleen's. He had caught the slamming of the door.

'Women, eh?' he grinned, and slapped Peter's chest with his rolled-up newspaper. 'Maybe we're better off without them, eh, Father?'

He strode on, unaware of how close Peter had been to punching him in the mouth.

TWENTY

FOR SIOBHAN, THE tone of events seemed to have been set by the catastrophe of the new porch. After that, the whole working day was bedevilled with upsets and minor disasters. At one farm she managed to skin her knuckles tethering a bull before giving it an injection; on the road between Cilldargan and Wicklow she detected a stammer in the rhythm of the Land Rover's engine and discovered, a mile from the nearest filling station, that she had run out of petrol. There was also the matter of an old sheepdog she had known for years which actually bit her; the extreme nuisance of a whole box of vaccine being smashed when a horse stepped on her bag, and the maddening discovery of a hole in one of her wellingtons as she waded through a puddle of nastiness outside a cow shed.

By four o'clock she felt like going home, but there was one more call to make. Eamonn Byrne's pigs were unwell, and he was very concerned.

'They're itching something terrible, Siobhan,' he told her as he followed her round the pig pen. 'They're all the time scratching themselves up against the slats and up against each other, and when they're not doing that they're just lying about looking miserable.'

Siobhan took blood samples from all of the pigs and labelled the specimen bottles with the pet name of each animal.

'That's all we can do for now,' she told Eamonn. 'We should have the results in a couple of days.'

She began packing up her equipment.

'You seem to be taking this awful serious,' Eamonn said.

'It's probably nothing, but I just want to be sure.'

Eamonn was not placated. 'Be straight with me, Siobhan. Am I going to lose them?'

It was not a question she could answer. 'Your pigs haven't been vaccinated against Aujesky's Disease, have they?'

Eamonn looked puzzled.

'It's a virus. It attacks the animal's nervous system.' It was also known as pseudo-rabies, but she didn't want to tell him that and throw him into a panic. 'I'm concerned because there's been an outbreak in Cilldargan.'

'Is it fatal?'

'It can be.'

Eamonn looked at his pigs. 'They might just be lumps of bacon on legs to anyone else, but they mean the world to me, Siobhan.' He patted a huge sow tenderly. 'Isn't that right, Mary?'

From somewhere outside a woman called to Eamonn. She sounded irritable. She called again as Eamonn and Siobhan emerged from the pig pen. Siobhan was startled. Standing in the doorway to the house was an attractive young woman, wearing nothing but a towel wrapped around her.

'Eamonn, is it asking too much to get a bit of hot water around here?'

Eamonn gave her a sheepish smile. Siobhan stared, dumbfounded.

Eamonn followed the girl into the house. Siobhan trudged back to the Land Rover. After a day like she'd had, she supposed a bizarre note like that was the fitting conclusion.

That evening, before Fitzgerald's started to get busy, Brendan and Padraig spent some time trying to talk Assumpta into helping with the forthcoming Ballykissangel Festival. Assumpta was unmovable. She didn't want to help.

'I told you already, Brendan, I'm too busy here.'

'Ah, come on, Assumpta, get into the spirit of things, it's only once a year.'

The bar door opened. Peter hovered uneasily at the entrance. He and Assumpta exchanged a glance. Assumpta looked at Brendan again.

'I run the pub,' she said, 'not a child-minding service.'

Padraig groaned. 'Where's your community spirit?'

'Right here, behind the bar, where it's staying.'

Brendan turned to Peter. 'I think a little divine intervention's required. Father, will you tell Assumpta we need her to help out at the Festival?'

Peter looked uncomfortable.

'Oh, no,' Assumpta said, 'I won't be bullied into anything, least of all by a priest.'

Peter turned and addressed Brendan and Padraig, but the real target of his message was standing behind the bar. 'The whole point,' he said, 'is that we want willing and enthusiastic volunteers. It's no use asking people who have no interest.'

Brendan and Padraig exchanged a wary look. Assumpta looked stung.

'Come on,' Peter said. 'Drink up, Brendan, the meeting started five minutes ago.'

The Festival Committee – Quigley, Niamh, Brendan and Peter – were meeting in the dining-room at Quigley's house. When they were all finally seated around the dining table, Brendan, the supplier of timetables, handed round the photocopied sheets of paper.

'This is just a rough timetable of the day's events,' he said.

Everyone studied the schedule.

'What's the gap after the Irish dancing?' Peter asked.

'That's Brian's contribution,' Brendan said.

They all looked expectantly at Quigley. 'Don't keep us in suspense, Brian,' Peter said. 'What have you got up your sleeve?'

Quigley already looked pleased with himself. He got to his feet and picked up a roll of paper from the sideboard. He slowly unrolled it to reveal a poster.

'QUIGLEY DEVELOPMENTS IN ASSOCIATION WITH "BABBLING BROOK" PRESENTS – THE LILY OF BALLYKISSANGEL.'

The wording was illustrated with a tacky drawing of an Irish 'Colleen'. The others exchanged troubled glances.

'You're all familiar with the "Rose of Tralee" competition?' Quigley said. 'Well, this is the Ballykay version.'

Peter looked uneasy. 'A beauty contest?'

'It's more than that, we're searching for the new face of "Babbling Brook".'

Brendan shook his head. 'I'm not with you, Brian.'

'I've managed to get sponsorship for the event from a company that bottles spring water. They're holding regional heats to find a beautiful girl for their advertising campaign, so we're covering this area.'

The rest of the committee looked uneasy.

'Correct me if I'm wrong, Brian,' Peter said, 'but isn't our Festival supposed to be a celebration of Irish culture?'

'Absolutely, and what could be more cultural than a celebration of Irish beauty?'

Now the others looked openly sceptical.

'The competition's open to any girl,' Quigley continued, 'provided she's under twenty-four and a native of Ballykay.'

'Pity,' Brendan said, 'I had my money on Padraig.'

'And you'll be judging it, Dad?' Niamh said.

'No. Representatives from "Babbling Brook" will make up the panel. I'm going to compere the event.'

Brendan snorted. Quigley glared at him.

Peter said, 'I still fail to see how a beauty contest will help promote culture in our community.'

'A winning beauty means publicity,' Quigley said patiently, 'and good publicity ups the tourist stakes for Ballykay. Just think of the potential,

Father. Look at what the Rose Festival has done for Tralee.'

Quigley took a slug from his tumbler of whiskey, smiling to himself. The others continued to look uncertain.

†

Siobhan dropped into Fitzgerald's later that evening to relay the gossip about Eamonn and the female in his life. Assumpta listened while she served drinks. Further along the bar, Padraig and Brendan were deep in a conversation of their own.

'There she was,' Siobhan said, 'this glamorous bit of stuff, all teeth, and legs up to her armpits.'

'Sure it wasn't a horse?' Assumpta said.

'This was no horse, believe me. Standing there, acting like she owned the place.'

'Maybe he's got himself a housekeeper now!'

'I've never known Eamonn to be involved with a woman,' Siobhan said. 'He's more interested in his animals.'

Assumpta giggled. 'Maybe he finally struck lucky. There's hope for us yet, eh, Siobhan?'

'Speak for yourself.'

Assumpta took two pints to the other end of the bar and put them in front of Brendan and Padraig. Brendan handed her a note, which she took to the till.

'A beauty contest!' Padraig said, looking shocked.

Brendan nodded. 'What's his angle this time, I wonder?'

'White slave traffic?'

Brendan looked doubtful. 'You need beautiful young virgins for that.'

Assumpta was returning with Brendan's change when she suddenly stopped dead, her mouth half open as she stared across the bar towards the door. The others followed her gaze. Eamonn stood in the doorway with a glamorous young woman at his side. She wore a short slip dress that showed off her long, tanned legs. Assumpta looked at Siobhan, who nodded.

Eamonn stepped up to the bar. The girl followed him. She looked a little uncomfortable.

'Evening, everyone,' Eamonn said.

A small chorus returned the greeting.

Assumpta came forward. 'What can I get you?'

'The usual for me please, and . . . ' Eamonn looked at the girl.

'A mineral water,' she said.

Eamonn noted the expectant faces at the bar. 'I don't think I've introduced you all, have I?' He turned and swept his arm grandly towards the girl. 'This is Naomi. My niece from Dublin.'

Naomi smiled. Within minutes a small group had gathered, all intent on making the newcomer welcome.

Siobhan remained apart from the men at the bar, observing them with interest. In no time at all, she noticed, young Naomi was holding court. Siobhan inched a little closer to hear what was being said.

'So how's life in the Big Smoke?' Padraig was asking.

Naomi shrugged. 'It's, you know . . . Dublin.'

'Dirty and noisy,' Brendan said wryly. 'A seething hotbed of crime and corruption.'

Naomi smiled uncertainly. 'It must seem like that to country people,' she said.

Brendan didn't know whether to laugh or be offended.

Niamh came in and stood further along the bar. 'Give us a glass of lager, will you, Assumpta?'

'Coming up.'

'How are rehearsals going, Niamh?' Siobhan asked.

'Spectacular.'

She was training a group of schoolchildren for the Irish Traditional Dancing segment of the festival. Her job would have been easy, had it not been for the presence in the group of Con 'Genghis' O'Neill. Con's mates were easy to control, but he simply did not want to dance. It seemed, to Niamh, that he didn't want to be involved in group activity of any kind. She viewed his disruptive tactics and his refusal to fit in as a failure on her part. Tonight she didn't want to talk about it. She just wanted a chance to stun her mind for a while.

In the corner by the window the men were laughing at something Naomi had said.

'You'd think they'd never seen a woman before,' Siobhan said.

Niamh looked over to where Naomi was sitting. 'Who is she?'

'Eamonn's niece,' Assumpta said.

Niamh's expression betrayed a mixture of envy and curiosity. 'Last time I saw legs like that,' she said, 'they were standing in a nest.'

Peter entered tentatively, making his first social visit to the bar since Assumpta threw him out. Brendan called him over.

'Father Peter, have you been introduced to Naomi? She's down from Dublin to rough it with us for a few days.'

Peter shook Naomi's hand. 'Is this your first time in Ballykay?'

'Not at all. I was born here.'

'Ah, you're a local then.'

'Hardly. It's the first time I've been back since I was a month old.' She gave Peter a flirtatious little smile. 'I hear great things about you.'

'Ah.' Peter shook his head. 'You shouldn't believe anything you hear in this place.'

'Depends on who you're listening to,' Assumpta said.

Peter appeared to ignore that. 'What d'you plan to do while you're in Ballykay, Naomi?'

She shrugged. 'Maybe you could offer a few suggestions?'

'Well, we've got our Festival on Saturday, you must come to that.'

'Yes,' she nodded, 'it's always amusing to see these little country traditions.'

Assumpta flashed a look at Peter, then stared at Naomi. 'You'll love it,' she said. 'We still burn witches at the stake.'

Naomi's smile froze a little, but she hung onto it.

As the group closed around Naomi again Peter took Brendan on one side.

'I just spoke to Ambrose a minute before I came in. He's worried about the strain this business with Con O'Neill is putting on Niamh.'

Brendan nodded. 'It's a shame. She's doing a grand job with those kids, but Con won't play along, and he creates havoc every chance he gets.'

They glanced along the bar to where Niamh was starting on a second glass of lager.

'Rather than commiserate with her,' Peter said, 'I'd like to do something useful, like helping the situation in some way. What's the story on O'Neill, anyway? I gather he lives with foster parents, because he hasn't any family.'

'Oh, he's got a family, but they don't want him.'

'How come?'

'According to his teachers at Allenstown, his parents split up and dumped him on his grandfather.'

'Then why is he with foster parents?'

'The old man died six months ago,' Brendan said.

'Poor kid. He must feel like everyone's deserted him.'

'Even more so, now his gang are settling down here.'

'So what do we do, Brendan? How do we get him involved in the Festival?'

Brendan shrugged. 'We'll just have to leave him out of it altogether.'

Peter wasn't happy with that. For the moment, however, he had no alternative to offer.

twenty-one

WHEN PETER WALKED into the general store the following afternoon he found Siobhan deep in conversation with Kathleen. They stopped long enough to say hello, then got straight back to the gossip. Peter went to the crisps display and picked out a packet.

'Apparently she's taking part in this spectacle of Quigley's,' Kathleen said.

'Is that so?' Siobhan stuffed her shopping into a bag as she listened.

'It's a disgrace. Young women cavorting about on a stage, displaying their wares for all to see.' Kathleen turned abruptly on Peter. 'I'm surprised at you of all people, Father.'

Peter stared at her. 'Me?'

'You're on the Festival Committee, it's your place to try and prevent this kind of vulgarity, not encourage it. I'm sure Father MacAnally wouldn't approve.'

'Father Mac's on sabbatical, as well you know,' Peter said, 'and this beauty contest is nothing to do with me, I assure you.'

Peter put his money on the counter and left.

'Her of all people,' Kathleen said, taking up where she had left off, 'you'd think she'd have some shame.'

Siobhan was intrigued. 'What do you mean?'

Kathleen lowered her voice. 'Born on the wrong side of the blanket, if you get my meaning.'

'Who to?'

'Eamonn's youngest sister, Rosaline. It was a real scandal at the time.'

'Naomi?'

Kathleen nodded with authority. 'Rosaline and Eamonn had a terrible falling out over it, so she took the baby and moved to Dublin. She brought shame on the good name of that family.'

'Where's Rosaline now?'

'Last I heard, she moved to America and was living in sin with a plumber from Cork.'

'And Eamonn hasn't spoken to her in all these years?' Siobhan said.

'Not a word.'

Wheels were starting to turn in Siobhan's head. 'So why has Naomi turned up all of a sudden?'

'Exactly.'

The two women looked at each other, the question hovering between them.

At the top of the hill, meantime, as Peter walked towards his house munching his crisps, he saw Eamonn waiting on his doorstep. He looked very anxious, but that tended to be one of his standard facial expressions.

'This is a pleasant surprise, Eamonn. What can I do for you?'

'I need your advice, Father.'

Peter nodded. 'Go on.'

'How does the Church view pigs?'

'Um . . . ' Peter thought for a second. 'To be honest, I'm not aware it has any particular standpoint. Why?'

'Well, when they pass on . . . '

Peter surreptitiously shifted his bag of smoky bacon crisps behind his back. 'I'm sorry, Eamonn. I didn't realise yours had – '

'They haven't, but I'm preparing myself for the worst.'

'I see. Well, I'm sure that if it does come to that, I could come over and say a few prayers.'

Eamonn nodded, looking greatly relieved. 'That's all I wanted to know. Thank you, Father.'

Eamonn headed off down the hill towards the pub. Peter stuck another crisp in his mouth and fumbled for his key.

'Father Clifford.'

He turned. It was Siobhan.

'Have you a minute, Father?'

'Of course.'

'I was wondering if I could take a look at the Parish Register?'

'Sure. Drop by later and I'll sort it out for you. Anything in particular you're looking for?'

'I won't know until I find it.'

She turned to go.

'Any news on Eamonn's pigs?' Peter said.

'I'm still waiting for the results of the blood tests.'

'Poor old Eamonn.'

Siobhan walked off a few steps and stopped. 'I don't suppose there's a patron saint of swine?' she said.

'No,' Peter said firmly, 'but all nominations will be gratefully received.'

†

Niamh got back to the classroom early after lunch so she could arrange the afternoon's work before the children came in from the playground. As she entered she saw Con O'Neill rummaging about in a corner.

'What are you doing in here?'

He looked startled. 'Nothing.' He got to his feet, watching her nervously.

As Niamh went closer she saw her handbag on the floor beside his feet. She snatched it up and went through it. Her purse was missing.

'Give it here,' she said.

Con made to run off.

'Oh, no, you don't.'

She grabbed him by the arm.

'Get off me!' He struggled and tugged, trying to free himself. 'Let me go!'

'You're not going anywhere until you tell me what you've done with my purse.'

As Con continued to wriggle and jerk the purse slipped from under his jumper.

'Right!' Niamh picked it up, keeping a firm hold on the boy. 'I've had just about enough. We'll see what the Guard has to say about this.'

Back at home, Ambrose had removed his uniform jacket and switched on the TV. He was about to settle down comfortably with a sandwich and cup of tea when he heard the front door slam.

'Get off me!' a boy's voice yelled. 'Get off!'

'Ambrose! Are you here?'

The living-room door opened and Niamh strode in holding Con O'Neill firmly by the arm. Ambrose shot to his feet, peeved by the intrusion.

'What's going on?'

'I caught him red-handed,' Niamh said. 'He was stealing my purse.'

'I wasn't!'

Ambrose looked at the boy, then at his wife. 'Niamh, a quick word.'

She released her grip on Con and followed Ambrose into the hallway.

'What are you doing, bringing him in here?' Ambrose demanded.

'You've got to give him a talking to.'

'I'm trying to have my lunch.'

'This is serious,' Niamh insisted. 'Sort him out.' She marched to the front door. 'I'll be back in an hour.'

She went, leaving Ambrose standing in the hallway. With his jaw set hard, he strode back into the living room and saw Con rummaging through his record collection.

'Come away from there!'

The boy turned. 'I only wanted a look.'

'Well you can't. Sit down.'

Con did as he was told. Ambrose remained standing.

'I shouldn't have to tell you that stealing is a very serious business. Do you know what happens to thieves, Con?'

The boy just looked back at him.

'They go to prison.' Ambrose paused to let it sink in. 'Is that what you want?'

Con got up, crossed the room, knelt in front of the pile of records and began thumbing through them again. Ambrose watched him and decided he should say nothing. The boy wasn't behaving like a hooligan. He was more like a compulsive browser.

'My Da went to prison,' Con said, without looking up.

Ambrose was caught by the softness in the boy's voice. Perhaps it was a hint of underlying gentleness. Perhaps it wasn't. In Ambrose's experience, a tough, unruly shell was often the kind of cover adopted by isolated, sensitive individuals.

'What did he go to prison for?'

'All kinds. Nicking stuff, mostly.'

Ambrose began to feel a little awkward in the authoritarian role. 'You've got to understand, Con, that stealing isn't big or clever.'

Con paused with an LP sleeve in his hands. 'Have you ever nicked anything?'

'Indeed I have not,' Ambrose said.

Con read aloud from a label on the back of the record sleeve. 'Property of Cilldargan Public Library.' He looked at Ambrose, then back at the sleeve. 'Nineteen seventy-nine?'

Ambrose snatched the record. He looked at the label. The boy had read it correctly.

They looked at one another. Ambrose shrugged and made a glum mouth. An important barrier had been removed.

Ten minutes later they were both sitting on the floor, eating sandwiches and surrounded by LPs. 'In God's Country' by U2 was on the player.

'You've some good music here, for an old person,' Con said.

Ambrose was flattered. 'I've always been something of a musical trendsetter,' he said. 'I was the first kid in Ballykay to buy a Bay City Rollers record.'

Con looked at him, his face a blank.

'And this was the first album I ever bought. I was only ten.' He held up an album by The Nolans. 'Brilliant. They don't make them like this any more.' He handed the album to Con to look at. 'I'd have loved to be a musician, but I've no real talent for it.'

Con smiled. He was beginning to relax. He pointed to a fiddle hanging on the wall. 'Do you play?'

'Would it be stuck up there on the wall if I did?'

'Can I have a look?'

Ambrose hesitated.

'I won't nick it, if that's what you're worried about.'

Ambrose got up and took the fiddle and bow off the wall. He handed them to Con.

'It was a twelfth birthday present from my parents. They were hoping I'd turn out to be a musical genius but it's been hanging on walls ever since.'

Con held the fiddle carefully, turning it in his hands, running his fingers along its contours.

'What about yourself?' Ambrose said. 'Can you play?'

Con shrugged. 'A bit. My granda taught me. He was a brilliant fiddler.'

'Give us a tune, then.'

Con shook his head bashfully.

'Go on,' Ambrose coaxed him. 'You can't be any worse than me.'

Con put the fiddle under his chin. Slowly he drew the bow across the strings, tuning up.

'I'm a bit out of practice,' he said. 'I don't have a fiddle. Used to play granda's, but it disappeared after he died.'

He began to play a little tune, unevenly at first, gradually getting better as he gained the feel of the instrument.

Ambrose was touched to the heart. When Con had finished he said, 'Would you like to borrow this fiddle?'

Con stopped playing. He didn't look sure.

'Would you?'

'Yeah,' Con nodded. 'I would.'

'All right then,' Ambrose said. 'But only on one condition.'

Niamh arrived at the front door ten minutes later, just as Con was leaving. He was carrying the fiddle.

'I'll see you later,' Ambrose said.

'Yeah,' Con nodded. 'Thanks.'

Niamh stood back and watched Con march off along the street. She pointed to the fiddle case. 'What's he doing with that?'

Ambrose smiled and tapped the side of his nose. For the moment, no other answer was forthcoming.

†

Siobhan had meanwhile viewed the parish register, following which she made a telephone enquiry. The call was eventually returned and her query answered. As a result of all that she was now gunning the Land Rover up to Eamonn's farm.

Eamonn was pushing a wheelbarrow across the yard as she pulled up. He dropped the handles of the barrow as she strode towards him. She looked grim.

'It's bad news, isn't it?' Eamonn said.

'You could say that.'

'I knew it. My poor pigs are finished.'

'It's nothing to do with your pigs, Eamonn. This is about your niece.'

Eamonn suddenly looked evasive. 'What do you mean?'

'Come on, Eamonn, fess up. I'm on to your game.'

Eamonn stared at the ground for a moment, shaking his head. He looked at Siobhan. 'You'd better come inside.'

In the cluttered, old-fashioned kitchen they sat at the table, surrounded by pieces of farm machinery and bags of animal feed on the floor. Eamonn told Siobhan everything. He finished by telling her that Naomi's real name was Finnoula.

'So Quigley's rigged this beauty contest?'

Eamonn nodded. 'He says she'll win because she's more glamorous than any of the girls around here.'

'I might have known that sleaze bucket was up to no good.'

'Fair play to him, Siobhan, he didn't force me into it.'

'He didn't need to, he knows you're short of cash.'

Siobhan got to her feet. She was furious.

'Promise me you won't say anything,' Eamonn said, following her to the door. 'Please, Siobhan?'

She marched out across the yard to her vehicle, too mad to promise anything.

Later that evening she sat in the pub and listened to Peter, Padraig and Brendan discuss the pros and cons of the beauty contest.

Padraig said he could see no harm in it.

'Me neither,' said Brendan.

'Well . . . ' Siobhan sighed. 'You're men, you wouldn't.'

Padraig grinned. 'Come on, Siobhan, what's wrong with showing a little admiration for the female form?'

'I'm not even going to dignify that with an answer, Padraig. The whole thing's a joke.'

'I'm not entirely comfortable with it either,' said Peter.

'Well, I'm all for it,' Assumpta said, 'if it helps improve business in Ballykay.'

'What?' Siobhan was shocked.

'The Rose Festival helped put Tralee on the map,' Assumpta pointed out.

Siobhan snorted. 'Thanks for the support.'

Assumpta was unrepentant. 'I run a business, I can't afford to knock anything that might help me.'

'Help you?' Siobhan's voice rose with indignation. 'Would you wake up, Assumpta? Beauty contests are organised to make money out of stupid, vain women and dirty old men. They're just glorified cattle markets.'

'In your opinion,' snarled Brian Quigley, who had just walked into the bar. He walked up to Siobhan and looked her over. 'What do you know about beauty contests?'

'Children, please,' Brendan muttered,

'Let's face it,' Quigley went on, 'it's been a long time since you qualified for a beauty contest of any kind, if ever.' He turned to the bar. 'Large whiskey please, Assumpta.'

Siobhan was mortified. She got off her stool and walked out of the pub without a word.

Peter glared at Quigley. 'There was no need for that, Brian.'

'She shouldn't dish it out if she can't take it back. She's only trying to make trouble.'

'You're well out of order,' Peter said, 'and you know it.' He turned to the others. 'Shouldn't one of us go after Siobhan?'

Assumpta shook her head. 'I think she'll want to be left alone right now.'

Brendan said he would call in on her on his way home.

Assumpta banged down Quigley's drink in front of him. 'Mind you don't choke on it, eh?'

Quigley put his money on the counter and proceeded to drink his whiskey with unhurried composure.

Brendan turned to him. 'You must have been the star pupil in charm school, Brian.'

'Thank you.' Quigley beamed with equanimity.

Assumpta moved along to where Peter was standing and leaned close to him. 'He's lucky I'm on this side of the bar or I'd lump him one,' she murmured.

'Yeah,' Peter nodded, 'the thought had crossed my mind.'

Assumpta gave him a big warm smile.

As one rift starts, Peter thought, another one heals.

twenty-two

SIOBHAN WAS ON the sofa at home, making short work of a bottle of whiskey. Her eyes were red and swollen from crying.

When the doorbell rang she ignored it. It rang again. She paid it no heed. On the fifth or sixth long ring, however, she felt constrained to shout.

'Go away!'

The ringing persisted.

'Go away, will you!'

'Siobhan!' Brendan shouted. 'Open this door before I break it down!'

He began hammering on the door with his fist.

Siobhan swore under her breath. She got up, opened the door, and came back to the couch with Brendan behind her. She sat down and poured herself another drink.

'Just a small one for me, please, Siobhan.'

She handed Brendan the bottle. 'Help yourself.'

He took a tumbler from the cabinet and poured himself a large measure. He sat down in an armchair by the couch. He asked her if she was all right.

'Why shouldn't I be? Sure, I love being humiliated in front of my friends.'

'Pay no mind to Brian. He didn't mean it.'

Siobhan looked down into her glass and nodded her head sadly. 'Maybe. But he's got a point.'

Brendan took a deep swallow of the whiskey. 'You're just feeling sorry for yourself, Siobhan.'

'God knows I'm no oil painting.'

'That's just the drink talking,' Brendan said. 'You know you're a good-looking woman.'

She gave a deep, shaky sigh. 'Says who?'

Brendan looked at her awkwardly. He was in a corner. 'Well . . . ' He took another deep swallow, nearly emptying the glass. 'Me, for one.'

Siobhan looked up at him. The effect of too much booze was beginning to kick in. 'You're just saying that to make me feel better,' she said.

Brendan drained his glass, then filled it again. He got up and sat beside Siobhan, placing a comforting arm around her shoulders.

'We've been mates for years, have we not?' he said.

Siobhan nodded.

'Well then, you know I wouldn't lie to you about something like this.'

There was a pause while Brendan struggled to find more of the right things to say.

'You're an attractive woman and the only person who doesn't know it is you.'

A strand of Siobhan's hair had fallen into her glass. She lifted it out, shook it, and gulped back the whiskey.

'D'you really think so?' she said, and belched softly.

'I'm telling you,' said Brendan, on a roll now. 'Looks and brains, that's a deadly combination in any woman. Sure, I can't believe someone hasn't snapped you up already.'

'I've had my fair share of offers,' Siobhan said coyly.

'I can well believe it.'

'Oh, Brendan . . . '

He was aware of danger approaching, so he patted her hand and started to get up. 'Best be on my way, then.'

Before he could stand, Siobhan seized her opportunity and hurled herself on top of him. The next thing Brendan knew, he was smothering in her passionate embrace.

He awoke to birdsong. It seemed to be coming from the wrong side of the room. He opened his eyes, blinked a couple of times, and realised he wasn't in his own bed.

Recollection began to filter through.

He raised his throbbing head and looked over his shoulder. Siobhan was sleeping contentedly next to him.

'Oh my God . . . '

He got out of bed quietly, gathered up his clothes and left.

Later that morning, as he stood next to Peter in the school hall, watching the children thunder their way through a jig under the supervision of Niamh Egan, Brendan was overcome simultaneously by the noise, the pain in his head and the weight of alcoholic remorse.

'Can I have a word with you somewhere quieter, Father?'

They sat on the steps outside and Brendan told Peter the whole story. He admitted that he was still shocked at the speed of his descent from friendly condolence to ravening lust.

'One minute I was trying to offer a little friendly comfort, the next – '

'Yeah, I get the picture,' said Peter. 'Has Siobhan said anything?'

'She doesn't need to. It's all in the eyes with women. That's why I'm avoiding her.'

Peter looked at him despairingly.

'It was just, you know how it is . . . ' Brendan stopped, realising Peter probably didn't know. 'We had a bit to drink, and one thing led to another.'

'But you think Siobhan might have ideas about something more permanent?'

'I think she's in love with me.'

'You can't keep avoiding her.'

'I just don't want to hurt her feelings.'

Peter nodded. 'That's all the more reason why you should say something.'

Brendan shook his head. 'I can't.' He stood up. 'I need a good night's sleep before I do anything.'

'Coward,' Peter said.

'Knackered coward,' Brendan said.

Later, as Peter walked back along the main street towards St Joseph's, he saw a large van outside Fitzgerald's unloading soft drinks. Assumpta was putting some of the crates into her own van.

'What's all this?'

'My contribution to the Festival,' Assumpta said, sliding the last crate into the van.

'It's very generous of you.'

'Sure it is,' she said. 'I'm all heart.'

'Have you got a minute?'

'Does it look like it?'

'I really need your help,' Peter said.

'Oh, that bad, is it?'

They went inside and Assumpta poured Peter a mug of tea. He stood by the doorway with it as he told her what had happened between Siobhan and Brendan.

'Would you talk to her?' he said.

Assumpta was taken aback. 'It's not my place to. What happened between Siobhan and Brendan is their business.'

'We can't just stand by and watch them fall out over this.'

'Things might work out between them.'

Peter didn't agree. 'These kind of complications always end up ruining friendships.'

'It happens. Sometimes it can't be helped.'

Their eyes locked for a moment.

Peter said, 'I hate to see people I care about get hurt.'

Assumpta relented. 'All right, I'll speak to her – when I get a chance.'

'Thanks, I really appreciate it.'

Assumpta smiled. 'What are friends for?'

†

Early next morning, the day of the Ballykissangel Festival, Brian Quigley left a big bunch of flowers on Siobhan's doorstep. Tucked in among the flowers was a card. It said, 'I'm an ass. Humble apologies, Brian.'

Shortly afterwards Siobhan returned from an early breech delivery at a farm out past Cilldargan. She found the flowers and picked them up. She didn't see the card flutter away on the breeze. She sniffed the blooms, smiled, and inwardly thanked Brendan for his kindness.

She went in, put the flowers in water and checked her telephone messages. There was one that concerned Eamonn. Siobhan left the house again and drove up to his farm.

He was mucking out his pigs as Siobhan rounded the corner into the pig pen. She was smiling.

'Good news, Eamonn, your pigs are clear.'

His jaw dropped open. 'I don't believe it! Music to my ears!' He turned to the big sow. 'Do you hear that, Mary? Look, she's over the moon, Siobhan.'

Siobhan looked at the pig, which hadn't moved since she came in. 'Yes, I can see that, Eamonn.'

'So what is it they've got?'

'A strain of the flu virus. The symptoms can be similar to Aujesky's Disease. I'll get them started on a course of antibiotics straight away. They'll be as right as rain in no time.'

Eamonn stood there nodding, looking thoughtful. 'You know,' he said, 'I reckon all this was my punishment for getting involved with Quigley's little scheme.'

Siobhan rolled her eyes.

'In future,' Eamonn said, 'I'm keeping my nose clean. Pretty girls mean trouble.' He patted Mary's head. 'At least you know where you are with an old sow. Eh, Siobhan?'

†

By eleven-forty-five the stage was set for the Festival. Hundreds of seats had been laid out on the school playing field and people were beginning to arrive in substantial numbers. Brendan and Peter stood to one side of the performance platform, watching the proceedings.

'Well, here we go,' Brendan said.

Peter gave him a sidelong glance. 'Have you spoken to Siobhan yet?'

'No.'

'Are you going to?'

'Yes,' Brendan said firmly. 'Later. Later.'

He turned and saw Siobhan approaching. Assumpta and Padraig were with her.

'Oh no,' Brendan said.

He strode away in the opposite direction. Peter called after him, but he didn't look back.

Within ten minutes the entertainment was under way. Padraig stood beaming proudly as his son Kevin recited a poem. Nearby, Con O'Neill was staring anxiously at the platform. Beside him Ambrose smiled his reassurance, but the boy still looked worried.

In the refreshment tent Brian Quigley was talking to a tall, bearded businessman called Dessi McMichael.

'I hope, after all this,' McMichael said, 'my daughter isn't going to be disappointed, Brian.'

'No worries,' Quigley told him.

'Finnoula's been through a lot for this contest – living with that man and his pigs.'

'Well, she had to be local,' Quigley reminded him. 'Anyway, she looks a million dollars. Trust me, Dessi. She'll walk it.'

Back on the platform Niamh's dancers were into their routine, accompanied by a proper Irish country band. The audience loved them. Niamh stood alongside the platform, relieved the day had come, relieved they were doing so well. She grinned and blushed as Peter, over on the edge of the crowd, gave her an enthusiastic thumbs-up.

Peter's next wordless communication was to Assumpta. It consisted of a waggle of his pointing finger between her and Siobhan, and a questioning lift of his eyebrows.

Assumpta's return gesture was a firm shake of the head and a semi-exasperated look that said 'give me a chance'. A moment later she nudged Siobhan, mimed a drink, and Siobhan immediately nodded. They got up and headed for the refreshment tent.

As the dancing ended to uproarious applause, there was a drum roll and Brian Quigley stepped onto the platform, carrying a clipboard. He stood in front of the microphone and said a few opening words, none of which were heard by anyone. He turned and glared at Donal, who was in charge of the PA system. Donal ducked down and flicked a switch.

Quigley started again. 'Ladies and gentlemen. Welcome to the Lily of Ballykissangel contest, organised in conjunction with "Babbling Brook", the unique taste of pure Irish spring water.'

'Shove your water!' a man shouted. 'We want to see the girls!'

Quigley ploughed on, smiling relentlessly. 'It promises to be a most entertaining event, so please put your hands together for our first contestant, May Houlihan. Big hand for May.'

Assumpta was sitting on the grass beside the refreshment tent. Siobhan came back from the tent with their second drink. She handed a glass to Assumpta and sat down beside her on the grass. With a little alcohol inside her, Assumpta now felt she could tackle the delicate business she had come over here to conduct.

They clinked glasses. 'Right,' Assumpta said, 'come on now, Siobhan, what's the gossip?'

'Gossip?'

'You've been keeping something to yourself. I can tell.'

Siobhan looked at Assumpta, and her look said it all. She was dying to tell someone.

'Well?'

Siobhan leaned close. 'Don't breathe a word to another soul.'

Assumpta crossed her heart.

Siobhan leaned even closer and said, 'Eamonn's niece, Naomi, is an impostor.'

Assumpta stared at her. 'What?'

'She's not who she says she is.'

Assumpta was confused. 'What are you talking about?'

They both glanced at the stage where the counterfeit Naomi, at that moment, was making a big production of strutting her stuff.

'I did a little research,' Siobhan said. 'The real Naomi is a nun, works with the Little Sisters of the Poor in Liverpool. Has done for years.'

'So who's she up there on the platform?'

'Finnoula McMichael. Her father runs a big shipping company in Dublin, he's an old buddy of Brian's. She wants a modelling career, so they struck up an agreement. If she wins the competition, Quigley gets himself a major building contract.'

'And winning this will help her?'

Siobhan nodded. 'If she gets through and wins the final. First prize is a huge modelling contract to help promote that piddle.' She pointed at a poster advertising 'Babbling Brook'.

'I don't believe it,' Assumpta said, but clearly she did.

'Quigley reckons there's no competition. As far as looks go, she's a dead cert.'

'Is that a fact?' Assumpta got to her feet, fuming. 'Well, we'll see about that.'

'No.' Siobhan laid a hand on her arm. 'Wait till she's pronounced the winner. Why spoil the fun?'

They finished their drinks quickly and moved determinedly towards the stage. The judging was over and everyone was waiting for the result.

'And here comes the Chairperson of the judging panel,' Quigley said.

A woman came forward and handed him an envelope.

'Let me do it,' Assumpta whispered.

'Not a chance,' Siobhan said. 'I've been looking forward to this.'

'Well, the moment we've all been eagerly awaiting,' Quigley said, tearing open the envelope, 'the result of the contest.'

Assumpta and Siobhan stood close to the side of the stage, poised for action.

Quigley pulled out the folded sheet of paper and held it aloft without looking at it. 'Written on here is the winning name.'

A hush fell over the crowd.

Quigley smiled evenly and with great assurance. The contestants stood anxiously behind him, fingers crossed, smiles fixed in place. Sitting at the back of the crowd Dessi McMichael was tense, chewing the corner of his lip.

Still smiling, Quigley unfolded the paper. 'The winner is . . . ' Quigley's face stiffened for a moment and the smile nearly died, 'Deirdre Patrick.'

Assumpta and Siobhan looked at each other, thunderstruck. Then they started yelling and cheering along with everybody else.

McMichael got out of his seat, visibly angry.

The winner stepped forward, wearing her best dress now. She was a simple, natural beauty, the wholesome opposite of the sophisticated, over-made-up Finnoula.

Quigley was managing to hold up. 'And now, Deirdre, your prize,' he announced. 'You will go forward to the national heat in the search for the new face of "Babbling Brook". Oh, and a free hair-do at Lilian's Premier Styling Salon. Well done.'

He handed over the envelope and shook Deirdre's hand.

†

When the excitement of the beauty contest had died away, Brendan walked out onto the platform and spoke into the microphone.

'Now back to the musical programme. We are about to enjoy a contribution from one of our visitors from Allenstown, Con O'Neill, who's going to play a little something guaranteed to get your feet tapping.'

Brendan stepped aside. The audience clapped.

There was no sign of Con.

Niamh, watching from the side of the stage, looked across at Ambrose sitting in the audience. He shrugged.

The audience wondered what was happening. Brendan looked around anxiously.

Suddenly Con walked onto the stage, clutching the fiddle. He looked very nervous. Ambrose waved and gave him an encouraging thumbs-up.

There was a renewed ripple of applause at the boy's entrance, then silence fell.

Con put the fiddle under his chin and began to play 'The Darling Girl from Clare'. His nervousness was so severe that he could hardly manage to draw the bow across the strings. The sound he produced was shaky and uneven. In the audience, Ambrose whispered 'Come on, Con,' and stared at the platform with fierce intensity, willing the boy to overcome his nerves.

Niamh nodded to members of the band, who needed only the slightest encouragement to get involved. The boran player started up a drumbeat, then the tin whistle joined in, and then the accordion.

Con looked round, startled. The boran player nodded to him. Con started playing again, more confident now, his foot tapping the rhythm. The whole band joined in as he began an inspired assault on the old tune and whipped it up to such a tempo that several people in the audience got up, kicked back their chairs and started to dance. Sitting there watching, Ambrose had tears in his eyes.

The lively music continued as Quigley walked across the field, away from the stage. He saw Dessi McMichael and his daughter walking towards McMichael's car.

'Dessi!' Quigley called. 'Wait up!'

McMichael stopped. He turned to face Quigley and made a throat-slashing action. He turned away again and bundled the girl into his car.

As Quigley stood there, speechless, the Chairperson of the contest judges approached him.

'A wonderful show, Mr Quigley,' she said. 'We've got ourselves a real country beauty. Exactly what we're looking for.'

Quigley smiled bleakly. He saw Assumpta and Siobhan standing a short distance away, grinning at him. He waved to them, believing Siobhan had been mollified. But she shook her head at him.

'Beauty's in the eye of the beholder, eh Brian?' she shouted.

He stared at her, deflated.

Peter and Brendan came across the field, heading for the refreshment tent. When Brendan saw Siobhan he took a grip on his courage.

'Siobhan,' he said, 'would you mind if we had a quick word?'

Assumpta took Peter by the arm and pulled him away towards the platform, where Con and the band were still playing and even more people were dancing.

'Come on, Father,' Assumpta said, 'have a go. Pretend you belong.'

Brendan cleared his throat noisily. 'There's something I have to say to you, Siobhan.'

Siobhan put her hand on his arm, silencing him. 'Brendan, you're a great pal, you know that, and I think the world of you. But that's all. I don't want to hurt your feelings, but I have to be honest. I'd much rather stay friends.' She smiled, squeezed his arm consolingly, and said, 'I'm sorry.'

Brendan stared at her as she walked away. He was astounded. After a few yards she turned and shouted, 'Thanks for the flowers. They were a lovely thought.'

Brendan blinked at her, mystified, feeling the need of a good stiff drink.

TWENTY-THREE

SOMEWHERE AROUND eleven-thirty, while locals were still in Fitzgerald's talking over the more outstanding Festival events, a fire broke out in the home of Kathleen Hendley. Kathleen herself was alerted by the smell of smoke and ran out into the yard in her nightdress and dressing-gown, squealing hysterically. But already a couple of people leaving the pub had seen the flames leaping in the sitting-room window and igniting the curtains, and they had raised the alarm.

Within minutes a fire-fighting operation was under way. A human chain, running all the way from the riverbank up to the roadway in front of Kathleen's house, passed brimming buckets to where Peter stood by the open doorway, throwing water at the heart of the blaze. Brian Quigley arrived and inserted himself in the chain next to Peter.

The heat was blistering, but Peter kept throwing on the water as fast as the buckets came at him. In fifteen minutes the fire was under control. By that time, however, the house was virtually gutted.

In Fitzgerald's, Dr Ryan and Assumpta did what they could to comfort the distraught Kathleen, who kept howling that her house was ruined and her things were destroyed.

The most shocking truth came to light when Assumpta suggested that things might not be as bad as they seemed. Kathleen told her not to be stupid, she had seen the flames, hadn't she? But on the bright side, Assumpta insisted, with the insurance everything could be replaced, the compensation would make the place like new.

At that, Kathleen went off into gales of fresh wailing, and it dawned on Assumpta and the doctor that on top of her other misfortunes, Kathleen had no insurance.

In the morning Peter joined Padraig, Brendan and Niamh as they wandered through the burnt-out house, surveying the damage.

Padraig knelt at the skirting board, examining an electrical socket bristling with adapters and plugs. Peter squelched his way across the blackened sitting-room.

'She'll need a new carpet. Furniture. Wallpaper.'

Padraig held up a plug. 'My guess is the fire started here. Look at that.

Round-pin plug. I thought they'd sunk with the dinosaurs.'

'Kitchen's in a hell of a state,' Brendan said, coming through. As Niamh came in behind him they heard a shocked howl from the doorway.

'Here she is,' Niamh whispered.

'Be tactful,' Peter told the others. 'It's bad enough for her, without us adding to the gloom.'

Kathleen appeared, wearing an assortment of clothes that were clearly not her own. Assumpta came in behind her and stood beside Niamh.

'Oh, look at it,' Kathleen moaned, 'look at it. It's all ruined.'

'Actually, Kathleen, it's not that bad,' Peter said brightly. 'I mean it looks bad – on the surface, that is – but underneath, it's fine.'

Quigley, Liam and Donal came clattering down the stairs.

'New carpet,' Quigley was saying, 'new bed, paint job. And about time. It's like a slum up there.'

'A slum!' Kathleen squeaked indignantly.

'Dad!' Niamh snapped.

Quigley stared at them, flustered. 'Kathleen. Sorry. I didn't know you were here.'

Kathleen howled, flustering him even more.

'Just leave it to me,' he said. 'I'll turn the house into a palace. Won't cost you a penny. I'll do a nice little estimate for the insurance company . . . '

Kathleen howled louder.

'Dad!'

'What have I done now?'

'She doesn't have any insurance!'

'How was I to know that?'

'Hello?' Father Mac called from the kitchen. 'Anybody there?'

'Father Mac!' Kathleen yelped. 'He mustn't see the state of the place! Don't let him in!'

At that moment he appeared. 'My God,' he said, looking around him, 'what a mess. Poor Kathleen, what a thing to have happened.' His attention switched briskly as he spotted Peter. 'Ah, you're there, Father Clifford. I was on my way to see you.' He turned to Kathleen again and patted her shoulder. 'There, there, pull yourself together. I'm sure the insurance will take care of everything.'

On the way out, Peter explained the problem to Father Mac. He didn't look too sympathetic.

'Did Kathleen think the Lord would provide?'

'She says she can't afford insurance,' Peter said. 'There's not much profit from the shop.'

They walked to where Father Mac's car was parked. 'Well, when it comes to hard cash,' he said, 'we've either got an insurance policy, or we have to turn to our fellow man. Which is why I'm here, Father Clifford.'

'Oh, I see.'

'I'm at my wits' end to know what to do about it.'

'It's pretty obvious, isn't it?' said Peter.

'Is it?'

'We've got to raise money for her somehow. I've called a meeting – '

'Not Kathleen! The parish church!'

'The parish church? Why?'

'It'll fall round my ears, one of these days. It's one of our oldest problems. So I'm afraid I have to ask all my curates for a contribution towards the cost of refurbishment.'

Peter felt the news like a pain at his heart. 'I'm very sorry, Father MacAnally, but I haven't a penny to spare just at the moment.'

Father Mac opened the door of his car. 'I don't think you understand me, Father Clifford. I came here to explain the circumstances. I didn't come to beg.'

He got into the car and drove off, leaving Peter fuming on the pavement.

A few minutes later, as Ambrose got into the police car to drive Kathleen to her sister's, a battered old car, caked with mud, drew up outside Fitzgerald's. The driver got out. He looked every inch the hill farmer, down from his mountain without a wash or a shave. He scratched his chin idly and stood looking up and down the main street. Then he spotted Brian Quigley go to his Range Rover and put something in the back.

'I don't believe it!'

Quigley turned at the sound.

The man came forward, grinning. 'I do not believe it! The world's about the size of an orange! I've never been to this one-horse town before. I didn't even know it was on the map. And who's the first person I bump into?'

Quigley stared at the scruffy figure for a moment, then recollection dawned. 'Mossy Phelan.'

'As large as life and twice as ugly.'

'I wouldn't have known you,' Quigley said.

'And you're heavier than when I last saw you.' Phelan held out his hand. 'How are you, Brian?'

Quigley accepted the hand warily and shook it. 'I couldn't be better,

Mossy. And you?'

Niamh came across the road. 'Excuse me. Dad, I won't get around to doing your lunch today. I need to sort some stuff out for Kathleen after this meeting we're having.'

Quigley told her not to worry about it. Niamh nodded politely to Phelan, then walked away.

'She called you Dad,' Phelan said. 'Your daughter. That's not Niamh, is it?'

'Yep.'

'Niamh! She was only a little girleen when I last saw her.'

'Yes, I know.' Quigley was suddenly all business. 'Listen, Mossy, I've got a lot to do this morning. I'll see you again some time.'

'And that's it, Brian, is it?' Phelan looked wounded. 'Twenty years, and it's not worth sharing a drink? And the pub just across the road?'

'They're not open yet.'

'They'll make us a cup of coffee, Brian.'

'Well . . . ' Quigley sighed. 'All right, but I haven't very long.'

'That'll be long enough.'

They were the first customers in Fitzgerald's that morning. Quigley sat at a table. Phelan asked Assumpta for two cups of coffee and brought them from the bar. To outward appearance, Quigley looked like a man wishing he was somewhere else, with someone else. Phelan, on the other hand, was good humoured and expansive.

Quigley put the cups on the table and sat down.

'You look prosperous, Brian. Doing well, I can see.'

'Could be better.'

'That's what we all say.'

Quigley had been appraising Phelan's shabby clothes and his uncared-for look. 'Life's been a bit hard on you, has it, Mossy?'

'Ah, now, Brian boy, don't let appearances fool you.' Phelan winked.

'And I don't remember you coming from Kerry.'

'I come from wherever I want.'

They sipped their coffee, and slowly they began to reminisce. They talked in a shorthand that Assumpta could not pick up. 'Limerick, seventy-six, a stormer . . . You were the cutest, cleverest man I ever knew, Brian . . . Could have taken on the world between us, and beaten it . . . '

They stopped talking at the sound of an electronic warbler. 'Wouldn't you know it,' Phelan grunted, fishing out a mobile phone from his inside jacket pocket. 'I thought I'd switched this thing off. God be with the days when the only way people could find you was by pigeon post.'

Quigley went to the bar to get two whiskeys as Phelan answered his phone, making an odd picture, a dishevelled unshaven countryman with a yuppie tool stuck to his ear, its aerial waggling as he spoke. Without appearing to do so, Quigley followed the conversation.

'Mossy Phelan here. Sean!' Phelan lowered his voice dramatically, but Quigley could still hear. 'Everything all right? What? At this stage? Oh, for God's sake . . . He said he had the money. He's a shyster, that man, I always knew it. Well, what else can we can do, we'll have to pull out!'

Quigley picked up the two glasses of whiskey from the bar and waited with them, letting Phelan finish his conversation.

'You ring them, Sean, will you? Tell them why. Yes, it is a pity. It's a hundred and fifty grand of a pity. If only he'd given me a bit of notice.'

Quigley came back to the table as soon as Phelan switched off the phone and put it back in his pocket. He put the glasses on the table and sat down.

'Something wrong?'

Phelan grunted. 'A hundred and fifty grand split three ways wrong. I'm down fifty thousand quid.'

'That's a lot of money.' Quigley emptied his whiskey into the coffee.

'Listen, Brian . . . ' Phelan pushed back his chair. 'Thanks for the crack, but I've got to go.'

'Your whiskey,' Brian reminded him, as if he might be on the verge of committing sacrilege.

'I'd spew it up.'

'Drink it. Calm yourself.'

'God dammit!' Phelan shook his head. 'I've been dreaming of it. Fifty thousand quid dancing in the heel of my hand.' He picked up his glass and swallowed the whiskey in one go. 'It's not only the money, Brian. It's the cuteness of it.'

'The cuteness of what, Mossy?'

Phelan appeared to consider whether he should say any more. 'Ah, sure . . . ' he shrugged, 'what's the harm. There's a dog running at Enniscorthy this evening. Black Dazzler. Not another dog to touch him in the race. He's owned by this gang of English sharpers, real cute hoors the lot of them.'

Assumpta interrupted to put Quigley's change on the bar.

'Thank you.'

He waited until she was out of earshot, then nodded for Phelan to go on.

'They're going to ring it,' Phelan said. 'Run this pudden of a dog instead. They're going to put their money on the second favourite, Tarbert Warrior. They needed capital, so I was invited in. But I couldn't handle twelve thousand quid. So I called in a couple of friends. Put in four thousand each. Now one of them has pulled out.'

'You could still bet your four thousand,' Quigley said.

'I'd look very handsome in a concrete overcoat, wouldn't I? They want to control the betting.'

Quigley nodded slowly. 'So what's the chances of ringing a dog these days?'

'The answer's in the name, Brian. Black Dazzler. Black. No other markings. One black dog is just like another black dog.'

'What about the tattoo, the number in their ears?'

'You tattoo the same number inside the ringer's ear. That's it. They've no other markings to go on.'

Quigley thought it over. 'Sounds good,' he said.

'Was good.'

People began crowding into the pub for the emergency meeting called by Peter.

'Come on.' Quigley swallowed his whiskey. 'Let's get out of here.'

'Ah, no, Brian, I'm on my way.'

'Come on!' Quigley snapped.

They stepped out onto the pavement.

'Four thousand?' Quigley said. 'And a hundred and fifty thousand split three ways?'

'Oh, God,' Phelan sighed, 'it still makes my mouth water. Fifty thousand quid.'

'Tell you what, Mossy, I'm not promising anything, mind, but I'm tempted to pick up that shortfall.'

'I'm in no mood for jokes!'

'I'm not joking,' Quigley said.

'Brian, if you're serious, you might be a life-saver. And I mean that in every sense of the word. But I'll have to check it out first.'

'So will I, Mossy.'

Phelan took out his mobile phone and hit the redial button. At that moment Niamh approached the pub.

'Dad?'

As Phelan waited for his call to be answered, he stretched out his free hand to Niamh.

'Mossy Phelan,' he said, introducing himself. 'An old friend of your father's. I knew you when you were just a girleen, and you've grown up to be a fine woman. You've got a few years on me, but I'd chase you down the bohereen any day of the week.' He paused, listening to the phone. 'No, not you, Sean.'

He turned away and started to mumble into the phone.

Quigley inched nearer, trying to hear. Niamh tugged his sleeve.

'Look, Niamh, I'm busy right now.'

'What's going on?'

'Nothing that would interest you.'

'Aren't you coming to the meeting?'

'I've changed my mind. You can tell me about it.'

He nodded for Niamh to go into the pub. As she went, Phelan switched off his phone.

'Sean had already told them we're pulling out,' he told Quigley. 'So he's got to call them back, check if they'll give us another chance. We've got to wait.'

Quigley told Phelan to leave his car where it was. They could drive up to his house and have a drink there in comfort while they were waiting to hear from Sean.

'And while we're waiting,' Quigley said, 'I can do my own bit of checking.'

At the house Quigley sat Phelan down in the sitting-room with the racing on the television and a large glass of malt in his hand.

'I'm going to the hall to make a phone call, Mossy. I won't be long.'

Quigley came back five minutes later. He was smiling. 'Black Dazzler,' he said. 'Sounds like a hell of a racer.'

Phelan nodded. 'If you're going to ring a dog, ring a good one.'

'Which makes Tarbert Warrior a very good bet indeed.'

Mossy's phone rang. 'Sean, too,' Phelan said, pulling out the phone. 'His timing is great.' He held up crossed fingers as he thumbed the green button. 'Mossy Phelan. Yes, Sean.' He listened. 'Good man yourself! What's that? Well obviously.' He covered the mouthpiece. 'The money, Brian. When can we have it?'

'As soon as I see your money,' Quigley said.

'Hang on, Sean.'

Phelan pulled out a wad of notes from his inside pocket and slapped it on to the table. Quigley didn't have to count it. He nodded.

'We can get the money now.'

Phelan spoke into the phone again. 'All under control, Sean. In Enniscorthy, yes. When? Seven o'clock?' He looked enquiringly at Quigley, who nodded. 'We'll be there.'

Phelan switched off the phone and dropped it in his pocket. He raised his glass. Quigley raised his.

'The old team, Brian.'

'The old team, Mossy.'

TWENTY-FOUR

THE BILL FOR NEW carpets, furniture, paint and wallpaper at Kathleen's house came to two thousand and fifty pounds. That was the best deal obtainable, and it was thanks to Padraig's contacts that it was on offer at all. Everyone agreed it was a decent figure. The only problem was that vigorous collecting around Ballykissangel had raised only one hundred and fifty pounds.

'So how do we turn a hundred and fifty quid into two thousand?' Assumpta asked as they cleared the decks in Kathleen's place, ready to redecorate.

'A miracle?' Brendan suggested.

Siobhan pointed to Peter. 'There's your man.'

Peter shook his head. 'Don't look at me. I flunked miracles at the seminary.'

'We'll have to hurry up,' Niamh said. 'Danny O'Sullivan's delivering the furniture on Monday – COD.'

'And at this rate,' said Peter, 'we won't have the cash to COD with, will we?'

They scraped the walls in silence for a minute, then Siobhan said, 'There's a dog running at Enniscorthy tonight. As near a certainty as you can get, so it won't be much of a price. But it would boost the kitty a bit.'

'I don't think it's appropriate for me to become involved in gambling,' Peter said.

Siobhan looked at him. 'Why do you have to get involved? Any one of us can place the bet.'

Peter shrugged. 'True.'

Brendan asked what the dog's name was.

'Black Dazzler,' said Siobhan.

†

Late that afternoon, after Quigley had eaten the dinner Niamh had cooked, she asked him for a donation to Kathleen's restoration fund. He resisted. He said he had already donated the services of Liam and Donal.

Niamh pressed him, and eventually he parted with a cheque for fifty pounds.

'So now you've got a total of two hundred pounds,' he said. 'It won't get you far.'

'We know that,' Niamh said. 'So we're going to put it on a dog. At Enniscorthy. Tonight. Siobhan says it's a certainty.'

'What dog would that be?'

'Black Dazzler.'

Quigley couldn't hide his shock. 'Listen,' he said, 'I want to tell you something in confidence. Do you hear me? Don't put the money on Black Dazzler.'

'Why not? Siobhan says it's – '

'Siobhan could be wrong. We're not dealing with an exact science here. Just take it from me, Black Dazzler is not the dog to back in that race.' He leaned forward and lowered his voice, as if someone might overhear. 'The dog to back is Tarbert Warrior. In the same race.'

Niamh looked deeply puzzled. 'How do you suddenly know so much about dogs?'

'Just do what I'm telling you,' Quigley said. 'Back Tarbert Warrior. And keep my name out of it.'

That evening Peter sat in the confessional at St Joseph's feeling anger, resentment, and several other emotions he was not supposed to take in there with him. Earlier, Father Mac had shown up and practically demanded a contribution to the Parish Church fund. Peter explained, again, that he had no money to spare, and furthermore he didn't foresee himself having any to spare for some considerable time. Father Mac ignored what he said and announced that he would expect a substantial contribution by the end of the week.

Re-running the exchange in his head, Peter got so incensed again that he failed to hear someone come into the confessional. It was only when a female throat was cleared that he shook himself and slid open the hatch.

'Bless me, Father, for I have sinned.' It was Niamh's voice, talking in a near-whisper, and rather fast. 'It's been a week since my last confession – listen, Father, earlier today I heard something. I haven't been able to get it out of my mind.'

'What is it?'

'Black Dazzler.'

Peter sighed. 'I'm hearing confessions.'

'This is a confession,' she said. 'I was talking to – someone. And he told me, in the strictest confidence, that Black Dazzler is going to lose the race tonight. And that we're to back a dog called Tarbert Warrior.'

'This person is saying that the race is fixed?'

'That's my impression, Father.'

'That's a very serious matter,' Peter said stuffily. 'Who is this person?'

'I can't tell you that.'

'I see. Could you stop him?'

'No, Father.'

Peter was silent for a few moments. 'Listen,' he said finally, 'Siobhan's putting the money on the dog, so why don't you tell her?'

'I can't, Father. I promised. Anyway, it'd be better coming from you.'

'I'd remind you,' Peter said, 'this is confession, and I'm bound by the rules. And there's something called absolution . . . ' He heard the door shut on the other side. 'Oh well,' he sighed, 'see you next week.'

No further penitents were waiting, so Peter left the confessional a few minutes after Niamh had gone. He found Brian Quigley sitting alone in a pew.

'You're the last person I expected to see.'

'Don't worry,' Quigley told him, 'I'm not here to renounce my sins. What had Niamh to say to you? Did she talk about the race?'

Peter stared at him. 'Brian, I heard her confession.'

'I'm not interested in her confession – did she mention the dog?'

'I can't tell you!'

'I'll take that to mean yes.'

Peter groaned. 'I give up. There used to be a time when you wore a dog-collar – '

'Enniscorthy,' Quigley interrupted. 'This evening. Tarbert Warrior.'

'You wouldn't change your mind and let me hear your confession?'

'Listen, Father,' Quigley said, 'just recognise a good turn when it bites you. And if any of this gets out, I'll deny it.'

He slid out of the pew, strode down the aisle and was gone, leaving Peter with a lot to think about.

†

A good crowd was gathered for the evening meeting at Enniscorthy and the stand-up bookies were doing good business.

Quigley and Mossy Phelan entered the stand and climbed the steps to the top.

Peter, Assumpta, Niamh, Padraig, Brendan and Siobhan were down on the ground, close to the action. They moved among the crowds, watching the dogs parade, eyeing the starting prices on the bookies' blackboards. Peter was edgy, knowing that the moment of truth was at hand.

'There's Black Dazzler!' Padraig said, pointing.

Brendan nodded. 'He's black all right – let's hope he dazzles.'

Siobhan gathered them into a huddle at the front of the stand for a policy recap.

'OK, pay attention. We each of us go to a different bookie. And we watch each other. See if we can place the bets at roughly the same time – we've got to keep the price up as long as we can.'

She handed out wads of money to Assumpta, Niamh, Padraig and Brendan, and kept one for herself.

'Thirty pounds for each of you. Forty for me. And forty for you, Father Clifford.'

He shook his head. 'I'm not betting.'

'We need to cover all the bookies,' Siobhan told him. 'Without you we'll miss one out.'

Peter was adamant. 'I can't get involved in gambling.'

'It's for Kathleen's sake!' Assumpta said.

'That's not the point.'

'Listen,' Siobhan said, 'it's not a big problem, I'll deal with it. So off we go then.'

They started to move off. Niamh nudged Peter hard in the ribs.

'Wait!' he yelped.

They all stopped and looked at him.

'I think we should put the money on Tarbert Warrior,' he said.

Assumpta blinked at him. 'What?'

Peter looked at Siobhan. 'I'm sorry, I'm not going against your judgement.'

'It certainly sounds like you are,' Assumpta said.

'I'm not,' Peter insisted. 'But . . . I don't know how to say this.'

Siobhan helped him out. 'You've heard something, Father, is that it?'

'I'm not at liberty to say.'

Padraig asked if he'd had a mystical experience.

'A vision?' Brendan suggested.

'Ah!' Padraig winked. 'A tip in the confession box!'

Assumpta looked questioningly at Siobhan.

'Well, information is information,' Siobhan said, 'and it may be a lot better than mine. Tarbert Warrior it is, then.'

'Thank you, Siobhan,' Peter said.

'Oh no,' she said. 'Thank you. I'm glad to be rid of the responsibility.'

Peter took a deep breath, looking at the money in Siobhan's hand. 'Oh, well,' he said, 'in for a penny, in for a pound. Give me the forty quid.'

Siobhan handed him the stake. 'All right, team! Away we go!'

Niamh gave Peter's arm an encouraging pat. He tried to look reassured.

A few minutes later the loudspeakers announced the names of the runners and their trap numbers. To Peter, the names Black Dazzler and Tarbert Warrior seemed to leap out from the others, unwisely drawing attention to themselves.

He took his place in line in front of his appointed bookie. He looked along the row of boards. The team appeared to be in place and on schedule. When it was his turn he gave a nervous little cough.

'Forty pounds to win. Tarbert Warrior.'

The bookie winked as he tore off the ticket. 'Squandering the church funds, Padre?'

'I'm trying to build a new cathedral.'

The bookie took the money and handed Peter his ticket. 'Nothing like good works to give a dog a boost up the bum.'

Quigley and Mossy Phelan were meanwhile taking an overview of events from their position at the top of the stand. Phelan was studying the bookies' boards through binoculars. Away to their left, on the bend, the dogs were being put into the traps.

Phelan lowered the binoculars. He was frowning. 'There's been a bit of a shift in Tarbert Warrior's price,' he said. 'Some money's gone on at the last minute.' He threw a sharp look at Quigley. 'Did you have anything to do with that?'

'What? I'm not a fool,' Quigley blustered.

'I hope not. We get paid at starting price. Someone's going to be very unhappy about this.'

Quigley shifted uncomfortably, forcing himself to stay expressionless.

The traps clanged open and the race was on. As the dogs tore round the track Peter made a tiny sign of the cross. The announcer called the order of the dogs as they rounded the bends and hammered into the straight.

It became clear, very quickly, that this was a one-dog race. The dog was Black Dazzler. The crowd yelled their encouragement at the favourite and he responded by lengthening his lead until he was six yards ahead of the next dog.

As Black Dazzler passed the line Peter's face was a mask of tragedy. High above, at the top of the stand, Quigley's expression was stiff with identical despair. He turned to look at Mossy Phelan, and discovered he was nowhere to be seen.

Niamh looked stunned. Assumpta, Siobhan, Padraig and Brendan all registered deepest disappointment. They turned as one to look at Peter, whose face was buried in his hands.

TWENTY-FIVE

AT TEN MINUTES past one the following afternoon, Peter's phone rang. He came downstairs slowly, nursing a mug of coffee and a hangover, fully dressed but scarcely ready to face the world. He picked up the phone.

'Father Clifford speaking. Oh, Father Collins, yes. No, no, I'm fine, just a bit husky today.' As he listened, the look of pain around his eyes intensified. 'He wants it for what? New vestments. What, for himself?' He nodded a couple of times. 'Well, thank you for letting me know, Father.'

He hung up.

The night before, drinking to ease the pain had seemed a useful and even an urgent measure. Now Peter felt worse than ever, and his remorse was intact. The phone call, however, had at least given him something else to think about.

Ten minutes later he walked into the bar at Fitzgerald's. The other members of the betting syndicate were there. They turned to look at him, much as they had looked at him the night before at the dog track when Black Dazzler scorched past the winning post. Dr Ryan was there, too.

Peter stepped up to the bar and ran his tongue around his dry mouth. 'I want to apologise to everyone,' he said, 'and especially to you, Siobhan. I'm sorry. And I hope I won't be so stupid again.'

'Ah, sure, betting's always a matter of tips and whispers, Father,' Siobhan said.

It was a huge relief to realise that he had already been forgiven. Padraig asked him if he fancied a drink.

'Mineral water, thanks, Padraig. I'm practising for next Lent.'

'Doc Ryan's managed to raise another hundred pounds,' Assumpta said.

Peter nodded. 'Well done, Michael.'

'Straight flush,' Siobhan said.

The remark mystified Peter. Then he noticed that Siobhan, Brendan and Padraig were playing poker on the end of the bar. Padraig and Brendan chucked in their hands.

'Two pair,' Padraig muttered.

Brendan shook his head. 'First time in weeks I get a full house . . . '

Padraig was sympathetic. 'It's like playing the Cincinnati Kid.'

Dr Ryan was intrigued. 'Did you ever think of playing cards for a living, Siobhan?'

'That's it!' Brendan said.

Padraig frowned. 'What is?'

Brendan slapped the bar. 'A poker tournament!'

'Start again,' Padraig said. 'My brain hasn't caught up yet.'

'We organise a poker tournament. Sure Siobhan'll turn that hundred pounds into a thousand.'

'Hold on now . . . ' Siobhan looked wary.

'Yeah,' Padraig said. 'Great idea. What have we got to lose, anyway? What do you think, Father?'

'I'm no authority on gambling.'

'That's true,' said Brendan.

'It's too short notice,' Assumpta said, trying to be practical before enthusiasm outstripped reality. 'It's Wednesday already.'

'And we need the money by Monday,' Niamh said. 'How could we get word around?'

'Ring up Gamblers Anonymous,' Padraig said. 'Sure the county's full of gamblers.'

'We'll spread the news,' Brendan said, getting the bit between his teeth. 'They'll come from miles around!'

'And where,' Assumpta asked, 'would you be thinking of holding it?'

'Here, of course.'

She shook her head.

'Think of the business,' Padraig told her.

'Think of my licence,' she replied.

'And think of my reputation,' said Siobhan.

Dr Ryan pointed out that Ambrose wouldn't stand for it.

'It's for charity,' Brendan said. He turned to Assumpta. 'Say you're closed to the public for the day.'

'I'm not allowed to do that.'

Brendan appealed to Niamh. She was already thinking.

'Well . . . '

They were all watching her anxiously.

'His day off's Sunday,' she said. 'And he hasn't visited his old mother for months.' She smiled. 'It can be his contribution.'

'Right,' Padraig said. 'A vote. All those in favour?'

He raised his hand. So did Brendan, Niamh and Dr Ryan.

'I'm waiting for someone to ask me,' Siobhan said, visibly peeved.

Brendan, deliberately misunderstanding her, said, 'Will you vote, Siobhan? Please?'

Siobhan sighed and raised her hand.

All eyes were on Peter.

'You know I don't approve of gambling,' he said.

They waited. He put up his hand.

Assumpta was the only one who hadn't agreed.

'My future could depend on this,' she told them as they waited.

Niamh said, 'Trust me.'

Reluctantly Assumpta put up her hand.

'That's settled then!' Padraig announced, shouting without the need. 'This Sunday! The Ballykissangel Poker Tournament!'

Amidst the small jubilation, Peter threw a look of genuine concern at Assumpta. She shrugged.

Over the following two days the word was spread as far and as wide as the team could manage. Padraig talked to customers at his filling station and people in the street. He also handed out flyers advertising the tournament.

Assumpta told all the customers who came into the pub and she passed on the word to the delivery men, with the request that they tell anybody they met on their travels around the county.

Siobhan passed on the word to farmers and left them flyers as reminders.

Brendan spread the news to staff at the school, and with the aid of the school fax machine he disseminated the flyer information clear across the county educational system.

Dr Ryan told patients.

Meanwhile, the restoration of Kathleen's house went ahead, with everyone involved spending every minute of free time on their appointed tasks, working into the night to get the job finished.

At nine o'clock on Friday night, Father Mac walked into the paint-smelling sitting-room. Peter was up a stepladder painting the ceiling, his head covered with a baseball cap. Padraig knelt by the skirting board, working on the rewiring.

Father Mac looked around. 'Coming along nicely, Padraig,' he said. He strode to the ladder and stood with hands on hips. 'Father Clifford.'

Peter came down the ladder. Father Mac took him to the far side of the room and spoke quietly, though sharply. 'What's this I hear about a poker tournament?'

'It's for Kathleen.'

'On a Sunday.'

'Yes . . . ' Peter winced apologetically. 'I know.' It occurred to him that Father Mac would probably have liked to be involved.

'And I hear you were seen betting at the dog track the other night.'

Peter nodded sheepishly.

'So that's where the money goes, is it?' Father Mac tilted his head and stared indignantly at Peter. 'Money that could be better used to refurbish our parish church?'

'Oh, I agree, Father MacAnally. If indeed the money is being spent on refurbishing the church.'

Father Mac stiffened. 'What's that supposed to mean?'

'Now, understand . . . ' Peter lowered his voice, 'I give this no credence, but I did hear the money was going on new vestments.'

Father Mac actually blushed. 'Isn't that revolting!'

'It is,' Peter agreed.

'Malicious rumours.'

'That's what I thought.'

'The lengths to which some people will go . . . ' Father Mac stood back, stiffening with resolve. 'I'm glad you told me, Father. We must scotch this rumour, right away.'

He turned and hurried out. Peter smiled. So did Padraig.

†

On Saturday an encouraging number of people arrived at Fitzgerald's to sign up for the poker tournament. Ambrose, watching the activity from across the road, confided to Niamh that he wished she hadn't got involved in the tournament.

'Why not? I'm not the strong arm of the law.'

'You're its wife.'

'I thought we agreed you'd see nothing, hear nothing? So why don't you go and . . . ' Niamh rummaged in her head for something he could do, ' . . . see what the mountainy men are up to?'

She moved off towards the pub.

'Niamh!'

She paused long enough to throw Ambrose an accusing look. 'Do you want Kathleen to come back to an empty house?'

Ambrose had no answer for that. He frowned at his wife, and swallowed.

Trade was brisk. Niamh hung up her coat and got behind the bar.

Assumpta was showing Brendan a clipboard with a page of signatures on it. Peter stood nearby, looking worried.

'It's doing a lot better than I expected,' Assumpta said.

Brendan nodded approvingly. 'Twenty-four players. Excellent.'

'Five tables. So that's four tables with five players, and one table with four.'

'I'll help you get set up in the morning,' Brendan said.

He moved off down the bar to join Padraig. As Assumpta turned from the bar Mossy Phelan stepped up beside her. She recoiled at the unkempt sight of him, then remembered he had been in a few days earlier with Brian Quigley.

'Can I help you?'

'God, but you're a fine-looking woman,' Phelan said, showing her his yellow teeth.

'Thanks,' Assumpta said, deadpan.

'You wouldn't be in the market now for a decent man, would you?'

Assumpta took corny onslaughts like that in her stride, but Peter found it offensive.

'No, no,' Assumpta said, 'I wouldn't be in any market, decent men or not.'

'Anything that would interest you?'

'How can she resist?' Peter said.

'Janey Mac!' Phelan exclaimed, mock astonished. 'Sure, you've got a priest for a bodyguard! That beats Madonna any day.'

Assumpta smiled tolerantly. 'What do you want?'

'I'd like to sign up for this tournament thing. I'm mad about a game of cards. Thirty-one. Whist. Solo. I love it.'

'This is a poker tournament.'

'Poker. Oh, they're all the same.'

'Yes, but we're talking serious money here,' Assumpta said.

'Money's always serious. How much money would you be talking about?'

'At least a hundred quid.'

Phelan took out a thick wad of notes and riffled them. 'Would this be enough?'

'You're a lucky man,' Assumpta told him. 'We have one last place. What's your name?'

'Mossy Phelan.'

Assumpta wrote down his name on the sheet, then on a stick-on label which she handed to him. 'There you are. Make sure you're wearing it tomorrow.'

Phelan took the label. He glanced beyond Assumpta to the other end of the bar where Brian Quigley stood, staring back at him.

As Assumpta moved off Phelan said, 'Now don't you be wasting your time on these priests, my dear. Sure they're all theory and no practice.'

Quigley came along the bar and stood directly in front of Phelan. 'I never expected to see you again,' he said.

Phelan laughed. 'What's the good of revenge unless you're not around to enjoy it.'

'I'll get you for this.'

'Which is worse, Quigley? Losing the money, or being made to look like an eejit?'

'Don't be so sure you've got away with it yet.'

Phelan sniffed. 'You got away with a lot of strokes in your time, Quigley. I bet your daughter Niamh would be interested to hear about them – including cheating me out of a grand.'

Quigley was growing red around the ears.

'Did you think I'd forget?' Phelan said softly.

Quigley grabbed his shirt and brought up his fist. 'You dirty – '

'Ah, ah, steady now . . . ' Phelan nodded to where Niamh was watching with a worried scowl on her face. Quigley stepped back, his fist still bunched at his chest.

'Till tomorrow then,' Phelan said cheerily, and waved, backing away. He waved again, to Assumpta this time, then turned and left.

Quigley walked along the bar and stood for a while, looking at no one, letting his temper settle. When his colour finally subsided to normal he told Niamh to give him a large brandy.

twenty-six

PETER ARRIVED at the pub as the poker tournament was about to begin. The place was packed. Contestants could be distinguished from spectators by their labels, worn variously on their jacket lapels, shirts and hat bands. Quigley was at the top end of the bar, glaring into his glass. Niamh stood beside him. Siobhan was there, too, looking very tense, having a pre-contest drink and being morally supported by Assumpta, Brendan and Padraig. Assumpta saw Peter come in and waved him to their corner of the bar.

'Peter, would you say something to Siobhan.'

He nodded. 'Hello, Siobhan.'

'I'm serious. She's nervous.'

'I'm not nervous,' Siobhan said. 'I'm panicking.'

'Siobhan,' Peter said, 'we have every faith in you. And even if you do lose, what difference does it make?'

'People will never talk to me again.'

'People are not like that,' Peter insisted. 'Look at me. They've forgiven me.'

'Don't bet on it,' Brendan muttered.

'Siobhan, it'll make no difference at all,' Assumpta said.

Padraig agreed. 'But have your ticket booked to Holyhead, just in case.'

Assumpta looked at her watch. 'Better start getting all these people together.' She took a small bell from behind the bar and shook it. 'OK, everybody. Will all contestants please take their places.'

There was rumbling and clattering as players took their seats at the tables and spectators jockeyed themselves into comfortable viewing positions.

Brendan leaned on the bar, a stance that gave him a perfect view of Siobhan as she settled into her chair. 'Listen,' he said, 'has anyone thought what Kathleen will say when she finds out the money's been raised by gambling?'

'Ah,' Padraig said, 'well spotted.'

'She probably won't accept it. Tainted money.'

'Give it to me then,' Padraig said, 'taint me, taint me!'

'Father Clifford can launder it,' Assumpta said.

Peter stared at her. 'What?'

'Drop it in the box with one hand, take it out with the other.'

'I certainly will not. That would be dishonest.'

Padraig grinned. 'Isn't it nice to meet a priest with integrity?'

Mossy Phelan sat down ready to play at the table nearest the door. He caught Quigley's eye and gave him an amiable nod. Quigley stared back coldly.

Brendan leaned over to where Niamh was standing beside her father. 'Ambrose safely out of the way?' he murmured.

'First thing this morning,' Niamh said, 'with a face like a nine-day clock. His Ma's delighted, she'll have her boy to herself for a whole day.'

Assumpta pushed her way out into the middle of the room, ringing her little handbell again. 'Welcome, everyone, to the Ballykissangel Poker Tournament.'

The assembled crowd cheered and clapped.

Assumpta waited until they were quiet again. 'You all know what it is in aid of – refurbishing Kathleen Hendley's house, because we don't want to lose our local shop.'

There was more clapping.

'Which is why,' Assumpta continued, 'we're asking the winner to generously donate ten per cent of his, or her, winnings to the cause.'

A few contestants grumbled at that.

'Our local vet, Siobhan Mehigan, has generously offered to donate all of her winnings, should she win the tournament.'

That effectively shamed the rebel contestants, while the onlookers cheered louder.

'You all know the rules, but just in case there are any disagreements or arguments, Father Peter Clifford will be referee, and his word is law.'

This was news to Peter. 'Why me?'

'The dog-collar lends authority,' Brendan said.

'But I know nothing about poker.'

'We'll advise you,' said Padraig.

'I've got Mass at six.'

'Cut it short.'

'Are we all ready to start?' Assumpta called, and winced at the roars of affirmation. 'Right then! Ten, nine, eight, seven . . . '

Everyone in the place picked up the countdown to one, at which moment Assumpta rang her bell and the play commenced.

Quigley moved to where he had a good view of Mossy Phelan, who grinned and gave him a thumbs-up. Quigley put his glass to his lips and absently swallowed a large whiskey in three gulps.

†

For the first hour no clear winning form revealed itself. During the second and third hours, less skilful players ran out of money or courage and one by one they left the tournament. Then, as evening wore into night, the hard, instinctive poker players came to the fore and proceeded to do serious battle with one another.

As the number of players thinned so did the crowd of spectators. After his break for Mass in the early evening, Peter went back on duty as referee and stayed there, propped on the bar, bored rigid. Quigley stayed where he was, too, trying to spook Mossy Phelan, with no apparent luck. Phelan was shaping as the most dangerous threat to Siobhan's supremacy. He was a born poker player, and no amount of staring from Quigley could do anything to alter the fact.

By two in the morning Assumpta and Niamh were in whispered agreement that Phelan, to all appearances, had done better out of the tournament, financially, than Siobhan. It was hard to tell whether he was a better player, but he certainly had the edge when it came to extracting a cash advantage from his lead in a game.

As the number of players dwindled to five, all seated at the same table, no one could doubt that Phelan had the determination to make winning very difficult for Siobhan. He played a relentlessly aggressive game, talking all the time like a simpleton from the hills but playing like a pro from Nevada.

†

At five-twenty the next morning, Ambrose crossed the road from the police house to Fitzgerald's. He was dressed in casual clothes but still managed to look like a policeman. He tried the handle of the pub door and found it was open. He went in.

At the game table, with dawn light creeping across the bar, the five players sat ready for a fresh hand of seven-card stud. Mossy Phelan had clearly been doing well – he had money piled all around him on the table. Siobhan had done well, too, though not as well as Phelan. The other three – Taidh, Seamus and Connell, all from Cilldargan – had not done well during the past two hours. They were all but ready to fold. About fifteen spectators still remained, and in spite of fatigue and an occasional case of serious intoxication, all of them determined to stay until a winner was declared.

Ambrose hunkered down beside Niamh. 'It's not still going on,' he whispered.

She nodded. 'Looks like it'll never finish. Anyway, what are you doing here?'

'I woke up and you weren't there.'

'Don't worry, Ambrose, I don't have a job to go to.'

'Neither will I if this gets out.'

Connell dealt the first two cards to each player face down. The first deal of face-up cards gave Phelan a king, Siobhan a three. Even Ambrose, the newest spectator at the drama, knew that these were the two significant hands, the ones to watch. The clue wasn't in the cards, it was in the calm earnestness of the players.

'Let me see now,' Phelan said, scratching his dark stubble. 'I feel very lucky here. Tell you what, I'll open with fifty pounds.'

Sleepiness among the onlookers was banished. They drew closer, paying serious attention to the action. Phelan threw the notes in the middle of the table. Taidh folded. Siobhan hung in. After some hesitation, so did Seamus and Connell. They put in their money.

The second round of face-up cards was dealt. Phelan got a second king, Siobhan a second three.

'I'm telling you now, it's all flowing,' Phelan said in his sing-song whine. 'It'll take a hundred pounds to stay with me.'

That was too much for Connell. He folded. Siobhan checked her remaining funds.

'See you,' she said, putting in her stake.

Seamus did the same, but obviously against his better judgement. Phelan grinned happily.

On the third deal of face-up cards Phelan got a ten, so did Siobhan.

'Snap,' Phelan grinned. 'All right then.' The grin faded. 'Let's see the colour of your money. Another hundred.'

Siobhan, pale and sunken-eyed, looked at her cards, then her money, and decided to stay in.

'See you,' she said, and paid up.

It was time for Seamus to fold.

'Only you and me now, my love,' Phelan said softly.

The atmosphere was tense. Everyone gathered round the table.

The fourth round of open cards was dealt: Mossy got a ten, making two pair.

'Aha, boy!'

Siobhan was dealt a three, her third.

'Ho ho,' Phelan said, 'it's interesting now, wouldn't you say?'

'I'll raise it fifty,' Siobhan said.

'See you, my dear. See you all the way to the bank.'

The final card, face down, was dealt to each player. Siobhan got a king, Phelan a four.

'Another fifty,' Siobhan said.

Phelan yawned elaborately and stretched. 'I'm getting dog-weary of all this. I'm going to push it to the wire, see what you're made of. I will see your fifty, and I will raise you . . . ' He reached into the front of his shirt and took out a wad of notes held together with a rubber band. He did a quick thumb count and threw the wad on the table. 'One thousand pounds.'

The shock in the room was tangible.

'Now, let's see the colour of your eyes,' Phelan said.

Siobhan couldn't cover the thousand. She knew her hand could beat Phelan's, but his tactic effectively cancelled that advantage. Siobhan's supporters stared despairingly at the table.

'There's one thousand, nine hundred quid on there,' Peter whispered to Assumpta. Ambrose looked shocked – shocked enough to intervene in his capacity as a law officer. Niamh gave him a warning look.

Siobhan checked her money again and sighed. She looked at the glum faces of her supporters.

'I can't cover it,' she said.

'Indeed you cannot, my darling,' Phelan said.

He reached across for the kitty, and as he did a cheque fluttered down on the table.

'See him, Siobhan,' Quigley said.

Phelan was on his feet suddenly, eyes blazing. 'You keep out of this, Quigley!'

'No, I won't, Phelan.'

'No cheques allowed!'

'Referee!' Quigley snapped.

Padraig nudged Peter. 'That's you.'

'Me!' Peter shook himself. 'Yes! What?'

'No cheques allowed,' Phelan said. 'Am I right?'

Peter turned to Padraig. 'I'm not sure of the protocol.'

Padraig shrugged. 'It's up to you, Father. If you say cheques are allowed, then they're allowed.'

'Oh, right.' Peter considered the matter. 'The cheque isn't likely to bounce, Mr Quigley, is it?'

'Made out to cash, Father. As safe as the Bank of Ireland.'

'Well, in those circumstances,' Peter said, 'I'll permit the cheque.'

Phelan stared. He knew he had lost. 'A priest siding with Sodom and Gomorrah!' He scattered the cards and got up from the table.

There was cheering and jubilation. People slapped each other on the back. Siobhan was hugged all round. Peter and Assumpta hugged enthusiastically, then broke apart suddenly, realising what they were doing.

Phelan was still standing by the table. As Siobhan gathered up her winnings he took another wad of money from his shirt and held it up in Quigley's face.

The room went silent.

'There's a thousand here, Quigley,' Phelan growled. 'Are you man enough?'

He slapped the money down on the table. Quigley put his cheque book on the table beside the wad and wrote out another cheque. He threw the cheque on top of Phelan's stake. 'I'm man enough.'

'Straight deal,' Phelan said.

'Straight deal.'

'This has nothing to do with charity,' Ambrose said. 'I'm going to stop it.'

'No, Ambrose, no!' Niamh warned him. 'You can't! You stop this now and you'll never live it down.'

'I don't care.'

'I do care,' Niamh hissed in his face. 'Now, please. Go away out of here. Direct traffic or something.'

'There's no traffic at this time of the morning.'

'Find some!'

Ambrose started to argue, stopped, started from another angle, then gave up. He turned and walked out. Siobhan and Phelan were seated opposite each other. The stake lay on the table between them.

'Let the priest deal,' Phelan said. 'I know it's thick of me, but I don't think he'll cheat.'

'Me?' Peter looked panicky. 'I know nothing about the game.'

'Just deal them!' Phelan barked. 'Face up! It's a straight bet.'

'Oh . . . ' Peter shrugged. 'All right.'

He took the cards, squared them, and offered up a silent prayer before he began to deal.

Phelan got a three, Siobhan got a four.

Phelan got a nine, Siobhan got a six.

Phelan got an ace, Siobhan got a nine.

There was groaning and tension. Peter took a deep breath and continued to deal.

Phelan got a deuce, Siobhan got a nine.

Phelan got a jack, Siobhan got a ten.

Phelan got an eight, Siobhan got a seven.

A roar went up that rattled the windows. This time Peter and Assumpta shook hands.

Phelan stared malevolently at Quigley, who smiled at him sweetly, and picked up his winnings. Silence gathered as people watched Phelan, wondering what he would do.

He stared for several more seconds, watching Quigley light a cigar and walk to the bar, patting the wad in his breast pocket. Peter was ready to get between the two before any punches were thrown. But Phelan turned and walked slowly out of the pub.

The handshaking and back-slapping resumed.

†

Father Mac walked into St Joseph's at ten o'clock that same morning to find Padraig, Brendan, Quigley, Siobhan and Assumpta sitting in pews. They were all close to falling asleep.

'What's going on?' said Father Mac. 'It's hard enough to get some of you into church of a Sunday, but ten o'clock of a Monday morning . . . '

'We're waiting for Kathleen, Father,' Brendan said. 'To present her with money we've collected.'

'If I may mention it, Father,' said Assumpta, 'we're still open for a donation.'

'Oh. Yes, of course.' Father Mac dug out his wallet and withdrew a fiver. 'And was the collection successful?'

Assumpta nodded. 'Very successful, Father. Two thousand, nine hundred pounds.' She took the fiver from his nerveless fingers.

Father Mac was awestruck.

'The poker tournament, Father,' Padraig explained. 'Siobhan won it.'

Father Mac was shaking his head. 'Two thousand, nine hundred pounds in one night? That's very interesting. Siobhan . . . do you think I . . . could I have a word with you some time about . . . '

Before he could say any more, Peter and Dr Ryan came in with Kathleen Hendley between them.

'Here we are, everyone,' said the doctor.

They all stood and clapped politely.

Kathleen, for her part, looked bewildered. 'What's all this?'

'We've got a little surprise for you, Kathleen,' Peter said. 'While you've been at your sister's we've managed to put your house to rights. And . . . ' He nodded, cueing Assumpta.

'There's a tidy sum of money left over,' Assumpta said. 'Here.' She handed Kathleen an envelope.

'Your place looks like a palace now, Kathleen,' Quigley said.

'But . . . ' Kathleen had become misty eyed. 'Where did all the money come from?'

There was a moment of silence, then Assumpta said, 'I think Father Clifford had better answer that.'

They all looked at Peter.

He swallowed. 'A collection, Kathleen. The good-hearted people of this town all contributed.'

'And the parish church, don't forget,' Father Mac said. 'I made my contribution.'

'Oh, Father MacAnally!' Kathleen turned to him with something like rapture in her watery eyes. 'You shouldn't have. You're a very good man, an example to us all.'

Niamh appeared at the door and caught Peter's eye. She gave him a thumbs-up.

'Right, Kathleen,' Peter said, 'I think we are at last ready to show you exactly what the money has paid for.'

He offered Kathleen his arm, but she turned to Father Mac, who led her from the church. The others followed.

When they reached the open front door of Kathleen's house, Father Mac stood aside and let her enter first.

She stood on the new carpet in the brightly papered, freshly painted sitting-room and gazed around her, looking like a woman who had been given a sight of heaven. She walked round the room, touching the new mantelpiece, feeling the nap of the moquette on the chairs, stroking the polished surface of the table by the window.

While Kathleen fought to find words to express what she felt, Niamh hurried to close the door to the kitchen, where Liam and Donal, who had worked since dawn laying carpets and moving in furniture, sat on the floor propped against each other, fast asleep.

'Oh, Niamh,' Kathleen said, weeping freely, 'it's lovely.' She turned to Father Mac. 'It's a miracle, Father, so it is!'

Father Mac took her hand and patted it. 'The Lord provides, Kathleen.' The others grinned. Father Mac glanced at Siobhan as he added, 'We hope, fervently, that He will continue to do so.'

TWENTY-SEVEN

THE YEAR BEFORE, a pipe leading from Assumpta's main water tank in the loft had ruptured and caused a flood in the bar. The pipe had been repaired, after a fashion, by a Wicklow plumber who was no longer in business. Over recent weeks, the water pipes had been making odd noises again, worryingly reminiscent of the sounds they had emitted before the big downpour.

In addition to that, Niamh had observed that an old damp patch on the kitchen ceiling appeared to be getting darker.

It was never Assumpta's policy to ignore warning signs. In the case of the water pipe, however, she had been letting things ride because, for the time being, she couldn't afford maintenance work on that scale.

On Tuesday morning water began to drip through the kitchen light fitting. Assumpta called in Brian Quigley. She asked him to apply emergency measures, evaluate the damage and estimate the cost of putting the system right. While he rattled about in the loft, Assumpta used basins and jugs to catch the water, which now came through the ceiling in a steady stream.

After fifteen minutes Quigley came down the stairs, his hair awry, boiler-suit sleeves rolled up.

'That's it,' he said. 'The tank's empty.'

Assumpta came out of the kitchen wiping her hands on a towel. 'Can you mend the pipe?'

Quigley shook his head. 'Lead. As old as Methuselah's teeth and just as many holes. You'll need a new tank as well. That one's about to go any minute.'

'How much is that going to cost?'

'Well, the insurance will pay for the water damage.'

Quigley picked up a notebook and pencil he had left by his jacket. He scribbled on the pad.

'That's something, I suppose,' Assumpta said. 'How much, then?'

'Cash in hand?'

She nodded glumly. 'How much cash in hand?'

'Well . . . ' Quigley scribbled some more. 'If we cut out all the VAT on materials, ah, I don't know – say five hundred.'

'Five hundred?' Assumpta was dismayed. 'Where am I going to find a spare five hundred quid?'

Quigley started back up the stairs to get his tools. 'What about another poker tournament?' he said.

'Listen – can I open the pub?'

'No problem. It's connected to the mains itself. You won't have any hot water, though. And your toilets won't flush.'

'God help me,' Assumpta groaned.

At that moment a board in the ceiling came loose and gallons of water cascaded down into the kitchen.

Outside, a big black car came over the bridge and inched to a stop a few yards from the front of Fitzgerald's. Tom, the driver, had once been told that his bald head, tight mouth and steel-rimmed spectacles gave him the look of a Gestapo interrogator out of an old war movie. The remark had not been intended to flatter Tom, but he had decided to take it as an indication of the menace he could display, and he had worked on the effect.

Now, he sat expressionless in his dark suit and watched as his colleague, Jerry, a younger and rather handsome man, loaded a film in his Canon SLR and took a couple of trial shots of Fitzgerald's and the front of Kathleen's shop.

Tom turned his head as someone tapped on the driver's window. It was Ambrose in full uniform, his cap set squarely on his head. Tom touched a button and the window rolled down.

'Are you lost, gentlemen?' Ambrose asked. 'Or are you planning a heist?'

Without a word Tom reached in his pocket and produced a small black leather ID holder. He flipped it open and showed it to Ambrose.

Ambrose read the card and his face stiffened. He tried to smile, but it was too much of an effort. 'Right,' he said, and touched the peak of his cap, 'if there's anything I can help you with, I'm just at the house round the corner.'

Tom touched the button and the window rolled up again. He drove slowly away.

'Who were they?' Niamh asked, making Ambrose jump.

'Just passing through,' he said.

'They looked very serious.'

'I told them not to park here.'

'I'm away to Dad's.' Niamh nodded towards the police house. 'Do a bit of tidying.'

'Is your father up to anything at the moment?' A split second before Ambrose said that, he had looked at the big black car gliding up the main street.

Niamh narrowed her eyes at him. 'What do you mean?'

Again Ambrose tried to force a casual smile. 'You're right,' he said. 'When isn't he up to something?'

He walked off. Niamh went over to Fitzgerald's and leaned her bicycle against the wall. She went in. Assumpta was on the phone, talking in a low, confidential voice.

'Yeah, well,' she said, 'I'm interested now. Where? Sure, I know it. OK. See you then.'

Niamh came forward as Assumpta put down the phone.

Niamh was staring at the jugs, basins and towels littered about the kitchen.

'What happened?'

'Pipe burst. Your dad's upstairs sorting it out for me.'

'What a mess.'

'Isn't it? Just the way my life feels right now. Everything's collapsing around me. I want to get out of here altogether.'

'You don't mean that.'

'What is there for me here, will you tell me that?'

Niamh looked hurt. 'Do your friends mean nothing to you?'

'Of course you do, Niamh, but you have Ambrose.'

'There's not just me.'

'Well, apart from you, I don't think I'd be missed.'

'What's brought this on?'

'I had a letter today from a friend of mine, she wants me to come in with her and open a wine bar in Dublin.'

'You're not going?'

'I just might.'

Niamh decided that Assumpta looked as if she meant that. 'Listen, I'll come back later – I just wanted to have a wee chat.'

'Oh, I'm sorry, Niamh. What is it?'

'Later, Assumpta.'

As the morning passed the two newcomers, Jerry and Tom, made Ballykissangel aware of their presence, without revealing who they were. At ten o'clock they knocked on the door of Peter's house and told them they were holidaying in the area. Did he know of a golf course anywhere nearby? He directed them to the Cilldargan course, and when they asked about accommodation he recommended Fitzgerald's.

Ten minutes later, they were parked across the road from Sean Dooley's builder's yard, on the road north out of Ballykissangel. This time they were not advertising their presence. They were discreetly watching as Liam and Donal loaded a water tank onto Quigley's pick-up. As Quigley and Sean Dooley came out of the office Jerry took a picture of them.

'Come on, Quigley,' Dooley was saying. 'It's time we let bygones be bygones.'

Jerry's motor-drive whirred softly as he took another picture.

'There's too much bad history between us, Dooley,' Quigley said. 'I'll do business with you, but nothing more. Have we got a deal?'

'Sure we've got a deal.'

They spat on their palms and slapped hands.

Jerry took another picture.

†

Niamh freewheeled her bike down the path leading to her father's house. As she drew close to the back door she braked suddenly, noticing it was open. There was no sign anywhere of the Range Rover, which meant her father wasn't home. She couldn't recall him ever leaving the door open when he was out, either intentionally or by accident.

She got off the bike and leaned it on the wall. Up close, she could see the door had been jemmied open. She stood there for a minute, wondering what to do.

'Dad?' she called in a harsh whisper through the part-open door. 'Dad!'

She crept into the kitchen. Everything appeared to be in order, and there was no sign of anyone.

'Are you there? Dad?'

There was no one in the sitting-room either. Niamh made a swift inventory. The video and the television were both present. Then she saw the fireplace. The decorative false front had been jemmied open. She could see it, but she didn't know what she was seeing. It looked like some kind of secure door hanging open, where the hearth had been.

'Hello, Niamh.'

She turned and saw her father. 'Oh, thank God . . . '

He realised something was wrong. 'What the hell is going on?'

'Did you not see the back door?'

'What?'

'Nothing seems to be missing.' Niamh pointed at the fireplace. 'There's just this.'

'Oh, my God!'

Quigley knelt and peered into the empty gap behind the open front.

'What have they taken?'

'Money,' Quigley breathed. 'A lot of money.'

'I'll ring Ambrose.'

'No!' Quigley snapped. 'Don't tell Ambrose. Don't tell anybody!'

'But Dad . . . '

'No one!' Quigley shouted. 'Do you hear?' He stood for a moment with his eyes closed, calming himself. 'If you'll just excuse me, Niamh, I have to make a phone call to my accountant. In private.'

Niamh threw him a disapproving frown and left.

Quigley used the kitchen phone. He punched in the number and stood staring out of the window with the receiver pressed to his ear. The accountant answered on the second ring.

'Cathal Quinn here.'

Quigley identified himself.

'You just caught me,' Quinn said, 'I was on my way to a meeting with Sean Dooley.'

'To hell with him,' Quigley snapped. 'This is an emergency. I've been robbed.'

'What did they take?'

'Strong box.'

'How much?'

'Two grand.'

'Ouch.'

'Yeah,' Quigley grunted. 'And even more painful, they took the second set of account books.'

At that, Cathal Quinn went very quiet.

†

At ten past eleven Assumpta parked her van in front of the pub, which had a 'Closed – Be Back Soon' sign stuck to the door. She got out and after looking warily up and down the street, she opened the back doors of the van. When Peter appeared beside her she gave a little start.

'They told me what happened,' he said. 'Anything I can do?'

'You can help me in with these.' Assumpta nodded to the stacks of shrink-wrapped beer cans and crates of dumpy beer bottles filling the back of the van. 'Quick as you like.'

They took a pack each and carried them into the pub.

Liam was in the bar, picking up pipes. Donal was clumping around upstairs.

'I'll give you a hand,' Liam said, taking the pack from Assumpta.

'Thanks.' She turned and saw Peter heading into the bar with the beer.

'No!' she called to him. 'Into the kitchen!'

He diverted swiftly and went through the kitchen door, followed by Liam.

'There's a van full out there,' Assumpta told Liam. He went to the foot of the stairs. 'Donal! There's a load of beer down here!'

There was a crash as Donal dropped his tools and galloped down to join them.

Assumpta led Peter and Liam into a walk-in larder and told them to put the beer on the shelf.

'Why in here?' Peter asked.

'Why not?'

On the way back out through the kitchen Peter pointed to the damaged ceiling. 'What's this going to cost you?'

'More than I can afford,' Assumpta said.

Outside by the van, Liam suggested they make a chain to unload the beer. They began passing the packs from one to the other, Peter standing between Liam and Donal.

Ambrose suddenly appeared, smiling amiably. Assumpta looked startled.

'She's got you all working for her, Father,' Ambrose said. 'How does she do it?'

Peter shrugged. 'Don't ask me.'

'Ambrose!' Assumpta said, touching his arm. 'You're looking very well today.'

'Am I?' He noticed the packs they were moving. 'Continental beer, eh? We get a great variety of drinks these days, don't we?'

'Yes,' Assumpta smiled nervously, 'we certainly do.'

When the beer was all unloaded and stacked away in the kitchen larder, Liam and Donal decided to take their lunchbreak in the bar. Peter sat beside them. Assumpta put a half-pint of beer and a sandwich in front of him.

'The wages of sin,' she said.

He smiled at her. 'Very nice. Any time you want a van emptied, I'm your man.'

Assumpta suddenly noticed that Niamh was hovering just inside the door.

'Can we talk now?' she said.

Assumpta nodded. 'Come through.'

They went to the kitchen. Niamh stood by the table and took a deep breath.

'I think,' she said, 'I hope . . . I might be pregnant.'

'Oh, Niamh!' Assumpta reached for her to give her a hug.

'No,' Niamh said, backing away, 'please, please.'

'What's wrong?'

'I don't dare let myself hope. Not after the last time.'

'Have you been to see Dr Ryan?'

'I know it's stupid, but supposing he tells me I'm not pregnant?'

'What does Ambrose say?'

'I haven't told him yet. I couldn't possibly disappoint him again.'

Liam called from the bar. 'Assumpta! Customer!'

'Niamh, go and see Dr Ryan.'

Niamh made an uneasy, reluctant face.

'Do it! Promise?'

'I will,' she nodded. 'I will.'

TWENTY-EIGHT

THE LUNCHTIME CROWD were in Fitzgerald's. Liam and Donal were still working on the water supply. Assumpta was trying to cope on her own, which was harder than usual because she had no hot water for the glasses and had to bring kettles from the kitchen at steady intervals. As she looked up from pouring the third steaming kettleful into the sink she saw Padraig turn away from the bar.

'Where are you going?' she snapped.

Padraig was taken aback. 'To the gents.'

'There's a bucket just inside the door.'

'Right. I'll wave to it as I go by.'

'Use it!' Assumpta snapped.

'What?'

'I'll refill it from this tap when you've finished.'

'Oh, right.' Padraig's frown cleared. 'For a minute there I thought . . . '

Siobhan picked up her drink from the bar and approached Peter. 'Can I ask you a possibly hypothetical question?' she said.

'This reminds me of the seminary.'

'If someone asked me to apply to be a Peace Commissioner, what should I do?'

That morning, Sean Dooley, who in addition to being a builder's supplier was also a local politician, had told Siobhan that she had the qualities to make a Peace Commissioner, and she should apply.

'Is that the same as a Magistrate?' Peter said.

'No, they don't pass sentence. They just hear cases and decide if they go for trial or not.'

Assumpta had heard the exchange. 'And they want you?' she said.

Siobhan looked indignant. 'Why not?'

'You'd be too good for the likes of us, then.'

'Would I?'

Assumpta nodded. 'You couldn't sit in the pub playing cards and knocking back pints.'

'That might not be a bad thing.'

Peter glared at Assumpta and she moved away. 'Go for it, Siobhan,' he said.

They were interrupted by a polite cough. Ambrose was hovering.

'Could I speak with you, Father?' Ambrose nodded to the other end of the bar, away from the others.

'Yes.' Peter turned to Siobhan. 'Keep a judicial eye on my beer, will you?'

He followed Ambrose into the reception area.

'What is it?'

Ambrose shuffled his feet in silence. Peter waited.

'You're a priest, Father.'

'Yes.'

'Have you ever noticed that being a Guard is a bit like being a priest?'

'No, I hadn't noticed that.'

'Confidences,' Ambrose said, 'secrets . . . '

'What's the problem, Ambrose?'

'I possess confidential information that affects other people, but I can't say anything.'

Peter nodded. 'I see the problem.'

'Not that they mightn't deserve a bit of trouble, some of them.'

'I've often felt the same way,' Peter said.

'What would you do about it?'

'Say nothing.'

'No matter what?'

'There's no other option.'

'It's not easy, is it?'

'It's very hard.'

'Maybe it's the price we pay for living in a small community,' Ambrose said. 'It might be easier in a city.'

'I'm not so sure.'

'Bound to be,' Ambrose insisted. 'Assumpta's got the right idea.'

Peter frowned. 'Has she?'

'Oh . . . ' Ambrose checked himself. 'You're right, you're quite right. Niamh said to keep it confidential for the minute.'

'Keep what quiet?'

Ambrose laughed. 'You're better at this than I am, aren't you? Well, thank you for the advice, Father. You've been a great help.'

Ambrose waved cheerfully and left the pub.

Minutes later, as Ambrose was about to start on routine paperwork back at the police office, the front door opened, banged shut, and Niamh strode in.

'I want a straight answer,' she told him. 'Those two men. What are they doing? Why are they here?'

'What two men?' he asked mildly.

'Are they from the Revenue?'

Ambrose sighed. 'As far as I'm concerned, they're just tourists.'

'Are they after my dad?'

'Niamh, don't get involved!'

'How can I not get involved? He's my father! And he's your father-in-law. Remember?'

'I don't get a chance to forget it.'

Niamh snatched up the phone and tapped in a number.

'You should be protecting him,' she told Ambrose.

'I'm a Guard,' he said. 'It's my job, more, my vocation, my belief, that I was put on this earth to uphold the law. If people were above board, if people didn't hide things – '

The phone was answered. 'Dad?' Niamh said. 'It's me. Listen, this is a bit of a guess, but there are two strangers in the village. It's just possible that they might be from the Revenue.'

'Are you sure?' Quigley's voice sounded strained.

'No, I'm not sure, but I have my suspicions.'

'Thank you, Niamh. I'll, ah – I need to think about this.'

Niamh put down the phone and looked defiantly at Ambrose.

'Why did you do that?' he said.

'He's my father, Ambrose. What did you expect me to do?'

He shook his head. 'Just remember I've said nothing, one way or the other.'

Ten minutes after Niamh made the phone call, Quigley showed up in Fitzgerald's. He waited until Assumpta finished serving Eamonn Byrne, then he beckoned her to the end of the bar.

'Bit of a problem's come up, Assumpta.'

'What?'

'The nub of the matter is, I've got to be above board with the work I'm doing up there for you. It can't be cash in hand any more. It's got to be all the paperwork. Estimates. Receipts. Everything.'

'What?' Assumpta was horrified.

Quigley realised the others at the bar were listening.

'Well,' he sighed, 'I suppose everyone's entitled to know. A source of information informs me that it's just possible there's a couple of Revenue men nosing round the village. It's not clear what they're looking for – so I suggest we all keep our cards close to our chests.'

Horror had given way to shock on Assumpta's face. 'You're certain about this?'

'I've no reason to doubt my source,' Quigley said.

'Holy God!' old Eamonn said suddenly. 'Oh, holy God!'

To everyone's amazement he turned and ran out of the bar.

'He's left his bag,' somebody said. 'And his change.'

A similar reaction was about to set in across the road at Kathleen's shop. Father Mac, a bar of chocolate in hand, was leaving as Donal entered.

'I'll drop by again next week then,' Father Mac said. He nodded to Donal.

Donal touched a finger to his woolly cap, then pointed at the display behind the counter. 'A packet of them mints, Kathleen, please.' As Kathleen got the mints Donal said, 'Have you heard about the Revenue men?'

Father Mac stopped by the door. 'What Revenue men?'

'Two fellas hanging round the village. Mr Quigley told Liam and me about them.'

'Those two!' Kathleen's eyes widened as she remembered the men who had been in her shop. They had bought sweets and asked her how business was doing. 'So that's what they are! Revenue men!'

'What do they want round here at all?' said Father Mac.

Donal shrugged. 'No one knows yet. So, if you're doing anything, stop it.'

He took his change and left the shop, laughing at his own wit.

'Oh, dear God . . . ' Kathleen let out a little moan. 'You don't think it could be me, do you?'

Father Mac shook his head. 'What could they possibly want with you, Kathleen?'

'I've never been good with the books, Father. Oh, it's terrible they should hound a poor woman so.'

Father Mac reached for the door handle. 'Kathleen! I'm sure you've got nothing to worry about. We all bend the rules here and there, we wouldn't be human otherwise. Why even I myself – '

His face whitened visibly as he remembered something. He jerked open the door.

'Don't go, Father,' Kathleen howled. 'I need you to advise me.'

'Talk to Father Clifford.'

Kathleen watched him leave and hurry across the road to his car.

'I never talk to Father Clifford,' she whined.

Shortly afterwards, Siobhan decided the Revenue men were probably after her. She sat in Fitzgerald's, staring at her lager, the conviction growing steadily like a headache. From the corner table, Peter and Dr Ryan watched as a textbook case of auto-suggestion unfolded itself before their eyes.

'I'm sure it's me they want,' Siobhan said. 'Have you ever tried to persuade a farmer to pay you in a way that's accountable? Here's twenty in cash, he'll say, and not another word. And, sure, I've always found it easy to be tempted.'

'I know,' Assumpta said glumly.

Quigley, standing a short distance away, nodded sagely. 'One thing you can be sure of, that lot are interested in anything that would cause trouble.'

Dr Ryan laughed. 'Hands up the man who's never fiddled his tax, and I'll show you a saint.'

After a moment, Peter raised his hand.

'There's always one,' Quigley grunted.

The door opened and the two strangers walked in. The place fell deathly quiet. The younger one, Jerry, walked over to where Peter sat.

'Ah,' he said. 'The very man, Father.'

Peter looked terrified. 'Me?'

Jerry nodded. 'We're here on your commendation.' He looked around. 'Who is the proprietor of this place?'

Assumpta had to clear her throat before she could speak. 'I am.'

Jerry went to the bar. Tom stayed near the door, hands folded in front of him, his steel spectacle frames glinting in the sunlight from the window.

'Good afternoon, madam,' Jerry said smoothly. 'That decent man of a priest said you could provide us with rooms for the night.'

'Well . . . ' Assumpta had gone very pale. 'It's not really convenient.'

'We don't mind roughing it a bit.'

'Yes, well.' She swallowed hard and smiled. 'Fine.'

She led them away to the reception desk.

†

That evening, as Brian Quigley drowsed in a chair at home, the telephone rang. He leaned forward and picked it up.

'Yes?'

A man's voice said, 'Mr Brian Quigley?'

'Yes.'

'I've got something of yours.'

'What?'

'Books.'

'So? What about them?'

'Are they worth a thousand pounds to you?'

Quigley took a deep breath to steady himself before he answered. 'They might be.'

'I thought they might,' the man said.

'What, then? What are you proposing?'

'Get the money,' the voice said, 'and wait for another call.'

†

Next morning Assumpta called at the police house. Ambrose, in shirt sleeves, was at the kitchen table, reading the morning paper and drinking tea as Niamh brought Assumpta in. Assumpta carried Eamonn's plastic bag, and an envelope with his change.

'Ambrose. Assumpta to see you.'

'Assumpta.' He put down the paper. 'How can I help?'

Niamh started to clear away. Assumpta hesitated.

'I'm worried about Eamonn,' she said.

'Eamonn?'

'Yesterday he ran out of the pub and left these behind.'

'What are they?'

'Some cans of Coke and his change – he's not that free with money, is he?'

Ambrose was puzzled. 'How do you mean, he ran?'

'Just that. Ran! Like a scalded cat. I've been phoning him ever since and he won't answer.'

'Did something upset him?'

'I'm just guessing,' Assumpta said, 'but I think it was those men.'

Ambrose glanced at Niamh, who was concentrating fiercely on her chores.

'What men?' he said, all innocence.

'Those two fellas pretending to be on a golfing holiday.'

'Maybe they are on a golfing holiday.'

'Not at all,' Assumpta said. 'Sure everyone knows what they're up to.'

Ambrose glanced at Niamh again. 'Do they?' He became suddenly businesslike and stood up. 'Excuse me, will you, I need to get ready.' He held his hand out. 'But I'll take Eamonn's stuff from you, and I'll drop it in to him on my way back from Cilldargan.'

'Thanks,' Assumpta said. 'I'll be getting along then.'

She hurried out.

Ambrose glared at Niamh. 'You shouldn't have said that to your father. I'll get the blame.'

'For what?' Niamh said innocently. 'You told me nothing. Who are they, anyway?'

Ambrose grabbed his cap and stormed out of the house.

twenty-nine

CATHAL QUINN WAS racing along the road from Cilldargan to Ballykissangel, driving with one hand, using his mobile telephone with the other.

'A thousand?' he said. 'That's cheap at the price, Brian. Will you stop worrying? In the circumstances, it's the best thing that could happen. Anyway, I'm bringing the official books to you right now.'

Quinn's attention was drawn to something ahead. It was a police car parked halfway across the road. Two uniformed Guards were flagging him down.

'Hang on, Brian, I'll call you back.'

He pulled up and wound down the window. An officer leaned down.

'Mr Cathal Quinn?'

Quinn nodded.

'Would you step out of the car, please?'

At home, Quigley switched off the mobile and put it down. As he did, the house telephone rang. He looked at it as though it might explode. It rang again and he picked it up.

'Yes?'

'Go for a drive, Mr Quigley,' the man's voice said. 'Take your mobile phone with you. Oh, and don't forget the money.'

Quigley got in the Range Rover with a thousand pounds in an envelope in his pocket. He put the mobile phone on the seat beside him and started driving. After ten minutes the phone rang.

'Quigley.'

'Do you know St Bridget's Well?' the man said. 'Leave the money there at ten to twelve.'

'Leave the money at the well?' Quigley said. 'Just like that?'

'Just do what you're told.'

'Who is this?' Quigley demanded.

The line went dead.

He drove carefully for the next five minutes, timing his journey so he arrived at the appointed spot at a quarter to twelve. He had to park the Range Rover and walk across a stretch of moor to get to the well with its little shrine. At ten to twelve precisely, by his watch, he put the envelope with the money behind the figure of St Bridget at the top of the well, then made his way back to the vehicle.

He drove away at once. At two minutes past noon the mobile rang. He snatched it up.

'Quigley.'

'All sweet as a daisy so far, Mr Quigley.'

'What about my books?'

'I need to put some distance between us first. Keep your mobile on stand-by and wait for my call.'

'How do I know you won't rip me off?'

The man laughed softly. 'I'm an honest man, Mr Quigley. Unlike some.'

The line went dead again. Quigley put the phone on the seat. He believed he had detected something familiar in the voice, but he couldn't be sure. All that mattered, for the moment, was getting the books back.

Not far from where Quigley was driving, the two strangers, Jerry and Tom, were standing by their car on a stretch of country road. Behind their car was another, a blue saloon, occupied by three men and a woman, all of them plain-clothes police officers. Behind that was a police car with two uniformed Guards inside.

Jerry and Tom were gazing at the top of a telegraph pole. A man was up there working on the wires. As they watched, he gave them a thumbs-up.

Jerry turned and waved to the drivers of the two police cars. 'OK,' he called, 'off you go.'

The plain car pulled out, followed by the police car. They drove away.

'Now all we can do is wait,' Jerry said.

'How long, though?' said Tom. 'I get bored.'

'Don't tell me.'

Tom had an idea. 'Let's go back to the pub and worry the natives.'

Jerry laughed. 'Why not?'

†

Padraig was out at the front of his garage, fitting new brake-lights to an old banger. Brendan lounged beside him on a chair, mug of coffee in hand. Padraig's mug was on the roof of the car alongside a tape player, from which Brendan O'Dowda sang cheerily.

'I wouldn't have missed it for the world,' Brendan said. 'Quigley on the hop. Assumpta. Even Kathleen.'

'Siobhan,' Padraig added.

'Her, too. And I bet there's plenty more.'

Padraig turned with the pliers in his hand. 'Go on then – who's your money on?'

Brendan didn't hesitate. 'Quigley.'

Padraig nodded. 'Without a doubt. Ten-to-one on.'

'Mind you, the Revenue could look at you as well, Padraig.'

'What for?'

'Fixing cars. Cash in hand.'

Padraig looked sceptical. 'Would they bother?'

'What else have they got to do?'

Now Padraig looked troubled. 'You might well be right. That's the end of that then, till they've gone.'

He abandoned the job and began putting away his tools. A car stopped and the horn honked.

'Father Mac,' Padraig said, waving.

'Brendan!' The priest looked agitated.

Brendan went across. 'Yes, Father?'

'We need to talk.'

'Do we?'

'Summer camps,' Father Mac said.

'Yes?'

'Don't look so blank. There are two men from the Revenue lurking about. I sought a bit of advice last night, and we could both be in trouble.'

Brendan hopped into the car.

That afternoon, one of the few people in the village untouched by Revenue paranoia was Niamh Egan. She was too anxious about her physical condition to think about anything else. She had taken the step of providing Dr Ryan with the necessary specimen, and soon she expected to know the result.

The waiting was alleviated, at first, by household chores and by shopping. But as the morning wore on there was less and less to do, and she couldn't create things to occupy her because she was too worried about the test result. It preoccupied her into brooding immobility.

Then the doorbell rang.

It was Dr Ryan. He followed her into the sitting-room, noticing how defensively she was hunched, how tense her features were. She was ready for the worst.

'Relax, Niamh. It's good news. You are pregnant.'

She breathed in sharply. 'You're sure?'

'Absolutely certain.'

She still looked distressed.

'I thought you'd be happy.'

'I am. It's just because of what happened the last time, I'm so frightened, Doctor.'

'Niamh, so far as one can be certain in these matters, I'd say you should have no problems at all.'

'You're sure?'

'Quite sure.'

Tears welled at the corners of her eyes. 'I can tell Ambrose, then?'

'Of course you can. And I promise you here and now, I'll take extra special care of you.'

At last she was smiling. 'Thank you, Doctor.'

'It's Ambrose you should be thanking.'

Another person not particularly worried about the visiting strangers was Peter, who at that moment was mainly concerned about getting chewing gum from under a pew using a penknife. He worked diligently, dropping the liberated chunks into a paper bag. When that pew was cleared, he crouched and examined the underside of the others nearby.

As he moved along, still at a crouch, he spotted a paper grocery bag on one of the seats. He picked it up and examined it gingerly. He took out three accounts books. He sat down and opened them. The first inside page on each volume bore the title 'Quigley Developments'.

A note was taped to the first book. It read: 'Next time you play with your money, make sure no one's watching.'

'Father Clifford?'

He spun round in the pew, startled. 'What! Oh! Kathleen!'

He slid the books into the bag.

Kathleen's eyes were red rimmed. 'I've got to talk to you, Father.'

'Yes, of course.'

She sat beside him. 'Don't think this is easy for me,' she said.

'Is it confession you want?'

'No. It's just I'm sick with worry, Father. Those men from the Revenue. They're after me.'

'We don't know they're from the Revenue,' Peter said. 'Everybody's guessing.'

'They're Revenue,' Kathleen said darkly. 'I can tell from their eyes. Father, I'll have to go on the run!'

'Oh, Kathleen!'

'Head for Dublin, maybe,' she said. 'Where nobody knows me.

Assumpta Fitzgerald's got the right idea in leaving this godforsaken place.'

Peter frowned at that.

'What'll I do, Father?'

She began to weep forlornly. Peter gave her a handkerchief and sat there, watching her pity herself, letting his mind dwell on other matters.

When he had placated Kathleen as much as he could, and persuaded her to think again about taking off for Dublin, he put the bag with the books in it under his arm and went straight down to Fitzgerald's.

When he entered the bar, Jerry and Tom were sitting there on stools, fulfilling their intention of worrying the clientele. Jerry was asking Assumpta if they could have sandwiches.

'I hope you've got ham,' he said.

'Yes, we have ham,' Assumpta said, trying to act calmly.

Peter strode up to the bar. 'Assumpta!'

'I'm serving these gentlemen,' she told him.

'I'm sorry,' Peter said, his voice low, 'but I need to talk to you.'

'About what?'

'In private.'

'It's not the time – '

'Please!'

Assumpta scowled at him. 'It'll have to be quick.'

Peter followed her through to the kitchen, closing the counterflap behind him as he went, putting the bag with Quigley's books on top of the counter near Jerry. He glanced idly at the bag.

'Any chance of a glass of stout, Father?' he joked, but Peter didn't hear him.

Assumpta began making sandwiches as Peter hovered.

'What is it?'

'Is it true you're leaving?'

Assumpta rolled her eyes towards the ceiling. 'This place drives you mad. Say something, and you might as well post it on a wall.'

'Are you?' Peter insisted.

'Right now I've got something rather more urgent on my mind.'

She put down the sandwich knife and went to the larder door. She flung it open, revealing the stacked packs of canned beer. Peter looked at them, then at Assumpta.

'Beer,' he said.

'Yes.'

'What about it?'

'It's duty free.'

Peter frowned. 'What does that mean?'

'It was smuggled into the country. I didn't pay any duty on it.'

'You've broken the law.'

'I've got burst pipes and exploding tanks to pay for. I had to do it!'

'You had to. And you let me carry it in for you.'

'Don't be so pious.'

'It's dishonest,' Peter said indignantly.

'It's easy for you to talk. The Church looks after you. You'll never be short of a crust. Or a roof over your head.'

'There's more to life than that.'

'Is there?'

They stopped, looking dourly at each other, letting their tempers settle.

'Why didn't you talk to me about this?' Peter asked quietly.

'Whether I should sell bootleg beer?'

'You know what I mean – leaving Ballykay.'

Now it was Assumpta who frowned. 'What business is it of yours? I'm not one of your flock, I don't have to answer to you.'

'I care about you,' Peter said. 'I – '

He stopped himself. Assumpta looked at him. There was a moment of truth between them, unspoken but eloquent.

'Perhaps you're right,' Peter said, 'it is none of my business, but you and I are friends and I thought you might have considered my feelings . . . '

'But you are just a friend,' Assumpta said, her voice calm and controlled. 'You're no more important to me than any of the others. When I'm ready, you'll all know what I'm going to do.'

She went back out to the bar, leaving Peter looking miserable.

Later, he decided to secrete the account books in the garden shed at the back of his house, for safe keeping, until Quigley showed up. As he came out of the shed he heard Father Mac calling him. He went to the front of the house and found Father Mac and Brendan waiting for him.

'I'll get straight to the point,' Father Mac said. 'A small problem has come up that you might be able to help us with.'

'If I can.'

'Explain, Brendan,' Father Mac said.

Brendan stared at him. 'Me?'

'It's better coming from you.'

Brendan sighed. 'Father Clifford, you know I took the summer camp for Father MacAnally this year.'

'Of course he does!' Father Mac snapped.

'Well . . . '

'He accepted money from me without declaring it for tax,' Father interrupted.

'You suggested it!' Brendan said.

'Just tell him, Brendan.'

'Well, the last thing I want is to stand up in court pleading guilty to tax evasion, so – '

'Brendan wondered,' Father Mac cut in again, 'if you'd find it in your heart to say you'd taken the summer camp, as part of your duties as a priest, without extra payment.'

Peter thought for a moment. 'I'm sorry, no. I don't want to get involved in any of this.'

Father Mac looked insulted. 'Father Clifford, just listen to – '

'I will not collude, Father.'

'I see. That's your last word?'

'Yes.'

Now Father Mac looked wounded. 'You're too self-righteous for your own good, Father Clifford.'

'I'm a priest!'

'So?' Father Mac glared at him. 'What sort of excuse is that?'

Father Mac stalked off. Before Brendan followed him, he looked at Peter and shook his head.

'It's easy for you, isn't it? Either it's right or it's wrong.'

Peter watched them go and decided it must be his day for feeling rotten.

THIRTY

WHILE DRIVING AROUND, waiting for a call to tell him where his books were, Quigley decided to drop in at the home of Sean Dooley and deliver an ultimatum. It took less than a minute. He told Dooley that their deal over the water tank and pipes, plus any future dealing they might do, would have to be entirely above board, and no cash in hand.

Dooley told Quigley he was losing his nerve, he had no sense of adventure. Quigley ignored him and drove off again. At the foot of Dooley's drive Quigley's mobile phone rang.

'Yes?'

'Your precious accounts books,' the man's voice said, 'are in St Joseph's.'

'What? St Joseph's? Why did you put them there, of all – '

'This is Black Dazzler signing off.'

The line went dead. Quigley switched off his phone and dropped it on the seat.

'Mossy Phelan,' he growled.

Down in Ballykissangel, Ambrose was just pulling in at the kerb in front of the police house. As he got out of the car Niamh called to him from the doorway. He shut the car door and heard somebody else call his name. It was Peter.

'Yes, Niamh, yes Father.' He locked the car door. 'Just a minute, Niamh.'

Peter came across the road. 'Excuse me, Niamh.' He turned his back and went into a huddle with Ambrose. 'Who are those two men?'

Ambrose went shifty. 'What two men?'

'Everyone's in a panic. Kathleen's close to a breakdown.'

'That's not my fault, Father.'

'Maybe not. But you could help calm them. I mean, are these men from the Revenue, or whatever it is?'

'I can't say.'

'Or won't say!'

'Father, I'm only following your advice.'

There was nothing Peter could say to that, because it was perfectly true. Ambrose touched his fingers to the peak of his cap and turned to the house, where Niamh still waited at the open door, hopping impatiently from foot to foot.

'Ambrose,' she beamed.

'What?'

'Come here.'

He looked very wary. 'What is it?'

She threw her arms round his neck and kissed him hard on the mouth.

'I'm on duty, Niamh,' he said, flustered, misinterpreting. 'Can't it wait till dinner time?'

'I've got something very important to tell you,' Niamh said. 'Very serious.'

She pulled him inside and slammed the door. There was silence on the street. Then from inside the police house came a huge, tearing whoop of delight that rattled the windows.

†

Over at Fitzgerald's, Assumpta, Brendan and Padraig were glumly silent. At the other end of the bar Jerry and Tom killed time working on a crossword. Their mobile phone lay in front of them. Peter marched in suddenly, startling the group at the bar. He headed straight for Jerry and Tom. He put his elbow on the bar and leaned close, addressing them sotto voce.

'What are you two doing here?'

'Doing the crossword,' said Tom.

'Enjoying a cup of coffee,' Jerry said.

'You know what I mean.'

Jerry looked at Tom. 'Do you know what he means?'

'No.'

'What satisfaction do you get from upsetting a community and panicking a respectable woman?'

Tom stiffened. 'I never touched a respectable woman in my life.'

'What respectable woman?' Jerry asked.

'Kathleen,' Peter said, 'in the shop.'

Jerry looked bewildered. 'I only bought a bar of chocolate.'

'Ah, guilt and sin, Father,' Tom said. 'The world's full of it.'

'What?'

'And that's your department.'

Jerry nodded. 'Your problem.'

Peter looked from one to the other and nodded.

'Right.'

He turned and stalked out of the bar, heading for the back door. On the way, he pointed to Assumpta, then to himself, then to the rear kitchen. Assumpta, Padraig and Brendan, who were standing close to one another, assumed they had all been summoned.

A few seconds after Peter let himself into the kitchen, all three of them followed him in. Liam and Donal were already there, working on the pipes leading to the sink.

'Well,' Peter said ironically to the trio from the bar, 'I hope you didn't arouse suspicion.'

'What is it?' Assumpta said.

'Well, now you're all here – Brendan? I took the summer camp, OK?'

'Oh! Thanks, Peter, thanks a lot.'

'Now,' Peter continued, 'Assumpta, I've been thinking about that hooch you've got stowed in here.'

'What hooch?' Padraig said.

Peter opened the door of the larder and looked at Assumpta. 'Tell them.'

'It's duty free,' she said. 'I bought it cheap.'

There were understanding nods from them all, including Liam and Donal.

'You can stow it in my back shed,' Peter said.

Assumpta nodded slowly. She appeared genuinely touched by the gesture.

'Right,' Peter said. 'Let's shift it now, then.'

'We can't take it through reception,' Assumpta said. 'They'll see us.'

Padraig agreed. 'We need a diversion. Assumpta, is your van unlocked?'

She nodded.

'Good. Liam, Donal – as soon as we start the diversion, load this stuff into the van.'

'Yeah, great,' Liam said, always keen for an adventure, however slight.

'What diversion?' Peter said.

Padraig headed back to the bar. 'Follow me.'

Tom was making for the door as Padraig, Peter, Brendan and Assumpta came back.

'Ah!' Padraig shouted. 'Going out, are you?'

'Yeah,' Tom nodded. 'Why?'

'There's something I want to ask you, both of you.'

Tom came back to the bar and got on his stool again.

'What do you want to ask us?' Jerry said.

'Well, have either of you heard of a singer called Delia Murphy?'

'Yes,' Jerry said, 'I have.'

'Have you ever heard her sing "Three Lovely Lasses from Bannion"?'

'My Granny used to sing that song,' Tom said.

'Oh terrific, terrific,' Padraig said. 'You see, for ages now I've been trying to describe this song to Father Clifford – haven't I, Father?'

'Yes, yes you have indeed, Padraig,' Peter improvised.

'I want to tell him how the song goes,' Padraig said, 'but I can't remember it all.'

'I think I can – just about.' Tom was obviously keen to embark on any exercise that would relieve his boredom.

As he began to sing, Padraig and Brendan linked arms with him and they drew Jerry into the line-up. Peter stood listening with a rapt expression as they swayed their way through the lyrics, led by Tom whose memory improved by the second, as he flowed through the lyric in a wobbly tenor that sank occasionally, though only briefly, to a baritone. Behind the singers, Liam and Donal sneaked across reception carrying packs of beer. Four trips did it.

Peter applauded loudly and bought a round for the breathless ensemble. They were gulping down the top third from their glasses when Quigley stomped in. He saw Jerry and Tom and softened his approach at once.

He sidled over to Peter. 'You didn't happen to find any books in the church, Father?'

'There's all sorts of books in my church, Brian. What specifically were you looking for?'

'Books!' Quigley hissed. 'Accounts books. With my name on.'

'What were they doing in St Joseph's?'

Quigley's eyes widened. 'Have you got them?'

'Not here.'

'Come on, then.'

He went to the door and Peter followed him. Quigley paused, went back to Assumpta and said, 'I've got some business with Father Clifford. If Cathal, my accountant, calls in, tell him I'll be back soon.'

Assumpta gave him a look that expressed, quite clearly, what she thought of his pushy presumption, but he left without noticing.

Jerry and Tom had been watching and listening. They looked at each other. Jerry gave his partner the merest shadow of a wink.

Siobhan had meanwhile appeared, seeking a private moment with

Brendan.

'Do you want to come to a party with me tonight?' she asked him.

'Where?'

'Sean Dooley's.'

Brendan looked horrified. 'Sean Dooley?'

'They're running the eye over me,' Siobhan explained, 'to see if I'd make a Peace Commissioner.'

'I thought that was a joke.'

Siobhan sighed. 'That's what everyone else thinks – so do it for me, will you? I'm going to need all the support I can get.'

Brendan smiled. 'Oh, well . . . ' He nodded towards Jerry and Tom. 'It might not be a bad idea to ally ourselves with the Great and Good, while those two are on the snoop.'

At that moment Jerry's mobile phone rang. He answered it and listened. Tom stared at him expectantly. Jerry switched the phone off and shook his head.

'Not yet,' he said. 'But not far off.'

'All this hanging around,' Tom said softly, 'is driving me mad.'

Jerry yawned. 'Sing another song.'

'I've got a better idea,' Tom winked. 'Let's give the priest a hard time.'

They finished their drinks and left the pub, laughing.

Assumpta watched them go. She turned to Siobhan. 'Don't let anybody rob the till,' she said. 'I'll be back as soon as I can.'

She hurried out on to the street and saw Jerry and Tom drive off in the direction of the church.

'Assumpta!'

Niamh came across the road, smiling broadly.

'Yes, Niamh?' Assumpta was still half watching the saloon car.

'I am pregnant. Dr Ryan's confirmed it.'

'Oh, Niamh . . . ' Assumpta wrapped her arms around her. 'I'm so happy for you – and Ambrose.'

'He's dancing with delight.'

'I'm sure he is.'

'I'm just on my way to tell Dad,' Niamh said. 'Is he in the pub?'

'No, but I know where he is. Come on.'

At that moment Peter was leading Quigley into the gloomy little shed behind his house. Quigley stared at the packs of beer stacked up on the shelf at the back.

'Has the price of altar wine gone up?'

'It belongs to Assumpta,' Peter said. 'She over-stocked.'

'I believe you, thousands wouldn't.'

Peter pulled forward a couple of beer packs. 'The books are down here somewhere – hang on, hang on . . . ' He reached behind an old baize-covered card table leaning against the wall. 'I've got them.'

He brought out the bag with the books inside, just as Jerry and Tom appeared in the doorway.

'Ah, Father,' Tom said, 'we picked this up from the pub floor earlier. It fell out of your little bag there.' He handed Peter the note Mossy Phelan had put in with the books.

'Oh, thank you . . . '

Peter felt like a cornered felon, standing in front of stacks of bootleg booze with a bag of suspect account books in his hands.

'And a friendly warning, Father,' Jerry said, 'don't keep your accounts in a paper bag.'

Tom nodded. 'Funny books get funny looks.'

'As, indeed, does this shed,' Jerry observed. 'Right little Aladdin's cave in here, isn't it?'

'Oh, that's just for personal use,' Peter said, waving a casual hand at the beer, 'plus a few parishioners.'

Quigley could see they weren't buying that. 'It's for the party,' he said hastily.

Peter stared at him. 'Party?'

'What party?' Jerry asked.

Quigley blinked. 'Em . . . '

'My party,' Niamh said, coming into the shed with Assumpta behind her.

'Her party,' Quigley said.

Jerry turned. 'Your party?'

'It's a celebration,' Niamh said.

'Oh, nice,' Jerry smiled. 'What are you celebrating?'

'I'm pregnant. I'm having a baby.'

'She's pregnant,' Quigley said, his voice flat, his face expressionless, 'she's having a baby.'

'And Assumpta here is donating the drink,' Peter improvised smoothly. 'I've been storing it for her – right, Assumpta?'

'Yes.' She smiled sweetly to Jerry and Tom. 'You'd be welcome to join us.'

'Thanks,' Jerry said. 'We'd like to, but we've got something else on tonight.' His phone rang. He answered it. Somebody told him something. 'Right.' He switched off the phone and nodded to Tom.

'Excuse us,' he said to the others. 'Might see you all later.'

They hurried away.

Quigley was staring at Niamh. 'I'm going to be a grandfather. It's official?'

'Yes, Dad.'

Quigley hugged his daughter and kissed her cheek. 'Congratulations, Niamh,' Peter said.

She smiled at him over her father's shoulder. 'I'm putting you down for the christening, Father.'

'I'll be honoured.'

Quigley turned and picked up the accounts books, then followed Niamh out of the shed.

'Don't worry, Assumpta,' he said on the way out, 'I'll pick up the tab.'

'Thanks, Brian,' she grinned. 'That's a relief.'

†

Sean Dooley himself opened the door to Siobhan and Brendan. For a moment Dooley stared, unused to seeing Siobhan with her hair done and wearing a dress. As recognition dawned he smiled warmly, and nodded to Brendan, who was wearing his best suit.

'Welcome, Siobhan, and Mr Kearney.'

'My escort for the evening,' Siobhan explained. 'I hope you don't mind.'

'How could I possibly mind? You're very welcome, sir. Now, before I bring you in and introduce you to everyone, I've got a little present for you, Siobhan.'

He picked up a slender wooden implement from a table and handed it to her.

'Thanks. What is it?'

'A back-scratcher.'

The doorbell rang. Dooley went off to answer it.

'A back-scratcher, eh?' Brendan muttered. 'Now you know what's expected of you.'

A waitress came forward with glasses of sparkling wine on a tray.

'Take a drink and shut up,' Siobhan said, helping herself.

Brendan took a glass and glanced towards the door.

'Siobhan,' he hissed, 'look.'

Dooley had opened the door to Jerry and Tom.

Behind them on the step were two uniformed police officers.

'Garda Bureau of Fraud Investigation, Mr Dooley.' Jerry held up his identification. 'Could we have a word, please?'

Dooley put up no resistance. He led them across the hall to another room. As they passed, Tom nodded and smiled to Siobhan and Brendan.

Meanwhile, in Fitzgerald's, the stacked packs of continental beer stood behind a trestle table laden with plates of sandwiches and cakes. Peter hovered near Assumpta as she unpacked more cans and bottles of beer; Quigley stood near the reception desk, morosely cracking open a can; Niamh, Ambrose, Dr Ryan and Padraig were talking quietly by the bar, as were Liam and Donal. Kathleen sat at a table with Father Mac.

Even Eamonn had been persuaded to come down and wish Niamh and Ambrose well. It had been discovered, from fragments of intelligence gleaned by Ambrose and Siobhan on their separate visits to Eamonn's farm, that he had withdrawn suddenly from community life because he believed the Revenue men were in the district to punish him for defying regulations and using agricultural diesel in his car. Ambrose and Siobhan had done their best to assure him that his misdemeanour was not only minor but commonplace, and although he wasn't entirely convinced that he was safe from major prosecution, he had decided to come down for a few jars and help celebrate the forthcoming addition to the Egans' household.

Everyone was there – acquaintances, neighbours and friends of Niamh and Ambrose – and their pleasure at the couple's impending parenthood was entirely sincere. But the gathering lacked any atmosphere of celebration.

'I thought this was supposed to be a party,' Peter muttered, opening a bottle of Dutch lager.

'It would have been,' Quigley said, 'but the shadow of the Revenue men still falls.'

'I know,' Assumpta sighed. 'I wish everyone would hurry up and drink the evidence.'

'Why don't you put them out of their misery?' Niamh whispered to Ambrose.

'I didn't put them into their misery.'

'It's all so gloomy. I wanted a celebration. Instead I find myself in the Alamo. I've a good mind to come with you to Dublin, Assumpta.'

Quigley looked up. 'What's this?'

'I've got this opportunity,' Assumpta said. 'Partnership in a wine bar. I'm tempted.'

'I don't blame you,' Niamh said.

Eamonn stood back from the bar. 'What's Dublin got that Ballykay hasn't?'

'Better prospects of promotion,' Ambrose said.

'Theatres,' Niamh said. 'Cinemas. Clubs. Excitement.'

Eamonn thought about that. 'You're right,' he said.

'I wouldn't mind a bit of that myself.'

'Well, if you do decide,' Quigley told Assumpta, 'give me the word. I might take the pub off your hands.'

'If you're still in business,' Padraig said, making Quigley scowl.

The door opened and Siobhan and Brendan came in.

'Great news, everybody!' Siobhan cried. 'You can all relax. The Revenue men ain't Revenue men! They're the Fraud Squad.'

'And right this minute,' Brendan said, 'they're asking Sean Dooley some very searching questions about bribery and corruption and tax evasion. You name it, Sean Dooley's done it.'

The atmosphere lightened at once. 'That's what those men were doing here?' Assumpta said.

'Waiting for some raid to pay off,' Brendan said.

Quigley looked like a man waking from a terrible dream. 'You're sure that's all they were here for?'

Siobhan nodded. 'That's what one of the Guards told me.'

Padraig grinned. 'Did they bother you, Quigley?'

'Why in the name of God should they bother me?'

The party began to accelerate. Energy started to flow. There was relief, back-slapping, handshaking. As Brendan followed Siobhan to another group of people, he leaned over and whispered to Peter, 'You'll get yours in Heaven, Father.'

Peter looked across the room and saw Father Mac raise his glass to him. Peter returned the gesture with his bottle of Dutch lager.

Somebody turned up the volume on the tape player and people began to dance.

Niamh leaned close to Ambrose. 'You knew who they were all the time, didn't you?'

'All I know,' he said bluntly, smiling at her, 'is that I'm going to be a father, and I love my wife. Will you dance, Mrs Egan?'

'You're lucky I'm in a good mood,' she said. 'Come on.'

They joined the other dancers, watched by Peter and Assumpta. Peter nodded towards the happy couple.

'Is that what you're looking for, Assumpta?'

'No, no . . . ' She shrugged. 'Whatever I'm looking for, I'm not likely to find it here, am I?'

'You can find it anywhere.'

'Do you believe everything you hear?'

'Why not?' Peter said, clinking his bottle against hers. 'I'm a man of faith, aren't I?'